William Francis Butler

The Campaign of the Cataracts

being a personal narrative of the great Nile expedition of 1884-5. Second Edition

William Francis Butler

The Campaign of the Cataracts

being a personal narrative of the great Nile expedition of 1884-5. Second Edition

ISBN/EAN: 9783337423353

Printed in Europe, USA, Canada, Australia, Japan

Cover: Foto ©Andreas Hilbeck / pixelio.de

More available books at **www.hansebooks.com**

EX LIBRIS

THE REVOLT OF ISLAM.

THE

CAMPAIGN OF THE CATARACTS

BEING A PERSONAL NARRATIVE OF THE

GREAT NILE EXPEDITION OF 1884-5

BY

COLONEL SIR W. F. BUTLER, K.C.B.

AUTHOR OF "THE GREAT LONE LAND," "WILD NORTH LAND," "RED
CLOUD," ETC., ETC.

WITH ILLUSTRATIONS FROM DRAWINGS BY LADY BUTLER;
ALSO A MAP OF THE NILE FROM THE MEDITERRANEAN
TO THE EQUATORIAL LAKES

"In the flood of many waters they shall not come nigh unto him"

SECOND EDITION

London ·

SAMPSON LOW, MARSTON, SEARLE, & RIVINGTON

St. Dunstan's House

FETTER LANE, FLEET STREET, E.C.

1887

PREFACE.

ALTHOUGH the Nile Expedition stands alone in the magnitude of its effort, the immense theatre of its operations, and, above all, in the heroic name which will be for ever associated with its object and its failure, history will nevertheless regard all that relates to the tragic chapter of Khartoum as incidents in the train of events which first assumed visible form before the eyes of men on the 11th of July, 1882, at Alexandria.

Those events are still in process of development.

In the following narrative of the Expedition I have confined myself as much as possible to a personal record of the scenes that passed beneath my own glance.

Whenever I have been tempted to think that some other course of action—one more extra tug at the long line of our effort—might have saved all that was lost by so slight a margin, I have remembered the words of the two most heroic

soldiers of our age, at the moments of their
supreme disappointments—one speaking on the
evening that witnessed the defeat of his efforts to
carry the Turkish redoubts at Plevna, the other
writing the last message that ever came to us
from Khartoum. "It was the will of God."

.   W. F. B.

CONTENTS.

CONTENTS.

LIST OF ILLUSTRATIONS.

INTRODUCTORY.

WHERE AND WHY THIS BOOK IS WRITTEN.

T is the 20th March, 1885. I am writing these lines at a spot named Merawi, on the left shore of the Nile, in Nubia or the Soudan, as map-makers may determine, but in any case, a place about midway in the great river's length, and nearly 1500 miles from the Mediterranean.

EKS

B

All around lies the desert—the " Atmoor," as the Arabs call it—the great, lonely, waterless sea, terrible in the noonglare of day, beautiful in the moonlight of night, wonderful at flush of dawn and hush of eve ; but ever a waste where desolation has been cut deep into the face of earth—always a wilderness where the breast of the Great Mother is dead, and dry, and withered; where clay has burnt to ashes, and rock has calcined into cinder; where sight aches with distance, and sound finds utterance in winds, moaning over endless space; where earliest man has left his name in sand-swept pyramid, and buried temple—a vast, dead, withered world, with its unburied skeleton left bleaching under heaven —in whose depths the stars at night alone seem to have life.

Here, beside "seventy palm-trees," a small brigade of British troops sits "encamped by the waters "—the last of those columns which turned back a month ago from the noblest effort ever set before British soldiers, now the first and most advanced among the garrisons which hold the long line of the Nile, between the Third Cataract at Hanneck and the Fourth Cataract at Gerindid, waiting for the Soudan summer to come and go before the effort and the toil are again to be renewed—the effort and the toil only, for the cause has for ever passed away.

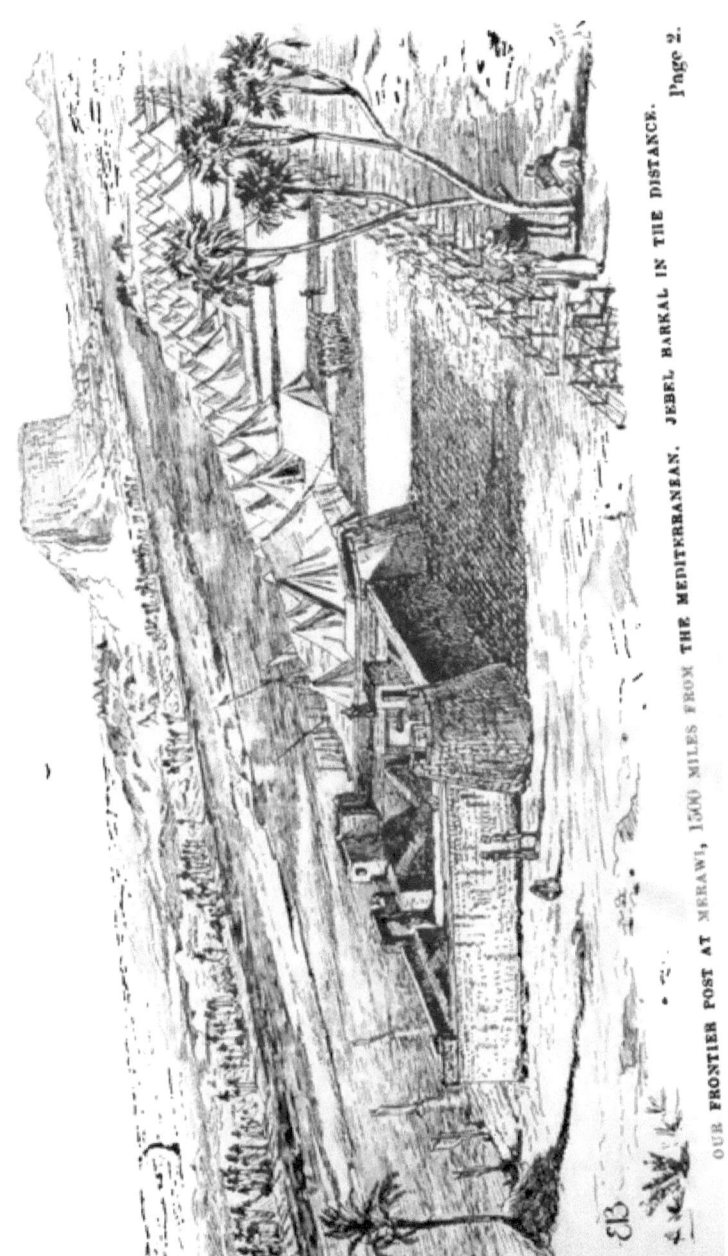

OUR FRONTIER POST AT MERAWI, 1500 MILES FROM THE MEDITERRANEAN. JEBEL BARKAL IN THE DISTANCE.

Page 2.

The prospect is not the brightest. The Soudan summer is yet a month distant; but even now the mercury rises in the afternoon to more than 100 degrees in the shade—or rather in such shade as we can best set up upon the sand. The river sinks daily into narrower compass, and more than two months have to go by ere the first symptom of increasing current will show itself in the broad sand-barred channel. April, May, June, July, August—five weary months before even the echoes of approaching movement will begin to make themselves heard—five months of vague waiting, with nothing certain save sun, sand, and almost insupportable heat. And then? Khartoum, perhaps. But Khartoum as a geographical expression—a point where two rivers meet in a wilderness—a name evermore of sorrow in our language—a tomb for ever in our history.

Nor, looking back into the past, is there much thought upon which the mind can rest with that satisfaction which toil and danger ever wear in memory when the final crown of success has set itself upon human effort. Everywhere through the past six months one sees time so filled with physical effort and mental expectation—with labour in torrent, in cataract, and in desert— with sun, and sand, and distance—with wrestlings against earth and sky, leagued, as it seemed, in

alliance against us—with march and bivouac—
with scouting by day and watching by night—
with fighting, with victory—and with failure, that
years, instead of months, seem to have passed in
that brief interval of time.

Beginning to-day, I hope to write, as time
permits and inclination prompts, some record of
these past six months, treating in detail only the
events and episodes in which I was myself an
actor, and as it was my fortune to have been an
actor of different degrees—at times set close to
the footlights—at other times standing in remote
backgrounds, where only palms and temples
and long reaches of river formed the scenery of
our enterprise, my story may at least be of use in
after time to give light to those who would tell
the full history which the future will demand, of
the best cause, the greatest effort, and the most
sorrowful ending that British soldiers ever went
forth to fight for.

In the months which saw the flotilla working
its way over the cataracts of the great river, I
was too constantly engaged in physical labour to
do more than set down a bare record of daily
distance and event. I could not attempt to put
in context the story which each hour was telling,
or to group into shape or sequence the quick-
running, but still long drawn-out threads, which
destiny was daily weaving into a mournful chapter

of our history. Even now I am conscious that it
is too soon to attempt the task; the echo of the
fall of Khartoum is still ringing over the desert;
the water that is flowing a few yards from where
I write was rippling by the walls of the wrecked
city but a week ago. It is little more than a
month since I carried into camp the bit of soiled
and torn paper, whose Arabic characters first
told us the fatal words "Too Late" had been
written across our gigantic effort. Is not the
mountain range all too near to allow us to catch
sight of the snowy summit, where Truth, like
Alp-top seen from Jura, rises clear over distances
of Time?

And yet the present moment offers many oppor-
tunities not to be thrown away, if this work I
would do is ever to be done. Having laid the
lines, and set going the works upon which the
health and welfare of those under my command
can best be secured during the coming hot season,
I have built myself an angular den of Nile mud,
on the north-east angle of a small native-built
fort—the fort all Nile mud too. When the
noonday sun hangs almost straight over this little
cabin, the temperature is some eight or ten degrees
lower inside the brown walls than it is in any
hovel of biscuit-box, or shanty of sail around me,
for like sailors wrecked on an uninhabited shore
we have raised sheds and lean-to's as shields against

the sun, and shelters against the sandstorms that
now, in this month of the Simoom, sweep the
desert from every point of the compass.   During
these hours of the hot day interruptions are few,
and mud wall and reed roof offer no inducement
to the mind's eye to wander off into distractions.
I look out at times through my three little loopholes, and see, beyond the blue strip of Nile—
beyond the yellow sand—the steep sides and flat
top of Gebel Barkal, the Sacred Mountain, rising
like a rampart isle above the waterless sea.   A
group of pyramids cut the lonely rim of the desert
a little to the left of the Sacred Mountain—there,
when the wolf was Rome's sole denizen, kings
and queens of Kush ruled and reigned; for these
pyramids and a few overthrown columns are all
that is left of Ethiopia's famous capital.   Now
and again the desert wind comes moaning around
the loopholes of my hut, making memory see
great distances of time as some sudden gust at
night will fan into glow, amid gray ashes, the
embers of extinct fires.   At times a little red-
headed dhurra bird will fly in through the door-
way, or a tiny brown mouse will peep out from a
wall-crack, intent on nest-building or biscuit
crumb; but even these, in their vast variety of
mouse and mountain, from present Soudan's
tiniest nest-builder to past wreck and remnant of
Ethiopia's oldest city, cannot do much to quicken

the hot and laggard hours on their dusty road. Here, then, too soon though it be, I will begin the story of " Too Late." What other words can sum in shorter and sadder sentence the history of the Great Nile Expedition? Too Late in its grand conception—too late in its immense effort, tried upon a theatre of unexampled magnificence —too late in its labour, its trials, and its sufferings —too late in all, even in the glory that remains to one name, and the sorrow that belongs to an entire nation.

CHAPTER I.

IN WHICH WE PLAN MANY THINGS AND BUILD MANY BOATS.

E must go back out of this Nubian desert to far-away England — back to a day in early August, just seven and a half months ago.   Late in the evening of August 4th I received the following telegram.   It ran thus—From Lord Wolseley, War Office, London. " I want to see you here to-morrow."

The reason was not stated, but there was no need of explanation.   For weeks previous the possibility of ascending the cataracts of the Nile between Wadi Halfa and Dongola, by boats built in England, similar in size and construction to those which had been used to carry our troops from Lake Superior to Lake Winnipeg in the Red River Expedition of 1870, had been a subject of frequent communication with the War Office, and only on the morning of this 4th August I had written and despatched the paper upon the navigation of the Nile Cataracts which is here noted.[1] The telegram told more than its words, and I read in it the announcement that the long-talked-of Expedition to Khartoum was at length about to be undertaken, and that the valley of the Nile was the route selected for the movement.

Who among us is without his anniversaries? What fly on the big wheel of life does not find himself brought round again to some particular spot on the Sun-circle, where, when leaves were green or trees were bare, he once felt the sunshine of success, and knew a day or an hour to be marked henceforth as a folded leaf in memory. This 4th of August was such a day in my life. On the morning of that day, in 1870, a small birch-bark canoe found itself at the head of a river-rapid—in sight of a far-spreading lake, upon whose waters a large Canadian canoe was coming along with the flash of many paddles, keeping time to the ringing measure of an old French *voyageur* boat-song. The small canoe had come a long way from the north seeking this larger

[1] See Appendix A.

craft through the lone wilderness of pine-forest, lake, and river-rapid, which then stretched in unbroken solitude between Lake Winnipeg and Lake Superior.

The large canoe had come a long way from the opposite direction. It was the advanced boat of the Red River Expedition, and it carried the leader of that Expedition—Colonel Wolseley, as he was then called. The smaller craft held a scout, who had worked his way through the Red River country to Lake Winnipeg, where, taking this birch-bark boat with a crew of five Indians, he had ascended the Winnipeg river, crossed the Lake of the Woods, until here, near the Falls of St. Francis, at the entrance to Lac la Pluie, he had found the object of his long search.

This, then, was the remembered scene which the 4th of August brought back to the writer of these pages—and to-day, as the mind recalls that episode looking across the intervening fourteen years, from the opposite poles of scene and circumstance which life in this Nubian desert gives—it is difficult to realize that all that world of waving pine-tree—moss-covered rock—lake-shore lapped with cool wavelets, all that vast fresh realm of shade, verdure, and crystal springs can co-exist on the same earth that holds the unburied skeleton of this dead Soudan world.

The day succeeding the receipt of the telegram

found me at the War Office, and in possession of
such information as could then be given. No
decision had yet been arrived at as to the actual
despatch of an Expedition to, or towards Khartoum,
but the contemplation of the movement of a strong
brigade of troops to Dongola by way of the Nile
was under consideration, and as this movement
would involve the use of boats suitable for the
passage of the cataracts which impede the course
of the river for a distance of more than 200 miles
between the great obstacles known as the Second
and Third Cataracts, it was necessary that I should
at once proceed to find, or to construct craft
suitable for the enterprise, and that in addition
to this proposed purchase, or construction of
craft designed specially for the work required,
I was also instructed to prepare lists of all
outfit, stores, food, and other supplies necessary
for the complete equipment of the boats and their
crews, during the long voyage into regions which
yielded only one requisite of life—water.

Associated with me in this work was an
officer who had also borne a part in the Red River
Expedition,[2] and whose judgment, experience,
and service, made him a most valuable auxiliary.

For the rest, time did not permit of detailed
instructions being given for our guidance. Previous correspondence bearing upon the subject

---

[2] Lieut.-Colonel Alleyne, R.A.

was almost limited to an application made by the military to the naval authorities, as to the length of time necessary to provide 400 boats similar to those used in the Red River Expedition. The reply to that inquiry was not encouraging. It would take from two to three months to provide 400 boats of the description named. It was true that a certain number of ships' boats could be obtained at once ; but no guarantee could be given either as to their fitness for the exceptional work required, or for the efficient condition which they might be in. Here, then, was the problem before us, simple enough in the extreme terseness of its main conditions. It is now the 5th of August. Can you build in England 400 boats capable of carrying 4000 men, with provisions for three and a half months, over the cataracts of the Nile between Wadi Halfa and Dongola ? Can you deliver these 400 boats, together with their sails, oars, masts, poles, and outfits complete, at the head of the Second Cataract, beyond Wadi Halfa, on the Nile, in time to enable troops to reach Khartoum if necessary, during the coming winter season, and return from Khartoum before the Soudan summer is upon them ?

You will have not only to build these boats, but to ship them from England, land them at Alexandria, carry them by train 350 miles to Assiout, thence, by river, 400 miles to Assouan,

thence up the First Cataract, and on to Wadi
Halfa, 220 miles further. From Wadi Halfa they
will have to be taken by train to the head of the
Second Cataract, and there, at a place called
Sarras, thirty miles beyond Wadi Halfa, they will
be delivered to the soldiers who are to work them
to Dongola. Such, in a few words, was the proposed task. Its essence, its inexorable essence,
was time. To-day, the 5th of August, and to be
of any possible use, at least 100 of these 400
boats should be at Wadi Halfa by the 1st of
November. Not a boat yet ordered, not a design
made, not a specification out, not a contract given,
not even a boat-builder spoken to. Three months
less five days, in which to design, order, build,
embark, land in Egypt, move by rail, embark in
steamers, carry 400 miles, launch, move by water,
drag up the First Cataract, tow to Wadi Halfa,
move to the top of the Second Cataract, and there
finally equip, at a distance of 1000 miles from the
Mediterranean, these 400 English boats. " Can it
be done ? " Yes, on one condition—that from the
moment " off " is spoken, all the countless pegs by
which the science of government pins down the
effort of the individual atom be for a time
removed, or loosened, so that a line can be run
straight through the densely-crowded streets of
the great city of " Departmental Administration."

The Nile is long, the cataracts are rough and

wild as rock and water can make them, the time at our disposal is hourly shrinking into smaller compass, but clear the course, and with God's help you will have the first of the 400 boats above the Second Cataract by the 1st of November and the last of them at the same starting-point ere the middle of the month has gone.

But although the inexorable essence of the task proposed was time, the word " off " could not yet be spoken.   It is true that every instant of every day was now precious, not to us alone, who were but the servitors of this work, but to the nation for whose name this work was being done.   It was literally true that each day, measured by the mere money value later on to be flung fruitlessly forth, was worth, and well worth, a million pounds.   It is true, too, that this article of time so precious to the nation and to its servants, had become precious because long months had slipped away in the debates, differences, and diagnosis, with which Authority, multiplied through many sources, has to filter its slow way into laboured execution.

And yet, even at this, the eleventh hour, the utmost sanction that could be obtained, was permission to proceed with inquiries, draw up designs, and stand ready for future action. Thus the evening of the 5th of August passed away in plan and forecast, and the 6th saw the beginning of our labours within the limits allowed us.

It would take too long to set down the various sources of information sought by us early on the 6th, from the highest office of Naval Administration in Whitehall, to the humble building-yards of Lambeth wharf, and the city offices of Glasgow shipwright firms, but by evening two facts had been made clear to us: 1st. That there were no boats either in the fleet, the dockyards, or the mercantile marine, that could be of any use in the proposed expedition.

2nd. That craft of the size and general type required by us could be constructed in large numbers by different building firms in a short space of time. Indeed, if the urgency of the case put cost second, and made rapidity of construction the first consideration, then the whole 400 boats might be built within four weeks from the date upon which the orders would be given. These important facts ascertained early on the 6th of August narrowed the scope of our immediate inquiries to three points.

1st. To decide design and specify the exact boat which should be built.

2nd. To determine the outfit necessary for this boat.

3rd. To ascertain the largest amount of building machinery which could be set going at a given moment upon the construction and equipment of the 400 boats required.

When these three principal points had been settled, there would then be time to arrange the countless details of delivery, shipment, transport to destination, &c., as well as to prepare for the future repair, supply of extra equipment, and safe progress of the boats on their long road to the Second Cataract. And now as to the first of the three points above stated—the exact boat which should be built.

The craft which could carry English soldiers into the distant waters of the Soudan Nile must fulfil many and varied conditions, not a few of them indeed being so opposite to each other that the attempt to realize those conditions in one structure might well appear hopeless of success.

Large enough to carry twelve men armed and equipped for a long campaign, and complete with food supplies for 100 days.

Strong enough to withstand the cataracts, rocks and rapids which impede for hundreds of miles the portion of the great river which was to be the theatre of our operations.

Light enough to be lifted upon the shoulders of men, dragged out of the water, and hauled across rock or sand-bar.

Stanch enough to weather the squalls and whirl-winds which frequently sweep the long reaches of the river from deserts which are sea like in their vastness—all this the boat must be that would attempt the task of forcing up the Nubian Nile, carrying soldiers into the Soudan.   But fifty other conditions were also necessary.   These boats would have to rely for progress against stream, upon oars, sails, poles and " track " or tow-lines, and of these essential requisites the supply must be sufficient to last for many months, and to outlive the wear and waste of innumerable cataracts, for as the desert banks yielded no food that could be calculated upon to supply the wants of the troops, neither did they give timber to repair damage to hull, or materials to replace lost or broken equipment.

This boat must sail well, pull easily, and draw only 20 or 22 inches of water when freighted with a load of four tons.   It must have keel for sailing, beam to give steadiness in the rush of rapids, freeboard to allow rowing, elasticity to bear the strain of transport, depth to stow the immense load it will have to carry.   It must be seasoned in every timber, for the Nubian sun is fierce, and the desert winds are parching.

Large but light, safe in cataract but swift in smooth waters, fast-sailing but easy to row, roomy but small of draught, strong but portable, heavy with cargo but light of build, stanch but elastic, slight but lasting ; truly a list of qualities

c

so opposite to each other that at first sight it might well seem there could be no possible point to which so many contradictory requirements might be paired down so as to meet in a single compromise.

And yet these opposite conditions were not the only difficulties which this boat would have to meet—the circumstances under which the opposing conditions would have to be worked, were of themselves opposed to success. You may trust a doubtful boat or a weak animal in the hands of men who are themselves experts in the different crafts of sea and land, and the skill of the sailor or of the rider will do much to neutralize the want or weakness in the mode of transport, but the tyro soon finds the weak spot in the tool he is set to work with. Of all our hard points to solve, this was perhaps the hardest—the boat that was to carry the men must also teach the men how to carry it.

It is the unhappy result of what we call our civilization that it has eliminated from the brains and bodies of our working classes most of the natural instinct of wild life—instinct of saddle-life, oar-life, gun-life, all those untaught faculties of healthy open-air struggle with the forces of nature which spring like indigenous plants from the true life of the peasant. The close-herded city coster, the factory hand or the mill operative

whose work is often the matter of a screw-head,
or the mechanical "feeder" of some patent pin-
machine—these will prove but sorry students
when face to face with the realities of that warfare
which man on the broad bosom of the open earth
has to wage with nature. This unknown quantity
of inexperience among the crews was perhaps
the most formidable among the long list of our
difficulties; there was only one way in which it
could be met, and that was by the provision
of some outside skilled assistance which would
train the young soldiers at the boat work.

Having seen what the ideal Nile boat should
be, and not be, we will proceed with our attempts
to find such a craft. By the evening of the 6th
of August we had found, as I have already said,
that it would be necessary to build our boats.
Shape, size, design, and exact specification had
then to be settled. We could not afford to build
in the dark, we must make sure that the big
load could be carried in the small boat, or all
the work would be for nothing.

There was only one way to ensure this. Let
us get together the exact load, the 100 days'
biscuit and meat, the groceries, tent, arms,
ammunition, and other equipment, and placing
them in various kinds of existing boats see how
far those existing types might be used as models
for our Nile boat.

Late on the afternoon of the 6th two telegrams were sent to Portsmouth; one from the Admiralty directed the naval boat stores in the dockyard to be ready at noon on the following day, the other from the War Office ordered the military supplies of arms and food to be at the same place and hour. Another telegram invited a few of the principal boat-builders of Portsmouth and its neighbourhood to meet us at the dockyard an hour later.

At noon on the 7th August we reached the dockyard, in company with an official from the Constructors' Department in the Admiralty whose assistance, beginning on this day, was continued without intermission to the end of our labours.[3]

Notwithstanding the unwonted orders telegraphed on the previous evening from such high centres of authority, there were but few evidences observable in the dockyard that our inquiries would be easily satisfied. A couple of large ship's-boats fully rigged, lay afloat in one of the basins, no stores or supplies of any kind had arrived, nor was any one to be found for a considerable time who could give us the slightest information upon any subject.

It was a very hot summer's day, the sun blazed down upon the big paving-stones, tar grew liquid on the roofs of boat-houses, water lay still and

[3] Mr. J. Dunn.

glassy in the great basins whose granite sides gave back the heat and glow as though the scene had been in Malta.

It was unfortunate for the rapidity of our experiment that biscuits should have formed a necessary item in the load to be got ready, for biscuits, although they form the most important article of the soldiers' diet in the field, are not a military supply, that is to say, they are a naval store and not an army one; hence, in order to meet our demand for 100 days' biscuits for our imaginary boat's crew, the Portsmouth commissariat had to ask the Naval Victualling authorities for the required quantity—1200 lbs.

This demand led to inquiry as to reasons; reasons could not be given, save such as the telegrams of the previous evening afforded—and they were of the vaguest nature. A refusal to supply the much-needed biscuits unfortunately followed, and thus, when in the full flush of anticipated experiment we reached the scene of our inquiries, it was only to find a ship's yawl and cutter lying idly in an otherwise deserted basin, and all prospect of a rapid settlement of our troubles completely dispelled.

There was nothing for it but to issue most urgent application for the supply of the requisite items of our cargo, and to await their delivery.

A glance at the two ship's-boats in the basin

sufficed to put them out of consideration. They were all too large and heavy for our purpose. An inspection of the boat-lofts followed. Ship's cutter, captain's gig, life-boat, jolly-boat, carvel-built mementos of Arctic exploration, clinker-built craft of various kinds were looked at and passed by. We were walking through a large store-shed among whose cross-beams and rafters many old and disused boats were stowed away. At last my eye chanced to rest upon a boat which seemed to promise an approach at least to the craft we sought. Taken down from the cross-beams, this boat proved to be a whale-gig, measuring twenty-eight feet in length, five feet six inches in beam, and two feet or thereabouts in depth. The interest in our search had by this time widened out, and there were many hands to aid the work of taking down the gig from its rafter perch and launching it upon the neighbouring basin. No doubt among the small crowd that now followed and watched our proceeding wild surmises were afloat. By this time the supplies of food, arms, and equipage were arrived or arriving, and their presence added considerably to the excitement. There could be no longer any doubt whatever something of a very unusual nature was contemplated.

In matters of this kind any previous existing apathy or unbelief is certain to give place to

wildest conjecture. At this moment, the principal heads or representatives of the boat-building
firms telegraphed to on the previous evening were
announced as having arrived, and their advent
added to the rumours. What could be the meaning of it all! Was it really true, it might well
have been asked among the crowd of bystanders,
that the First Lord of the Admiralty and the
Secretary of State for War were about to proceed
to sea in two open boats, with crews of eleven
men, fully armed, equipped, and supplied for
three months? Such was not, perhaps, the full intention concealed beneath these mysterious doings,
but something of similar magnitude might well be
developing, for was it not certain that the orders
issued late on the previous evening had come
from the inmost sanctuaries of the great twin
temples of Authority in Whitehall and Pall Mall.

But, to proceed with our experiment, which at
last seemed in a fair way towards realization.

When the cargo of military equipment and
food supply was all on board, twelve dockyard
men took their places in the gig, and she
floated out into the centre of the basin. The load
was too much for the little craft, but still she
floated easily. Add another four feet to her
length, a foot and a half to beam, ten inches
to depth, and boat and load will suit each other
exactly. Thus I wrote in a note-book, as we

watched the craft, with her dozen dock hands and high-piled cargo.

The boat-builders were watching the trial.

How long would it take to build ten such boats, but of the increased dimensions?

At first the builders had appeared half inclined to hold the business as one of those official outings that whatever might be its use, held to them small prospect of pecuniary benefit; but this question had the sound of money in it.

"In what length of time would you each engage to deliver ten boats of the lengths, breadths, and depths specified?"

Under conditions of payment that would allow double gangs of men to be engaged, the work could all be done within a month.

So far so good; if a single Portsmouth builder could turn out ten boats in less than one month, forty such men along the British coast would supply our wants, and by the end of the first week in September our 400 boats would be ready for shipment.

Back to London in the cool and quiet of the evening. All the scents of summer out for air and exercise in leafy lanes and along hedges thick with blossom. All the Hampshire hillsides hung with pictures of golden cornfields, set in green frames. Liss, Woolmer, Haslemere—how soft they sound, these Hampshire hills and Surrey slopes, lying away there, scented with summer dew, under the summer starlight—a thousand leagues beyond this blinding Nubian desert!

There is an old Celtic proverb which says that a pound of March dust is worth a king's ransom. It may be so; but things change their relative values according to locality, and it seems to me, writing in the depths of this Soudan sand-world, that one would barter, at times, the wealth of every Nile king of all the thirty-nine dynasties for a few ounces of dew falling softly over green-sward in the twilight of an English summer.

CHAPTER II.

IN WHICH WE CLOSE THE DOOR OF OUR ENGLISH WORK-
SHOP.

THE 8th of August came, but still no decision had been arrived at as to the reality of an expedition — and no positive order for actual purchase of boat or equipment could be given by us; but short of this, we went on as though everything had been settled—specifications were drawn up, designs made out, circular letters prepared for the various ship-building firms, estimates called for, and everything put into that shape which would allow the machinery of boat-building to be set

going in many places at the shortest notice.
Thus by the evening of the 9th, a large number
of builders were in possession of drawings of the
boat required; and tables, specifying exactly
every detail of size, material, equipment and outfit, were also given to them.

These drawings and specifications were prepared under the direction of the Admiralty official
already mentioned, from the measurements determined by us in the Portsmouth experiment.
From the same source, we were also supplied with
the names and addresses of the principal boat-
building firms at some twenty seaports round the
coast.

By the 10th August we were in receipt of tele-
graphic replies to our circular letters. A large
majority of the builders along the east, west, and
south coasts, had generally accepted our
proposals.

London and Glasgow had proved particularly
active in responding to our overtures; and
agents from the building firms on the Thames
and the Clyde were soon numerous in the
waiting-rooms of the War Office. During the
next two days our work went briskly on, letters
and telegrams poured in, personal interviews
were incessant; and by the evening of the
11th we could rest satisfied that, if once the
final word of sanction was given to us, we

could by a score or two of telegrams, set going a machinery which would produce from around the coasts of the island 400 boats, delivered at four great points, London, Portsmouth, Liverpool and Glasgow, within twenty-eight days. In order to keep at all level with the mass of correspondence which now poured in upon us, some clerical assistance became a necessity, for the interviews were so numerous that the detail labour of registering, copying, &c., could not be attended to.

It seemed, however, no easy matter to obtain the services of a clerk; the higher officials were of course already fully occupied and could not be spared. A very youthful junior was at length supplied to us, but whether dismayed by the ocean of unaccustomed work that had suddenly opened before him, or in the regular fulfilment of a previous intention, I am unable to say—but he vanished during the second night of his employment, and we saw him no more.

Late on the afternoon of the 12th August, I received a verbal order to repair to the office of a high Government official. The decisive moment had arrived. "I understand," said the high official, when I entered his room, "that you are charged with the work of boat construction upon an extensive scale?" I replied that we only awaited the actual order to proceed with construction; that our work of design and preparation had for some days reached that point at which it was compelled to halt, for beyond there only remained the realm of action.

"But," continued the high official, "do you really think that these boats can be built and sent from this country in the time I have seen stated —one month?" I replied that I entertained little doubt one month from date of order would see all, or nearly all, ready for shipment.

There was a slight pause, then the official took a half sheet of note-paper, wrote a few words upon it, and handed the paper to me. It ran thus— "You may proceed with the preparation of 400 boats." That was all, but it was enough. An hour later a dozen messages were speeding over England, and the Nile Expedition had begun.

Late as was the date on which the word of action had really come to life, there was something fortunate in the day which beheld its birth. The 12th of August clears the decks of the Great Ship of State—a good deal of congestion disappears about that time into remote Highland hills—London grows empty and workable; and the man who would drive anything through it will find it easier to do so after that date than before. It is true that in many great offices painters and charwomen are alone to be found;

but painters and charwomen are sometimes very hard-working and business-like people.

And now, for a week there went on without a single check all the pent-up work of the expedition. While the keels of the 400 boats were being laid from Peterhead round by Portsmouth to Glasgow, and masts, sails, oars, and lines were being prepared in vast quantities, we had time to turn our thoughts to the provision of other necessaries. Telegrams were despatched to Canada to secure the services of Indian and Canadian *voyageurs*. A steamer was sent to the coast of Guinea for African Kroo boys to act as boatmen; a stern-wheel steamer building for a South American Government in the yards of Messrs. Yarrow's, at the Isle of Dogs, was purchased, and the equipment of the Expedition in all the long list of its wants was pushed forward with work that often lasted from early morning until the small hours of the succeeding morning.

It was only to be expected that as these preparations got noised abroad considerable ferment should arise among the large class of nautical inventors, patent raft men, collapsible boat men, and other patentees and designers of the new and strange in the art of navigation.

It was impossible to deny admission to many of these honest believers in the possibility of effecting the object of the Expedition at a cost, which

although it invariably was found to gravitate towards their own pockets, was still, according to
the clearest evidence of assertion, incomparably
the best and cheapest for the country.

There was nothing in navigation or aquatics
which these rafts, barges, and ingenious craft
could not do; but as, in most instances, their
capabilities had never undergone more arduous
test than the placid reach of some local stream
had afforded, we did not feel justified in depart-
ing from our original model, even although, in
one instance, an inventor was the bearer of a
letter of introduction, which among other qualities of excellence attributed to the invention,
claimed for it that of being "able to float upon
damp grass."

Before the official sanction had been received for boat construction we had ordered a
trial boat to be built at Portsmouth. This work
was done with the utmost rapidity, and on the
18th August the specimen craft was ready for
inspection.

This time the trial was to take place at the
Ordnance Gun Wharf, and as time afforded
greater preparation, the loads were arranged as
closely as possible upon the actual lines which
the Expedition would require in all its details.
By noon on the 18th, two large service-waggons
drew to the Gun Wharf boxes of food, ammuni-

tion and stores, making a total weight of between six and seven thousand pounds. As this immense bulk of food and material was placed upon the wharf and one looked from it to the little craft moored at the foot of the stone steps close by, the impression grew strong in the minds of most of the beholders, that no power on earth could stow so much into so little.

The work of loading began; box by box disappeared, until at last the wharf was empty, and the boat was full; then twelve blue-jackets from a neighbouring ship of war took their places at the oars and the boat moved out into the harbour. She went gaily along, carrying a total load of nearly 9000 lbs.; she had a draught of only eighteen inches, and a free-board of sixteen inches; she pulled easily, and answered her helm quickly. So far for the test of rowing; now we will try sailing.

A steam launch towed us out into mid harbour; up went the two lug-sails, and bending to a fresh south-east breeze the first Nile boat sped on her way across the waves, under the shadow of Nelson's "Victory." Then coming round into the wind, she tacked and ran back towards the gravel beach under Fort Block House. One test more: we landed the men on the shingle beach, got out the "track" line, and began to tow the boat along the shore.

All was perfect—under oars, sails, and track-line, she carried her great load with ease, lay lightly on the water, and yet was stanch and steady withal. "You could take her across the Atlantic," said an old boat expert to me, as he looked at these trials. "She'll do."

We brought the boat back to the Gun Wharf, took out the load, and hauling her up on the wharf, put her empty on the scales. She turned just 1000 lbs. All the expectations we had formed were more than fulfilled. Our boat built in seven days, carried over four tons, and weighed less than half a ton. She sailed well, rowed easily, and tracked lightly. She could be lifted out of the water, and launched again with ease.

As I stood on the high wharf looking down at this, the first realization of our efforts, there passed across my mind a distant picture. It was of a great river flowing through a desert world, with buried temples and ruined tombs of forgotten kings standing at long intervals on sand-swept wastes. And, sailing there I saw this frail boat, and scores of others like it, with sails and oars flashing in sunlight, moving on through that immense land in the grandest effort our generation had seen—the saving of the noblest knight among us all. So was that day-dream.

And now? I look back: vaster is even still the vista. All the long river reaches, drawn by

D

imagination, lie dwarfed in the memory of the reality. Temples and tombs—toil and sweat of man are there, the sun, the sand, the endless distance, these are there; but, written across all is the Arabic sentence picked up among the rocks of Kirbekan, which first told us our mighty effort was in vain.

We had not waited for this confirmation of our calculations before giving final orders to many of the builders. So urgent seemed the need of rapid construction, that even at the risk of some uncertainty 280 of our boats were now well advanced in progress, but in order not to risk finding some grave defect of size or capacity in all of this number, they had been designed in three sizes, varying somewhat in length and beam. As we had now actually tested the capacity and quality of our boat, and had seen eighty cases of food supplies stowed away, there was no longer need of difference in sizes, and the remaining 120 boats, completing the total 400, were ordered by telegraph from Portsmouth, the date of delivery not to extend beyond the time already stated. Back to London again, to continue the work of organization and preparation. So far as that work was itself concerned it went briskly on during the remainder of the month of August.

The boats were growing in seaport and along

river estuary, from Dundee to Devonport, from
Glasgow to Greenwich; Woolwich was daily
getting ready our multitudinous equipment, and
so keen indeed had the boat-builders become
in the work of construction, that it was now
evident we could count upon the delivery of
more than 100 boats in the first week of
September.

It was strange that now, when the stream of
our effort was flowing along in an unbroken
current of success, when, by dint of exertion, it
might have been said we had pulled again out of
the abyss of lost opportunity, fully a month of
time, when we were daily saving even some hours
out of the close estimate of probable time
required—it is strange, I say, that this should
have been the moment selected by a great portion of the press, and by nearly all the recognized
leaders of opinion on African travel, to launch
their efforts against this Expedition.

There was scarcely a single item in the proposed scheme that did not become the subject
of ample censure as the month of August drew
towards an end.

Day after day, the columns of the London
press held letters denouncing or ridiculing our
arrangements. English boats to navigate the
Nile cataracts, what madness! long before these
frail structures could reach even their starting-

point, they would have warped and cracked out
of possibility of use, and perhaps it would be all
the better that they should thus by disaster in
preliminary stages of transport, save the wretched
men who were doomed to navigate them over
the terrible cataracts of the Nubian Nile, from
the certain deaths of drowning or destruction
by sunstroke which must otherwise await them.

Nor were these presages of disaster the out-
come of the valetudinarian critic who stands as a
self-appointed sentinel over the welfare of his
country, girt in the breastplate of a patent liver-
pad, and ever ready with pen at rest to launch
himself into the columns of his favourite organ.
He, of course, was fully represented, but he did
not fight alone. African travellers—Soudan explorers whose names were the household words
of Nile adventure—denounced our route, our
boats, and our proposals. Of course the faddist
was in full bloom. One day I met an engineer
officer in one of the office passages, with a huge
bundle of papers under his arm. "Do you see
this?" he said, pointing to his bundle; "what do
you think they are?" I could not tell. "Proposals to relieve Khartoum, and frighten the
Mahdi by flying balloons over the Soudan, starting them from Wadi Halfa," he replied. Nor
did our proposed food supply—by far the best I
had ever known on service—meet with better

treatment at the hands of the critics; one item in particular appeared to exasperate them. It had been observed in previous expeditions that prolonged use of tinned meats and dry biscuit produced among men a strong craving for preserved fruits in any and every shape. A considerable quantity of jams and marmalade were added to our boat ration to meet this desire. Unfortunately for us the newspaper critic would not swallow the jam; against this item his railing and his wrath were equally directed, and although the time of year was the season of the big gooseberry, he would have none of our preserves. It would have been well for us, however, if these had been the only objections which we had to refute.

It was about this time that there reached London a detailed report upon the cataracts and obstacles to navigation lying between Wadi Halfa and Dongola. This report, by far the ablest description of the river I had ever seen, was the work of an officer, who in the previous month of June had examined the cataracts with a special view to an expedition during the ensuing high-water season. Although his examination had been made before the project of a *small boat* expedition had been put forward, his report was not completed until after that project had been announced, and when the question was asked from England whether the naval authorities considered the scheme of 400 row-boats as being practicable for the navigation of the Nile beyond Wadi Halfa, the following reply was received :—

"Boats on the part of the Nile referred to, cannot be poled, because the water is too deep even close to the shore; propulsion by means of poles is an operation necessarily confined to shallow waters."

"Boats cannot be tracked by lines from the banks, because of the steep, precipitous character of the rocky sides of the river."

"Boats cannot be dragged or carried, because of the unfavourable nature of the ground."

"The stream runs so swiftly that rowing small boats or sailing them could not be relied on as a mode of progression. Moreover, the river is so rough in parts as to be quite unsuitable to passage by small boats."

There was more of similar import; but already those well-balanced words were quite enough to stagger the strongest in their faith in our boats.

What could I oppose to such testimony, full freighted as it was with the weight of highly-trained opinion, fresh from actual examination of the cataracts, the rapids, and the shores of the great river?

Nothing but an opinion; nothing but the memory of lessons learnt in a distant continent, under conditions differing totally from those of this Nubian river.

There is something in our human nature that, no matter what may be the strength of the conviction within us, makes us keenly sensible of seeming to occupy a false position. We may feel certain of being right, but we are conscious the balance of evidence is against us.

I had never seen these Nile cataracts ; I could only apply to them old principles which, at the best, were but inductive reasons, valueless in the eyes of outsiders, when set against the deliberate judgment of trained officials, studying the subject on the spot.

It is all past and gone now, and, writing this chapter, I have only to look out through my loop-hole window to see some sixty or seventy of these same boats, lying below on the shrunken Nile, as good and sound and fit for work as on the day they left the building-yards in England. Yet these very boats have not only ascended the cataracts lying between Wadi Halfa and Dongola but they have passed in perfect safety over the still more formidable torrents of the Shagghich rapids, which, before the advent of these English boats, had wrecked and utterly destroyed every flotilla that ever attempted to pass them.

But, although it is easy enough now to see how erroneous were the censures and criticism

passed upon our plans, it **was a** very different
matter to fight, all but single-handed, against the
flood of opposite opinion and hostile judgment
which was poured out, six months ago, against **us,**
alike by men who had known this Nile river
within sight of the Pyramids, and those who had
explored it to the Equator.   One might laugh **at**
the comment of the club critic ; but it was otherwise when some grizzly expert in African travel
launched his letters against us.   **I** could not
blind myself to the hundred differences that lay
between this proposed Nile Expedition and **the**
American one of fourteen **years** earlier—the
long transport to Wadi Halfa, the hauling and
dragging from steamers to trains, and from trains
to steamers, amid blinding heat **and** blistering
sun, the incessant possibility of accident along the
long line of sea, rail, river—cataract, river, and
rail—before even the starting-point could be
reached, and then ? For hundreds of miles the
great river, unknown, save that it was filled with
rocks and whirlpools, that its shores **were** wild
wastes of sand and granite, and that although
its banks had cradled the human race, and had
been the theatre of man's effort in the very dawn
of recorded history, no king or conqueror had
ever navigated its continuous waterway.

Ever before me, at this time, stood the fact that
this **matter** in dispute was not a mere question of

one being right **and many** being **wrong.** My **wrong,** if it was to be my wrong, meant the death of hundreds of men, the loss of millions of money, **the** utter failure in the eyes of the world of the most remarkable effort made by England in our generation. If the boats now being put together at **a** score of seaports were unfit to cope with the Nile cataracts ; if in that long series **from Semneh's** straight torrent to Hanneck's wild labyrinth of rapids there was a single ledge of rock, or rush of **water, high** enough **or** strong enough to bar **the** upward road against us, then I knew **that this** burthen of accumulated death and disaster would justly have been laid at my door.

Frequently during these late August and early September days, used I to long to have **the** trial over, the question set at rest. I tried to picture **the different** water-jumps on **the** long course **we** had to run, and to measure them in my mind's eye with some well-remembered scene in the Canadian or Columbian wilderness ; for after all, rocks and **water** and **angle of** descent must be the same whether pine-trees stand in rigid masses upon the American shores, or the lone sands of the Soudan spread away into endless distance.

But the verdict of the African expert was not always hostile. One day, when I was at work **as** usual **over** the details of the expedition, there entered my room a man, second to none in the roll of discoverers and explorers of this century. We had not met for years, for he had been long hidden in the interior regions of that great river, whose course he had been the first to follow to the sea.

" You are very busy, I know," he said, "and I won't stay long. I only looked in to shake hands and tell you that I have seen all these letters against the boats you are building. I have also read a description of the boats themselves, and, in my opinion, they are not only the right craft for the work you have to do, but they are the only means by which you can hope to do that work. I have tried boats like them on the Congo, and found them all right."

While thus, in three weeks' work, we had got almost within sight of the end of the labour of preparation, and the next week would certainly see the beginning of boat and store concentration, a great change had taken place in the magnitude of the proposed expedition. It was no longer to consist of one strong brigade of infantry, but of two brigades, supported by a large mounted force. Its avowed destination was no longer confined to Dongola. The goal was Khartoum. All these changes necessitated a double expansion on our part of craft and material, and before the 1st of September contracts for another 400 boats were given out, and duplicate lists of stores, supplies, and equipment ordered. These renewed orders had the effect of stimulating the efforts of the builders, who were desirous of completing their first order and obtaining a share of the second. So rapid was now the work, that by the end of the first week in September we had shipped 100 boats, the Yarrow stern-wheel steamer, the whole of the Woolwich equipment for the first 400, and food supplies for the 1st Brigade. By the middle of the month the last of the 400 boats, with their equipment, were on board ship at Glasgow, Liverpool, Portsmouth, and London, and our work, so far as England was concerned, was completed.

Run by events to a date in mid August, when the possibility of reaching Khartoum during the near approaching winter was reduced to one sole condition—Speed—there remained to those who had to ride this desperate race but whip and spur. So far, in the first month of the race in England, we had won a week upon the close-given estimate of time; nor, looking abroad to the wide area which had been reached in our preparations, was there yet reason for anxiety.

On the 5th of September, a steamer, carrying over 400 Indian and Canadian *voyageurs*, sailed from Quebec direct for Alexandria.

These men had been engaged and embarked all within three weeks from the date upon which the first telegram, authorizing their enlistment, had been received. Many among them had come from the distant shores of Lake Winnipeg, 2000 miles from the place of embarkation.

The steamer that had been sent to West Africa for Kroo-men was already at Sierra Leone, and might be looked for at Alexandria early in October.

As to the state of matters in the Nile valley, where so soon all the converging currents of our effort will centre, we could not as yet do more than endeavour to perfect and make ready, over the long line of communication between Alexandria and Wadi Halfa, the railway and steamer transport necessary for carrying to its distant starting-point our immense array of boats and stores.

Late in the month of August there appeared one morning an announcement in the leading London journal that the Government had decided upon taking a very important step. Recognizing the necessity of giving to the great task to which the nation was now committed all the strength that successful leadership long tried in distant and difficult campaigns could confer, the Ministers of the Crown had selected Lord Wolseley as Commander-in-Chief of the Nile Expedition. On the 1st of September, Lord Wolseley left London for Egypt, and with him went many officers who in previous campaigns had followed his fortunes.

By the middle of that month the work, begun on the 12th August, was completed : 400 boats had been built, delivered and shipped, and stores, munitions and food supplies were *en route* for Egypt. It was time for me to get across Europe to Alexandria to meet them on arrival ; so, at 5.30 p.m. on the 16th September, I closed the office door for the last time, shutting in and shutting out the piled up papers of boat designs, specifications, tenders, contracts, shipping reports, transport orders—orders for Red Indians—for Kroo-boys, models of new inventions, lists of requirements, comic cartoons of cataract and crocodile disasters, samples of Chicago beef and Tasmanian mutton, together with fifty other nameless odds and ends, splinters and shavings from the work-table of the past six weeks ; and, a couple of hours later was rushing along in the night express for Dover.

It was a dark, still night. All the lights of London were soon grouped into a dull red glow on the horizon. Over the Kentish hills the night wind blew cool and fresh. Rochester, Canterbury, Norman keep and Gothic tower, dimly visible against night clouds : even as long centuries ago, they rose before the sight of many an Eastern-bound soldier following this old crusader road to fight the Arab. Ah, we thought we had changed all that, laughed it out of our language, hissed contempt at the possibility of ever drawing sword in crusader cause again. Yet what is this that we have been doing in all these weeks of labour? Who is this far-off figure looming so large between the rifts in the dense leaguer which the Arab has drawn around Khartoum? We cannot save him with all this host, and all this piled-up treasure; but behold! our failure shall be his triumph—for God has raised a colossal pedestal in the midst of this vast desert, and placing upon it His noblest Christian Knight, has lighted around the base the torch of Moslem revolt, so that all men through coming time may know the greatness of His soldier.

CHAPTER III.

IN WHICH WE LOOK A LONG WAY AHEAD.

ROM Cornhill to Cairo is but a short trip to-day. Thirty or forty years ago it was a long journey. Thackeray travelling it about that time, managed to see a good many things along the route; but Thackeray could see a good deal, if he only sauntered from Cornhill to Chelsea. In olden time, anybody who wrote about Cairo—Grand Cairo as it used to be called—and left out the plague from his narrative, was liable to be looked upon as somewhat of an impostor. Egypt without the plague was Hamlet expurgated on the oft-repeated lines. If I recollect right, there was no plague in Egypt when the great satirist visited Cairo; but a convenient wave of cholera swept the Mediterranean about that date, and he was able to supply the omission when he reached Malta on his homeward road.

What has happened to the old plague? The doctors will tell you that sanitary science has routed it from its haunts; but we know, as a matter of fact, that Smyrna, Aleppo, Damascus, and a thousand other old plague-spots in the East, are just as drainless and as dirty as ever they were. No, the sanitary theory won't do.

One fact is certain, since steam has come in the plague has gone out. I believe it was a downright old Eastern Conservative that could not stand the radical blowing and spouting of steam penny whistles, but took itself off—(it knew a good deal about the taking-off business)—into some other planet, lying further away to the East, plagued to death by these Western innovations, leaving its old vacant Turkish slippers to a newer and less Conservative candidate, called Asiatic Cholera, who came fully prepared to undertake the off-taking business at reduced rates, and without partiality or favour to creed, class, or constituency.

Now there is this difference between the old plague and the new cholera, that the latter disease cannot possibly be invested with the same horrible but fascinating literary charm which its great predecessor ever possessed for English readers. A modern Defoe, face to face with the worst epidemic of cholera, would have no audience; but to be told of tens of thousands of dead Turks, or Syrians, or Egyptians being carried out of Smyrna, Aleppo, or Cairo—the victims of a scourge which for centuries always remained stationary in these far-away cities—was a very different matter to being informed about the ravages of a distemper which at any moment might be heard of in Belgravia or in Bermondsey.

So it has sometimes seemed to me that the great class of modern war-readers—the men, women, and children who now read and revel in descriptions and drawings of distant wars—who, in their clubs, mansions, houses, villas, shops, lodgings, and garrets, delight to be told in their daily papers of slaughtering of savages, sack of villages, bombardment of cities—would care less for this mental digest of battle if occasionally they got a little of war's grim reality mixed with their daily lives. That is, however, only a matter of opinion.

At the date mentioned in my last chapter, mid September, 1884, cholera had unfortunately appeared in France and Italy. Many scientific men had assembled to meet the intruder on his arrival at Marseilles, and to examine his credentials and report upon his claims to Asiatic parentage.

When doctors differ as to the particular form of disease under which an individual patient may be suffering, they usually keep to themselves the fact of their disagreement; but when they assemble to diagnose the collective capacity, cosmical germ, or whatever else they elect to call it, of some huge nebulous cloud of human distemper, their differences of opinion are published trumpet-tongued to the world.

At the moment of which we write, it happened that the germ theory of disease had taken very strong hold alike of the scientific and ordinary world. A German professor had discovered what he announced to be the true and *bona fide* cholera microbe, and a considerable portion of the well-to-do people in civilized society received the announcement with great satisfaction, rejoiced to believe that this bacillus theory—whatever it might mean—promised them some chance of escape from paying the old debt of nature in the terrible new coin of Asiatic cholera.

Meanwhile, however, the various governments concerned, not believing that the microbe theory had for ever settled the question, had drawn health cordons round their respective frontiers,

and had established quarantine more or less
rigorous upon travellers going from Western
Europe to Egypt. One route still remained open
—that *viâ* Trieste—and accordingly when the
Victoria Express had done its quiet, quick work,
and the Dover-Calais boat had done all that was
possible to prevent the inherent vices of the Con-
tinental world from invading England, and to
preserve the well-known virtues of Britain from
getting abroad into Europe, I found myself a
passenger in a *wagonlit* of surpassing discomfort
en route for Trieste.

Across Belgium, up the Rhine bank, over
Bavaria, into Austria, down the Danube valley,
through Vienna, up the Semmering, and down,
at sunrise, on the 18th, into the bay of Trieste—
just two sunsets and three sunrises since leaving
London, with a whole day to wash, and lounge,
and idle in Vienna.

No time to stop longer in this Austrian oasis,
amid the desert of German Europe.

Where did this delightful German-speaking
gentleman get all his quiet courtesy—his thought-
fulness of others, his dignified suavity of manner?
No wonder Napoleon could not abolish him, and
no wonder Bismarck wants to push him further
down the Danube—close contrasts are often
painful.

Out into the Adriatic, and down along the Dalmatian coast; into Corfu harbour, where island, mountains, sea, and people are all lying asleep in an afternoon of blue sky and golden sunshine. Out again into the Ionian Sea, along the isles and coasts of Greece, by peaks and promontories, past blue gulfs stretching deep into brown mountains, or held between curving capes where grey moles and castles of Venetian days look white in the light of evening; some of them seen in glimpses, more of them in fancy only as twilight falls, but all of them—Arta, Lepanto, Patras, Corinth, Missolonghi—"moaning with memories" that, like stars, are made visible at night.

The Austrian Lloyd's steamship, "Minerve," carries on her crowded after-deck a strange mixture of races—North Germans, aggressive, ugly, and rude of manner; Greeks and Sclavs of changing gesture and changeless linen; Italians and Hungarians of many types; cosmopolitan Pachas and nondescript merchants, making their way to Egypt, scenting afar off the Suttlers' harvest in the Soudan; Jews of all nations, but of a single type—these, with wives and children outlaid on the after-deck, oblige one to seek refuge upon the forecastle, where a nominally rougher, but immensely nicer and more interesting people, whose pecuniary resources have only permitted them a second-class passage, are to be found. Here, with three Italian and Dalmatian sailors—brown, honest fellows, who eat their dinner out of one big dish, and wash it down with a red wine drunk out of one huge bottle; here also, with a young Franciscan friar, an old Albanian chief, his hooded and "yashmaked" wife, and a couple of other Suliotes—red-slippered, buskined, linen-petticoated, and pistolled all over—I sat in perfect rest and contentment of existence, looking out upon the blue sea that washes the feet of Candia's snow-crested mountains. And now, while sitting here in this brief interval of calm between two periods of labour, it will not be amiss if, taking advantage of these few days' grace, I turn aside from our narrative to sketch the theatre of our coming effort, and tell the story of our object.

Beyond the Nile gate at Assouan, above the First Cataract, a vast waste of rock and sand spreads away into space apparently ended only by sunrise and by sunset. Burning by day, silent and shadowy by night, seared and seamed with long dead river channels, where water might have flowed in the drying of the universal deluge, piled with masses of rock, riven with strength of sun, and black from furnace breath of cycles of Simoom; opening out into measure-less, motionless expanses of yellow sand, vast as the sea and changeless as the stars, lies that great world of desolation called the Nubian desert.

Through all its length from south to north for full 1500 miles, a thin blue line of water holds its way, in itself a mighty river, but in relation to the desert, whose single rill of life it is, only a ray of starlight amid a vast void of night. To make up this single river, the downpour of dense tropical cloud masses, the full-fed springs of snow-capped mountains, and the rain-saturated swamps of immense equatorial regions have all given their aid. Nor has their united effort proved much more than sufficient to force through the long 1500 miles of rainless region the single current whose innumerable sources they nourished so abundantly in the great lakes, mountains and marshes of the far interior.

Of all the water children of the earth this Nile is by far the most wonderful. Out of the great mother's breast 10,000 nameless streams rush to feed the infant river. Around these countless life-springs of the "new-born giant," the grandest spe-cimens of animal nature have their homes, the lion, the wild buffalo and the elephant fill the forests with their voices, the Nyanzas are like oceans, the mountain kings wear their icy crowns right beneath the equatorial sun. Well has the great mother thus lavished upon her favourite offspring these choicest treasures of her bosom. No other, among her children, has ever done what this one has done. Cradled in the majesty of mountain-top and inland ocean, the river has itself been the cradle of human thought, order, law, art, and science—Roman borrowed from Greek, Greek from Assyrian, Assyrian from Egyptian, and Egyptian found in the ever-flowing waters and never-ending mysteries of his river the fountain of his inspiration.

Out of the south it came to him laden with life, bringing water out of sand, shade out of heat, life out of death, bearing all these things without rain-cloud ever darkening the sky, when the sun hung straight overhead, and the noon shadow of man had vanished from the fevered earth.

It was little wonder that the old races should fashion for themselves a God out of these wondrous waters, hewing their blocks of syenite, and building temples, pyramids, pylons, sphynxes and obelisks, to tell all future time the glory of their river.

I am writing these lines close by the shore of the Nile, not quite midway in the river's length from source to sea. In all those miles since the Mediterranean was quitted not one tributary stream has added its volume to the great river. I have lain down for some 200 nights on sand-bank or rock-shore, but never drop of rain or breath of dew has fallen upon my blanket, never a speck of rust has blurred blade or barrel, no trace of fog or mist have I ever seen above shore or water. When I first set out in early October the waters stood at their highest level, they are now shrunken to a fifteenth part of what they then were. It is now the beginning of May, and the river is almost at its lowest level, yet it is still a noble stream. Overhead the sun blazes in all the fierceness of the Soudan summer, the air crackles with intense dryness, the desert glistens like molten glass, so parched is the visible world that the surface seems in its thirst to conjure up fevered visions of pools and lakes of water, the mirage, the "Devil's sea" the Arabs call it, is abroad; the breath of the Simoom burns like a furnace blast, and at times tall spiral columns of smoking sand go whirling across leagues of desert; the birds seek the shade of our lean-to's, gasping for life. Another month like this, you say, and all that water must be dried up, the river has grown clear, the current is feeble, the volume shrinks daily, the sand-banks grow wider at the edges, and show higher in the centre, soon it must all be dry sand.

But even at the moment when sun is hottest, air driest, and water lowest, when literally the earth is at its last gasp for life, there comes, one night or morning, a swifter current in the channel, a darker colour in the clear green water—the great river is beginning to rise !

It is now the second week in May ; before the month has reached its end this change should have taken place. At first the saving tide comes with scarce perceptible increase, lapping the sandy edges of innumerable banks, and creeping a little higher upon the black and baked rocks, then growing daily stronger and stronger, rising higher and higher, until, in late August or early September, it pours along an enormous whirling flood of brown muddy water, submerging every rock and bank in its vast channel, blotting out its myriad cataracts, running smooth over its un-numbered rapids, and rolling down, level from bank to bank, that immense continuous fertilizing volume which, outspread over the Delta during three months, will give a year's life alike to master and to slave, 1300 miles below this Merawi stand-point.

And now turn from this sole life-giver, this river whose " single blessedness " of purpose rolls through a vast unblessed world, and look out upon the desert; you will not have far to go. Through all this immense distance it is ever a near neighbour, and through many a long mile the flinty rock or the yellow drifting sand end only at the water's edge.

Stop the boat, turn the camel aside, and walk

inland half a mile from the river, climb one of the million granite or sandstone hills, and look out upon the scene; eastward or westward, all the might of the desert is before you. It is only sand and rock, ash and cinder, drift and boulder lying spread out into a sky-line, sometimes of almost infinite remoteness, sometimes close at hand, sometimes set dark against lurid after-glows, sometimes lying clear cut against blue sky, or blotted out in the wrack of the Simoom, but always a scene that strikes the heart and brain of the beholder as never mountain mass or far-spread sea or fair expanse of gardened earth could do.

Dry and dead and withered though it be, the desert is still the grandest sight the eye of man can see on earth.

"Of what use is such a land?" I hear many worthy people exclaim. "You cannot have tall chimneys there. You cannot make cotton-cloth, nor work in steel, nor even grow wheat in that sea of sand, what good can there be in such a waste." So many people there are who go about through the world with their own particular two-foot measures in their hands, self-appointed measurers of the infinite, inspectors of the universe, two-foot rulers of creation. No doubt Rome under the last Cæsars had its two-foot measurers too, and the Greek of the lower empire held this

desert in very low estimation, and both thought
the Arab dweller a savage of the meanest capacity,
and yet somehow or other a day came when the
Arab from the desert broke to pieces the Greek
empire, and swept over the Roman world like the
Simoom of his own wastes.

And now Greek and Roman are gone, and half
a dozen later empires have followed them into the
tomb of Time—but the Arab is here still; this
desert is full of the salts of the earth. May it
not have been put here to keep fresh for some
later time the rod that has so often been the
scourge of the overseer, the measurer, and the
two-foot ruler of civilization ?

At what precise date the Arab from Arabia came
into these Nile deserts will never be known,
probably his chief migrations were made between
the eighth and eleventh centuries, the invaders
moving slowly from the sea-shore first into the
lands watered by the Abyssinian rivers, and
thence spreading out over all the Nubian wastes.

But at whatever period he came, he brought
with him across the Red Sea all his longings and
his hatreds—his longing for freedom, his untamed
spirit, his courage in battle, his patience under
heat, cold, thirst, hunger, and hardship, his fierce
impatience against the tax-collector, the usurer,
the master. He was hopeless to the man-tamer
in his old Arabian home, and now, too, he kept

unchanged his freedom, although whenever his
camels sought the rich pastures of the Delta
or the lower river it was to come into contact
with the most servile race on earth.

But long before ever an Arab had come into
this Nubian desert, the spirit of freedom had
been in it.   When Memphis was in its glory, and
the Nile rolled its yellow flood through Egypt's
living world of Palace, Tomb, and Temple, this
outside realm of Ethiopia was restless and defiant.
The land of Kush, as the region beyond the First
Cataract was called, was ever a thorn in the side
of Thebes ; a Sethi or a Rameses or a Thothmes
might march his hosts beyond the Cataracts, hew
a temple out of the rock, pull a Kushite city to
pieces, and take momentary tribute of gold, ivory,
slaves, and camelopards : but his triumph did not
last—Kush was soon in arms again, often following
close upon the retiring Pharaoh, and on more
than one occasion overrunning Egypt, and
seating a dark-skinned dynasty at Thebes.

Five hundred years go by, the Greek has come
upon the scene, but Ethiopia is to him what it was
to the Egyptian.   The frontier is now set at Syene,
Assouan (under Thothmes it was 250 miles farther
south).   Again, armies and expeditions are sent
out to punish the wild tribes, and again they retire,
leaving matters much as they were before.

The Greek goes, the Roman comes, but Ethiopia

is still the same. These wonderful milestones of empire could never be set much beyond Elephantine, as they then called Assouan. An Imperial army marched from the frontier fortress, which, still at Ibrim, like eagle's nest on lofty rock, marks the Roman eagles' southmost resting-place—passed the Cataracts, passed the Dongola of to-day, and here, at this sacred mountain of Gebel Barkal, defeated the armies of Queen Candace, and pulled down those very temples whose ruins dot the desert horizon over yonder beyond the palm-tops.

But there is another point of vision from which we get a glimpse at this land of Kush, just at this time of Rome's zenith power—a strange glimpse too.

Here is a scene that occurred one day about 1800 years ago—along " the way that goeth down from Jerusalem unto Gaza—this is desert." A rich traveller is journeying southwards, seated in his chariot. Around him are many soldiers and servants, for he is a man " of great authority under Queen Candace," of Ethiopia, " having charge over all her treasures."

He is reading aloud from a book which lies open before him, for he has come all this long weary way to seek Truth and to worship it.

Of the millions who read this Bible lesson, few care to ask whence came this first lord of Queen Candace's treasury on a quest so rare among men or ministers.

Queen Candace's capital was over there at the foot of Gebel Barkal, and yon lone group of pyramids cutting the sharp edge of the yellow desert and the overthrown columns and mounds at the base of the mountain are all that remain to-day of that once famous city. Gone now, the Queens and the Queendoms, the treasures and the treasurers—the desert wind blowing straight from the north, carries around our camp clouds of sand—sand of sun-crushed rock and wind-swept hill-top, pyramid sand, mummy sand — with perhaps a pin's head of the dust of forgotten empire in every league of storm—but the Truth which the great minister brought back from Jerusalem has since spread out over the world. No need to seek it now across blinding deserts. Right and left it stands as visible over the earth as yon sacred mountain is clear seen above this desert. Too easily found perhaps, to be sought after now, still less to be worshipped by minister or by man.

The Roman went his way—the early Christian came. How far up the great river the light spread into the dark continent will never be accurately known ; but Ethiopia had myriad churches when Gaul was still Pagan, and sandstone caves in the Nubian hills held Christian hermits when Druids were sacrificing in the oak glades of Britain. Of this Christian race the desert still holds ample testimony—testimony which even becomes more evident the farther we ascend the Nile. In the wildest regions of the Shagghieh rapids the remote isles of the Fourth Cataract hold crude brick churches of cruciform shape, and at times amid mounds of rubbish, or set to mark some Arab grave, one sees a broken column or shattered slab of marble, with the cross, or a Greek inscription still visible upon them.

It is certain that in those far-away regions a Christian kingdom long stood like an island amid the ocean of Mahommedanism, which, sweeping from the Red Sea and from the Mediterranean, spread over North-eastern Africa. Twenty years had not passed from Mahomet's death ere the Arab had overrun the Delta, and pushed his outposts to the Cataracts, but it was centuries before he conquered Nubia. Impossible though it may seem, the great wave of Arab conquest had reached Tours long before it touched Dongola. Mahomet was worshipped in Cordova before the white standard reached Kordofan; but Africa held no Norman race to raise itself as an iron shore against the Eastern flood; and once sunken beneath the tide of Islam, it could not lift its head again.

From the close of this Christian kingdom of Nubia to the beginning of the present century, the Soudan, as Ethiopia is now called, is without a history.

"Utterly waste and desolate from the tower of Syene to the borders of Ethiopia," it has lain a blank upon the map of the world. And yet the Arab conquest was not the darkest hour destined to pass over this dark country

In all the long list of victories gained by the great Corsican Captain, the battle of the Pyramids stands out in most striking form. From the field of Gizeh the broken remnants of the finest cavalry and the bravest soldiers the creed of Islam had ever produced, fled east and south. The southern detachment was pursued by Dessaix to the Cataract. There were no railways in those days, no telegraphs or steamboats, no preserved rations, nothing but Egyptian and desert life as the Arabs knew it; but all the same, neither Arab nor Mameluke could stop the march of those Frankish soldiers—and of all the inscriptions of victory which the temples of the Nile hand down to future time, there is none so simple or so grand as that which marks in the Temple of Philæ the limits of Napoleon's conquest.

From the head of the First Cataract at Philæ, the Mamelukes continued their retreat to a distant river-oasis, called Dongola. There, twelve hundred miles from Cairo, they set up their standard, and began the old life again—the life of fight and foray, which, for 600 years, they had followed in Egypt.

It would take long to tell the vicissitudes of fortune which followed the fugitives to their new home. Later in this narrative we may see on the theatre of their last exploits the closing scenes of their history. Enough now to say, that when twenty years later Mehemet Ali determined to undertake the conquest of the vast regions lying south of the Cataracts—stronger with him than the lust of conquest or greed of gold was the desire to follow to the death the last of the Mamelukes.

In 1819, an Egyptian army of invasion began its march from Wadi Halfa, under command of Mehemet's son, Ismail Pasha. The main army marched along the banks of the Nile—a fleet of 150 Dahabiehs and Nile craft followed on the river. After many delays and losses the boats passed at high Nile the cataracts between Wadi Halfa and Dongola; but the Shagghieh rapids proved an impassable obstacle, only nine boats, and these the lightest, succeeded in passing the Fourth Cataract; they were " dragged by the efforts of the entire population, impressed for the service, over the stones of the river channel "— the vast remainder left their bones on the wild rocks, and amid those terrible waters, where, for more than 100 miles the great river pours its flood down the winding stairways of Dar Monassir.

F

I have not space to dwell over the scenes of
this Turkish conquest, they were in their latter
stages at least, the old familiar ones which have
been so often recorded.

Skies black by day and red by night with the
smoke and flame of home and harvest; plunder,
destruction, outrage.—So came the Turk 500
years ago from his home beyond the Caspian, and
so it will be with him if to-morrow, or 500 years
hence, he has to go back again beyond the Oxus.

After conquering many provinces, and sending
expeditions East, South, and West from Sennar,
Ismail led his army back to Shendy (Khartoum
at that time did not exist). At Shendy there
dwelt a ruler named the Meg, whose *sobriquet*
of " Nim'r," or the Tiger, gives a glimpse of his
nature. History is conflicting as to the particular
form of insult or indignity which roused the Tiger
to his final vengeance; but the Arabs, who still
love to tell the story of the Meg's revenge, sometimes credit the Tiger's wife with the idea of the
crime.

While Ismail and his chief officers were deep in
sleep following a debauch in the midst of the
Turkish army, the shout and glow of fire broke
upon the camp. The Pacha's quarters were wrapt
in flames. Great contributions of grain and
forage had been levied upon the inhabitants, these
had been stored round the buildings occupied by

the Turkish Commander, and it was this straw which was now on fire. The straw or stalk of the Dhurra corn burns as no other straw can burn. In its flame is the quickness of parched grass, and the strength and heat of dry pine-wood. Great bundles of this stalk had been placed quietly at every door and window of the Pacha's dwelling—each outlet had been stopped. Caught in this flaming trap, Ismail and his chief officers were roasted to death.

When day dawned, the Tiger had fled to the Abyssinian hills. Mehemet Ali took a terrible vengeance upon Shendy a year or two after, but the Meg was never caught. Sixteen years later he is again at Shendy, and again he manages to get away into the fastnesses of the Abyssinian hills.

Since the date of the Turkish conquest, Soudan history can be easily told—war that has always been extermination, trade that has ever been in slaves, government that has always been cruel and corrupt—a narrowing area of cultivation, a wider wilderness of misery.

Like a stone flung into an abyss, the inquiry of the historical student soon reaches the depths of the Soudan question.

There is an episode in the history of Egyptian Nile Expeditions which deserves notice before we pass to the Soudan of yesterday and to-day.

About forty years ago, there came a Pacha and

his army up the Nile, bound for Khartoum. He was a son of Mehemet Ali's. On his road he halted for awhile in that wide reach of river where the Nile in a " sea-like stream " flows past the Tombs and Temples of Thebes. Here on the right bank of the river stands the most extensive, the oldest, and the most glorious ruin on the face of the earth—the great temple of Karnak. Here more numerous than at any other spot in Egypt, were to be seen those tall monoliths of red syenite, which, from the days of Imperial Rome down to our epoch, have formed the most remarkable trophies which Emperor, Pope, or People, could erect in their capitals. Karnak in its splendour, held four of these wonderful obelisks. We do not know how many stood erect when Abbas Pacha tied up his boat along the Nile shore, let us hope that time had mercifully laid low some of them.

Abbas had artillery with him. His gunners wanted practice. The tall and slender obelisks, standing half a mile away, were, to the Turkish mind, excellent targets placed there for his purposes ; and to-day if there is a red monolith standing erect at the end of that unmatched vista of pylon and pillar which the traveller beholds with silent awe, looking down the great hall of the Temple of the Sun, it is only because the aim of the Turkish gunners was not on a par with the savagery of their leader.

CHAPTER IV.

THE REVOLT OF ISLAM.

A ND now hav- ing looked at this Soudan, theatre of our coming effort, and lightly sketched the older history of the land beyond the Cataracts, it will be well if, still pausing before resum- ing the nar- rative of our expedition, we say something about events immediately preceding the present, time.

In that year of universal disturbance, 1848

there was born on a small island in the Nile,
midway between old and new Dongola, an Arab
child, destined to cause some commotion in the
world.

Time and place were alike fitted to give birth
to the leader of a revolt of Islam.   Beneath the
old monarchies of the Frankish kingdoms, the
internal fires of revolution were breaking into
flames.   Perhaps some echo of the struggles then
agitating these distant kingdoms came up the
long reaches of the Nile to the island of Konarté.

The father of the child was one Abdallah, a
boat-builder by trade, and it is possible that some
travelling merchant, or " Reis " of spoon-shaped
" Nugga " halting for repair of craft by the car-
penter's island, might have carried thither the
news that the infidels of the west had risen
against their masters.   But in truth there was no
need to bring from the outside world to distant
Dongola the news of rebellion—that kinship of
man must ever be a near neighbour to any spot
where the Arab has his dwelling.

The mother of the boy was named Amina, that
is all we know or are ever likely to know about
her, although it is more than possible that even
at this moment there are Arab men and women
in regions remote from Nubia who delight to tell,
or to hear, strange marvels about the mother
whose son has suddenly risen upon the long-

darkening horizon of their creed as the new light
of Islam.

It is possible, too, that as the boy grew into
youth, some neighbouring " Medressie," or passing
Dervish teacher, noticing difference of character
between him and his fellow-pupils, spoke of the
coincidence of his parents' names—Abdallah and
Amina—with those of the revered father and
mother of the Prophet. Much more we can fancy
in that simple life of the Arab on the upper river
shore, which I have so often watched when the
shadows began to lengthen over the eastern desert,
and the west was flaming with the glory of the
sunset.

While the boy was quite young, the family
migrated to a point on the river, some 600 or
700 miles higher up stream. Arab history in due
time, perhaps, will relate the reason of this
change; probably the boat-building business in
the long reach of smooth water between the Third
and Fourth Cataracts, began to feel the increasing
trade which in these years first passed from the
Red Sea to Berber, and a demand had arisen for
Murkabs and Nuggas on the wide, deep river
which stretched far beyond Khartoum into the
little-known south.

By the island of Abba, the boat-builder again
established himself. There the acacia and
sycamore grow to a size unknown in the drier

regions of the north, and there the old Dongola trade of boat-building was resumed.

Abba on the White Nile is the point of communication between Sennar and Kordofan, equidistant from Khartoum and from El Obied, its neighbouring ford, the only one in all Nile's length, is the direct route between the immense inland empire of Mahommedism in Africa and the shores of the Red Sea.

Year after year from distant desert kingdoms in the far interior, from Darfour, Wadai, and the Houssa regions of Lake Tchad, pilgrims passed, bound to, or from, the Sacred City of the Prophet.

What news they must have brought, those way-worn wanderers! News gathered at the remotest bounds of Islam, from Oxus and Ind, from Tripoli, Tunis, and Morocco, from Caucasus and Koosh, from Stamboul and Damascus, from Java and Malacca; and through all the news thus gathered at the Central News Mart of Mecca, there must ever have run the strain of evil tidings to the children of Islam—pressure of Muscovite on the north, of English in the east, of Frank in the west. Oh for a leader of the old type! Was there no warrior leader to go forth and head the Arab hosts again? Look around, this land of Africa was full of swarthy splendid soldiers. Alis, Kaleds, Mahomets, Othmans, Omars, Abdallahs, and Hassans by the tens of thousands; were they

not as dextrous of sword and spear as any warrior
that ever went forth to battle in the days of
the first Caliphs, against Greek phalanx, or
cavalry of Chosroe? and there were doubtless
many who shook their heads and said it was a
hopeless dream—the Infidels had the Evil One to
lead them, with the cunning of his craft. The
days of steel had gone by, it was no longer the
sword that gave victory, the " Venetian bullets [1]"
were more powerful than ever they had been, for
now they killed an enemy a thousand yards away.

But, on the other hand, had not this dark time
been foretold by the holy men of Islam. There
was to be a long night of defeat and persecution,
but it was to pass—the blood of the Imaums
had long called for vengeance—the dawn would
break upon the darkest hour of trial; the glory
of Islam would again arise; the prophet of the
prophet, the guide, the Mahdi would appear to
lead again the children of the desert across the
ruins of unrighteous empire. So the years went by.

From his cave in the isle of Abba, Mahomet
Achmet, the son of Abdallah, now grown to
man's estate—a sheikh, as well as a Dervish of
great repute—looked out upon the world. Many
holy men visited his retreat, listened to his words
of prayer and wisdom, and went their way to
spread the fame of his sanctity further through

---

[1] Name by which bullets were long known to the Arabs.

Islam. The lessons taught by the recluse of Abba Island were not new ones, however strange they may have sounded in the ears of the easy-going Egyptian officials in the Soudan.

"Adore God," he wrote; "hate not each other, but assist one another to do good. Let all show penitence before God, abandoning all bad and forbidden habits, such as the wicked acts of the flesh, the use of wine and tobacco, lying, bearing false witness, disobedience to parents, the non-restitution of goods stolen from others, improper signs with the eyes, slanderous language, calumny, the company of strange women, dancing and lamentations at the bed of the dead. Let your women be clothed in a decent manner, and let them not speak to unknown persons. Pray regularly, and give a tenth of all your goods to the public treasury of Islam."

But preach as he might, things grew no better in the Soudan, and the outlook of Islam was darker than ever. The Muscovite had come to the very gates of Stamboul. The English were drawing near the lower Nile. The French were spreading further along the northern coast of Africa, and never had the exactions, the tyranny, the oppression of the official been more grinding than now—the Egyptian ruler had sold his country to the Jewish bondholder, and the pound of flesh, extorted to the last grain, was being cut out of the very heart of Egypt. Truly the time had come. Behind the desert curtain the heart of Islam was beating strong and loud, the hour of revolt had struck, and the man was at hand.

In the month of May, 1881 people began to gather at Gezerah Abba in increasing numbers. A new prophet had appeared at that place. He preached one religion, one law, one ownership, one equality. There was one God he said, Mahomet was his prophet, and he, Mahomet Achmet, was the guide of Islam. Then began a revolt, which, whatever may be its end, has already set its mark in history. It is but four years since the strange flag with the cross and the Arabic prayers combined was first unfurled. Its followers were a few hundred Arabs carrying only swords and spears. How stands the struggle to-day? At least half a dozen Egyptian armies have measured their Remingtons and Gatlings against the swords and spears of the followers of the " false prophet"—the Remingtons and Gatlings are now in Arab hands, the Egyptian armies have been destroyed. Three times have English armies invaded the Soudan, and three times have they been withdrawn without result, save bloodshed and cost of millions.

Time after time men armed with swords and spears have assaulted in open desert British infantry in square ; and on more than one occasion these naked sons of the wilderness have done what the steel-clad cavalry of France could not effect at Waterloo.

It would take more time than I can give to trace the history of this revolt of Islam through these four years, but as my mind runs back over the chief acts in the long drama—the destruction of Hicks Pasha's army, the mission of Gordon to Khartoum, the destruction of Baker Pasha's army, the First Expedition to Suakim, the great Nile Expedition, the Fall of Khartoum, the death of Gordon, the Second Expedition to Suakim—I seem to grope through a desert of darkness in the attempt to find the reason of it all—the reason of it so far as we were concerned. What had we to do with this boat-building Dervish on Abba Island? In what deplorable manner did we manage to change sides and set ourselves against him? I remember, in August 1882, when the transports carrying the English army of invasion, lay in the harbour of Alexandria awaiting the movement on Ismailia, hearing one day our soldiers cheering vehemently; asking the reason for the enthusiasm, I was told it was because the Mahdi had defeated the Egyptian army with great slaughter in the Soudan.

Up to that date we were clearly on the Mahdi's side, his victory was looked upon as our victory; a year later the Egyptian soldiers who had fought against us at Tel-el-Keber were being drilled and organized at Khartoum by Hicks Pasha and half a score of English officers for an invasion of Kordofan, where the Mahdi then had his camp.

After that the sequence of trouble is clear enough —Hicks annihilated, Baker's army destroyed a few months later; Egyptian garrisons everywhere surrounded, all the pent-up Arab animosity of the sixty years of oppression and misgovernment at once let loose, and to heighten the exasperation and deepen the hatred of the revolt, the old creed quarrel between Christian and Moslem is added to the struggle by our appearance upon the scene as the allies or " subjects " of the Egyptians. One other matter, and that the mainspring of Soudan history in the past, remains to be noticed ere we come again to our story. It is the slave trade.

When the Egyptian conquest, in 1820, revealed the barrenness of the Upper Nile regions in gold, minerals, cereals, or vegetable productions of the earth, it opened up a new and apparently endless slave field.

Along the countless creeks and tributary streams of the great river dwelt negro tribes sufficient to fill the slave markets of Turkey, Syria, and Egypt for a century.

All through these decades of the thirties, forties, fifties, and sixties, herd after herd, drove after drove of wretched human beings were coming down the Nile, or wearily plodding the long "Arbain" roads that led northwards from the Soudan.

As year by year the Russian drew his cordon of conquest closer around the northern border of Turkish dominion, cutting off some Kurdish or Circassian province from the zone of slavery, the supply of slaves for the demands of Constantinople or Cairo had to be sought deeper in the equatorial regions.

It is now about twenty-five years since two intrepid travellers made known to the world that the interior of Africa, so long supposed to be a land of vast mountain ranges, was in reality a region of immense lakes.

Portuguese missionary priests had indeed told the same story 300 years earlier, but the knowledge of their discoveries had faded away in the sublime conceit of the eighteenth and nineteenth centuries, and in the commercial rivalries of nations.

With the knowledge of the equatorial lakes came the desire for further exploration. Baker followed Burton, Grant, and Speke, and at last the world knew the truth about the Soudan slave trade. But there was one thing which the world was slow to recognize, and that was the real source of all this misery. Not in Kordofan, not on the Bahr Gazelle, the White Nile, or the Blue

Nile, was the real cause to be sought, but on closer shores of the Mediterranean—amid the harems and households of the wealthy Turks. Kabba Rega or Tippoo Tib might indeed be at the Soudan end of the dismal Arbain road, but they were only the purveyors in ordinary to the thousand and one markets of Turkey, Egypt, and Syria.

Eleven years ago, there started from England, on a mission of civilization, conquest, and slave-trade suppression, a man who, even then, held foremost place among the brave hearts and noble souls of his generation.

No need to tell his story now ; the blow which cut short his life has stamped his memory deep upon the minds of his countrymen.

Cast in the prime of fighting life into the wide sea of Soudan misery, Gordon struck out in the years between 1874 and 1880, as a man would strike who, in the darkness of midnight, found himself assailed by numerous foes.

He flew from Abyssinia to Darfour, from Suakim to the great lakes. He fought Negro against Arab, Arab against Negro. One day he allied himself with some noted slave king ; the next, he was surrounding this slaver's stronghold, and thundering at his stockaded capital. He promoted, dismissed, rewarded, or executed with despotic power, but with strict impartiality.

His matchless energy gave him the mobility of twenty leaders. Like Napoleon, he distanced his escorts, and broke down his staff by the rapidity of his movements. He crossed deserts as though his camel had the wings of the simoom. He upset all the old traditions, and overturned the tables of Mecca law by supporting the Negro against the Arab, the slave against the master, and for the first time in its long misery the Soudan beheld strength and justice united in the hand of Government. All this went on for six years, —the slave trade was checked, the most noted traders were destroyed or driven out; but it was the check given to the current of a river by the sudden fall of an avalanche, the tide stopped for a time broke into unthought-of channels, soon to submerge all landmarks beneath it.

How long the black cauldron of the Soudan would have continued seething and simmering in its corruption, before boiling over in Arab revolt, it is impossible to determine, but it is certain that the rule of Gordon in the Soudan accelerated the day of retribution by years. Of this he was himself convinced.

" Things have come to such a pass," he writes in 1876, " in these Mussulman countries, that a crisis must come about soon." Again in 1879, he says : " If the liberation of slaves takes place in 1884, there cannot fail to be a revolt of the whole country." The revolt of the whole country began, as we have seen, in 1881. Everything was ready for it. "I had taught the natives that they had a right to exist. I had taught them something of the meaning of liberty and justice ;" thus Gordon wrote after the revolt had broken out.

What this insurrection really meant we have already seen. In a hundred proclamations we can now trace its objects. "The time of the Turk is over." "The line of their dominion is cut, and what God has cut, man cannot put together again." "We are men who love death as ye love life, and who count, in fighting you, on the great reward." "Death is dearer to us than our lives, and the very best of our possessions." These, if they stood alone, might well be passed by as empty words, but they did not stand alone. Many have been the surprises of war, and the hard logic of the battle-field has often dispelled the theories of the class-room, but never have the accepted canons of military art been more completely reversed than in this struggle of Arab Africa in the Soudan. History will make no mistake on this head. If Berber was not gained, if Gordon was not saved, the reason was because there were 30,000 Arabs whose deeds were equal to their words. If any man had said four years ago that it was possible for naked Arabs armed with

swords and spears to break into squares of
infantry armed with the most effective breech-
loading rifle, such a man would have been laughed
to scorn.

There is no need for us now to enter into the
question of whether the steps taken by Gordon
on his arrival in Khartoum in February, 1884,
were in exact accordance with the views of the
Ministers who had sent him to the Soudan. The
Soudan in London and the Soudan at home are
two very different things; all the phrases of
diplomatic correspondence, the verbiage with
which the sitter in the easy chair often en-
deavours to force himself and the world to believe
in his omniscience, are of small avail when
brought face to face with the realities of a state of
life such as the Emir Ali Mahommed-Abou-Iaad-
Esshawtrawhi-al-Albadi thus describes in a letter
to a friend at this time: " Know ye, my friend,
that the world is turned upside down, and that
henceforward there will be nothing but preparation for the Holy War, in the path of God—and
the spending of treasure and life at the pleasure
of God and His Prophet."

It was into such a scene that the most restless
spirit in the history of the nineteenth century
found himself introduced in the spring of 1884;
nor had he come to it as a stranger, knowing
nothing of its previous tumults, but as the man

who had been its master only a few years before.

Was it possible that the chief who had carried fire and sword for six years among the slave-kings; who had overrun Darfour, swept Kordofan, subdued Unyoro, and threatened Abyssinia, could have now remained a quiet spectator in such a scene of war? Gordon was no man's mouthpiece, no human telephone, so dear to the modern stool-sitter. Among his last words are these: " It was never our Government that made us a great nation. England was made by adventurers, not by its Government; and I believe it will only hold its place by adventurers." When he wrote these lines it is not unlikely that the memory of his own life was before him. In this England of to-day there had been no room for him. It was only in remote parts of the earth, and in the service of semi-barbarous states, that he could find scope for his greatness.

The man who on the vast horizons of Asia and Africa blazed like a sun, had been scarce known in his own land. Above the waste of yellow desert, near the pyramids of Gizeh, a great rock cut into the form of a human head looks across all the wretchedness of modern Egypt into the desert and the sunrise beyond. Men have named it the Sphinx. The drift of the desert has blown across it. That is all we know about it. Has it been left to mark the ebb of life from some vaster human ideal? Is it a lonely relic of a world now sunken beneath the sea of Time, still left looking into the sunrise waiting for some future resurrection?

So, when I think over the solitary figure of the great Celtic soldier, standing far out in the desert, waiting for the end, it seems to me that he, too, has been set there to mark for ever the real height he held among the children of his day.

Better that thus it should have been, than that, brought back by our little hands, he should have been lost to us again in the babble of our streets.

The vastness of this desert death fitted the lonely grandeur of his life, and evermore he stands looking across the centuries, the mark and measure of Christian knighthood, alike to the children of Islam, who dimly felt his power, and to the sons of modern unbelief who knew so little of his glory.

.   .   .   .

The last pages were written in the middle of May at Merawi. It is now early in October, and I continue this narrative under very different conditions from those which saw its commencement six months ago.

On the 26th of last May, I put the infantry garrison into our old boats once more, blew up the mud fort, and marched away with the mounted troops for Dongola.

The last sight of the distant place which had been our home during three months was a curious one.

With considerable difficulty we had kept back a crowd of hungry Shagghieh Arabs from forcing the line of cavalry and entering our abandoned fort, under the belief that it contained rich store of plunder. It was useless to tell them that the place had been mined, and that in a few minutes it would be blown into the air.

They seemed to consider the whole thing as got up to delay the moment when they would reach the expected treasures within. It is needless to say that these treasures consisted only of a few broken water-vessels, old boxes, and native bedsteads.

For some days previous, the bastions and the front face of the fort had been mined by the engineers. Seventy-five pounds of gun-cotton were put in the mines. All was now ready for the last boat of the Royal Highlanders to quit the shore.

When the Arabs saw the lighted match brought, they realized at last that an explosion was about to take place; and running back through the picquet-line, they lay down in hollows of the desert. Scarcely had the engineer officer who fired the fuses reached a place of safety when the mines exploded. A great cloud of smoke and sand burst from the front face, and out of it showers of baked mud and stones were projected on all sides. A loud detonation shook the surrounding desert. When the cloud partly lifted, the front of the fort was seen in three great breaches, having slid forward into the desert. In another second the Arabs, charging from every direction, went up the breaches like three assaulting columns, shouting and waving their arms amid the dust and smoke. They were soon hidden from sight; then we turned our horses' heads to the south, and began the march to Dongola. A mile away from the fort I stopped to take a last look; the cloud of smoke was drifting slowly across the desert. Gebel Barkal stood out on the northern horizon, and still above the fringe of palms the Pyramids and ruined Sphinxes of Nepata rose on the lone sky-line.

Those who have looked long upon the Egyptian Sphinx have thought that they could trace in that changeless face the semblance of a smile. Why should it not be there? These eyes have seen Persian, Greek, Roman, and Frank, come and go; and now across that stony vision the hosts of the Northern Islanders were passing away for ever.

We marched for ten days through heat impossible to describe. At times, terrific dust-storms swept the desert; at times the moon rose over the now quiet flowing river, as the moon can only rise in the desert and the Arctic regions—as though it seems to realize in those two extremes of the earth its own terrible extremes of ice and heat. This march, and a rapid visit to England, obliged me to put by my narrative.

Again appointed to command the new Soudan frontier—450 miles below the old line at Merawi —I now take up the story; but interruptions are frequent, and if the Arab flood which was set loose by the fall of Khartoum continues to flow north, it is not unlikely I shall again have to lay aside my manuscript.

CHAPTER V.

IN WHICH WE SEE MANY OLD THINGS.

OTWITH-STANDING these journeyings through distant Soudan regions, we have been all this while, so far as the thread of our personal narrative is concerned, sitting in complete rest upon the forecastle of the *Minerve*, while that overcrowded steamship held her way towards Egypt. At five o'clock on the evening of 24th September we entered the harbour of Alex-

andria. At the Gabarri Wharf two steamers
were lying, and as we passed near them, light-
coloured boats, that looked very small and slight,
could be seen held high in the crane slings as
they were being swung out from the decks of
the steamers to the wharf, where two trains
were drawn up to receive them. They were our
English boats. Not six weeks yet since first
ribs had been laid, and here were two steamers
already unloading at Alexandria, and the first
train timed to start for Assiout at midnight this
very night.

The Yarrow stern-wheel steamer, in her 700
and odd pieces, had also arrived. Bit by bit
we were gaining upon our estimate—another
week should see one hundred of our boats at
Assiout, 350 miles up the Nile. How hopeful it
all looked at sunset that evening as, after land-
ing, I watched the last boats being stowed upon
the trucks—securely packed in beds of coal,—
and protected with mats overhead as shelter
against the morrow's sun. Yes, it all looked
promising enough; but could one have seen a
sight some 1600 miles up the great river, upon
which the sun was looking at this moment, it
would not have appeared so hopeful to us.

This was the sight the sun saw about this
evening of 24th September, or within a day or
two of that date.

It is a vast landscape of rock and sand through which the river flows almost south. The Nile is in topmost flood, its red waters running all but level with the small margin of smooth shore which lies between the rocks and the river; slightly raised above this narrow margin stand a few mud-walled houses, with flat low roofs, low doorways, and small holes for light; little patches of green dhurra and cotton grow on the level margin, and a single group of palm-trees on the edge of the river breaks the vast monotony of black granite rock and waste of yellow sand beyond. The broad current of the flooded river is broken by a small diamond-shaped island lying nearer to the right bank (that upon which we have been looking) than to the left; and between this island and the right bank lies a wrecked steamer —a tiny boat to carry steam and paddles and machinery—but, big or little, her course is now run, for she lies hopelessly fixed upon a group of rocks that tilt her bows clear out of the quick-running stream.

So hopelessly wrecked is this small boat that all the crew have left her, and come over from the island to the houses on the right shore. Peace has been made with the villagers, and the Sheikh of the tribe has arrived from his village ten miles lower down stream. He, too, has assured the passengers and crew of safety, and has promised to provide them with camels for the continuance of their journey to Merawi, some seventy miles away, where the " Turk " still holds his last outpost in Arab-land.

This wrecked boat had left Khartoum ten days earlier, had passed the cataract of the " Wild Cows " and that of the "Wild Asses," had passed, too, the long rapids at Mograt Island, and was now entering the country of the Monassir Arabs, where for one hundred miles the Nile pours its waters through hundreds of rocky channels, amid whirlpools and torrents whose voice can be heard far over the bordering wastes of rock and desert: only at this the top-most stage of the river, might any steamboat hope to descend in safety these tremendous cataracts. How vain was that hope we have already seen ; the boat has been lost before the true cataracts of Monassir and Shaghieh have even been entered upon. Wrecked here, because the lesser channel between the island and the right shore has been followed instead of the main river which flows on the other side of the island. Whether this selection of the fatal passage has been made by accident or design will never be known until all the story of life and death is told, and then, perhaps, it will be found that the thing we call " accident " has but a small value in the final appraisement.

The wrecked party have landed on the right shore, and are now in the group of huts amid the lower rocks about one hundred yards from the river; they have been invited hither to talk with the Sheikh of the Monassir, and to arrange further payment for the camels which are to carry them to Merawi.

Around the mud houses, and down near the group of palm-trees, many Arabs are standing about; all have swords or spears; the party from the steamer carry no weapons, as the Sheikh has specially asked them to come unarmed—a strange request in a land where the lance or sword are as the canes and walking-sticks of civilization.

Suddenly, as the sun is going down behind the wild rocks at the back of the huts, there is a rush of armed Arabs; within the houses three Europeans are struck down with sword-blow and thrust of spear; without, at the group of palms another scene of slaughter is going on among the Egyptian soldiers and sailors of the wrecked vessel. It is all only the work of a few minutes, and then the sun has set, and the Nile rolls on its flooded course, bearing down to the wild rapids of Uss a few specks of death—all that earth now holds, save one, of England's garrison in the Soudan.

It has been said of man, that although he alone among the animals of the earth knows

that he has to die, he alone can laugh. If ever
it should come about that some more perfect
form of electric communication will show us what
the world is doing instantaneously in every part
of its vast spaces, perhaps the laughter of man
will not be so frequent. At all events could we at
Alexandria have seen the scene at Hebeh on the
Nile, on this 24th September, our prospects
would not have seemed so promising, nor our
satisfaction been so complete.

It was late at night when I got away from
Gabarri for Cairo; the trains with the boats
would start a couple of hours later. They were
timed to pass the Boulac Darcour station at nine
o'clock next morning. I would be able to see
them as they passed, and to judge how far the
railway journey had injured them, for among the
long list of foretold evils to our scheme, this
Egyptian railroad journey had not been omitted.

The Boulac Darcour station stands nearly half-
way between Cairo and the Pyramids, and marks
almost the ground where the right of the French
army rested when that never-to-be-forgotten
order told the flushed and triumphant troops that
forty centuries of history were looking down upon
their victory.

As I drove along the tree-shaded avenue leading from Cairo, on the morning of the 25th, I
encountered two horsemen, riding back from the

Pyramids.   One of them was the leader of this new Nile Expedition, an effort grander even than the great Captain of War could ever have allowed his imagination to conceive.

Near by, the Nile was rolling along in all the majesty of its flooded volume.   Two thousand miles up that great river lay the object of our effort.   A couple of miles away to the west long trains were already bearing our boats to launch them 250 miles higher up the river, and it was only six weeks since the first boat-keel had been laid in England.

The horsemen pulled up.   I got out of the carriage, and, saluting the general, briefly reported to him our progress.   "Put it all down exactly as it has happened," he said; "it will be a curious story to hear some day."

When I reached the railway station, the first train, carrying thirty-three boats, had come in. Not a boat had stirred; not a plank suffered injury; the officer in charge alone showed the effect of the journey.   Black as a coalheaver from the dust of the coal in which the keels of the boats were lying, he was now trying his best to wash himself white again.[1]

Satisfied that so far as the journey by rail was concerned, our boats could defy the wear and tear of a month's exposure such as this, I drove

[1] Lieut. W. Peel, 2nd Life Guards.

back to Cairo, and the trains passed on to their destination. But had I known that only on the preceding night the Egyptian army commissariat officials had despatched eighty waggon-loads of beans, lentils, and other food along this line of single rails to Assiout, blocking thereby the approach to the Nile at the latter place and delaying our boats for three days, I might not have felt so happily disposed to all my fellow-creatures.

I remained in Cairo during the next six days. Steamers arrived daily at Alexandria, and the despatch of boats and stores by train went on without check; but the beans and lentils still held their ground at Assiout, and it was not until the last day of September that the first river-steamer, carrying boats, got away for Assouan.

Modern Cairo is one of the saddest sights the world holds to-day. Amid its glorious tombs and in the ruins of mosques that recall the most brilliant days of Arab art, the lowest extremes of the humanity of three continents fight for a supremacy of theft.

If, in this maze of old ruin and modern café—this dying Mecca and still-born Rue de Rivoli—it was only Greek who met Greek in the tug of the modern shop, all the fact of the wretchedness of Cairine life might not be so apparent; but Greek and Jew, Armenian and Copt, Syrian and Levantine elbow each other in these crowded streets, while the native of the Delta seems to sit gazing with blurred ophthalmic vision—dazed among the rival rascals who are robbing him of his birth-right.

Behind all this modern Cairo there lies a won-drous city—a city of the dead. Monuments of forgotten cities that had passed away before ever Arab entered Egypt; ruins of Misrâh and Fostât; tombs of Abbasside Sultans and of Mameluke Beys; broken aqueducts, ruined mosques, and the headstones and white pebbles of unnumbered Arab graves.

Some Arab writer speaks of Cairo being twenty miles in circumference even when Sultan Selim took it, and, looking at the vast encirling ruins that to-day spread out into the desert around the modern city, one can believe the description.

There is a window on the west side of the Zuffren Palace in the citadel of Cairo, at which it is said Mehemet Ali spent the last years of his long life looking out over the unmatched panorama spread beneath. There is no other view in the world that holds so much history, and although the old Albanian ruler was too good a Turk to trouble his head much about the past, thinking perhaps, like his great prototype the first Selim, that the Pyramids were not worth a visit, still there is enough in the scene itself—city, river, verdure, Pyramids, and desert—to quicken the slowest brain that ever lay within a Tartar's skull.

Nor, looking at this view from the citadel rampart is there need to go back into the life of older Egypt to find food for thought. Between you and yon Pyramids most of the great ones of the earth have passed—Cambyses, Alexander, Cæsar, Antony, Amrou, Napoleon. Those twin pointed piles that rise so sharp and high against the red horizon have been magnets to draw the great iron-minded ones of history to their feet.

Selim, as we have said, would not go to the Pyramids. He was, perhaps, too busily employed during his five months' sojourn in Cairo, in the slaughter of 60,000 captives, and in loading 1000 camels with the gold and silver of the capital. He was the first Turk who entered Egypt.

But we must not linger here.

On the 1st of October I left Cairo for the south. It was pleasant to quit the modern city, with its mixture of stucco palace, wretchedness, and ruin ; its Shubbra road, where French fashion, harem life, and the abject misery of the fellaheen jostle each other in a confusion, which would be laughable if it were not hopelessly sad, and to get out into the peasant life of Egypt again— the fields of green maize, tall sugar-cane waving in the north wind, cotton, dhurra, and sweet-

11

smelling beans ; pleasant to watch this toiling fellah, whose power of turning sand into fruitful garden has made him the easy prey of the soldier and the usurer through 4000 years.   Poor fellow ! had he worked less at his " shadouf " and more at his spear-heads, he might have fared better in history ; and yet withal there is a strange lesson to be learned even in this " base native " who will only work and will not fight.   In all his history he has never fought ; he has never governed himself ; and yet he alone has kept his country. Nowhere else on the earth are you so certain that you see before you the people who were there one, two, three, four thousand years ago.   In Egypt there can be no doubt about it.   At the first railway station you come to you will see the same faces and the same figures which are familiar to you in the wall-pictures of a score of temples.

Nor are the wall-pictures the only evidence of this identity of race between the fellaheen of to-day and the builders of the Pyramids.   In the mummies of men and women, king and queen and priest mummies, taken from the Theban hills, or found at Memphis, can be read the undoubted proof that those who till and toil to-day were once the ruling race on earth.

So spake the Prophet when Thebes was in her glory, before Cambyses swept the temples of

Memphis: " And I will bring again the captivity
of Egypt, and will cause them to return into
the land of Pathros (Egypt), into the land of
their habitation, and they shall be there a base
kingdom."

The railway that runs to Assiout on the Nile
has the reputation of being the most uncomfortable
line in the world ; and certainly if heat, dust, and
delay have anything to say to discomfort, it would
be difficult to beat it.

The 1st of October was the beginning of the
Feast of Bairam.   All the tumble-down mud
towns and villages were holding festival.   Arabs,
fellahs, Copts, and Moslems crowded the hot
platforms.   At every sun-baked station the guard
of our train appeared to be under the impression
that the chief object for which we were perform-
ing this journey was to enable him to greet a
wide circle of male friends with repeated em-
braces ; a performance which, however satisfactory to the estimation in which he was held in
Upper Egypt, was by no means calculated to
ensure speed.

Now and again a lonely pyramid, standing
upon the edge of the western desert, caught the
eye, and sent thought back through the centuries,
from misery to majesty.

It was night when we reached Assiout.   Many
steamers were lying at the wharf, piled high with

our English boats. The block had ceased, and more than 100 boats were already *en route* for Assouan.

Here at Assiout our boats had reached the Nile. This broad blue river—blue in the moonlight that was now over it—was the same stream whose waters washed the walls of the goal of our expedition 1600 miles from this spot.

And yet here, 400 miles from the sea, our real race was not even begun—we were still 600 miles from the starting-point at Sarras. Across that void of 1600 miles between us and Khartoum, Gordon was on this night already looking for us. We know now that it was on the 1st of October he sent his steamers to await us at Shendy.

Next day I embarked in a small steam-launch, placed at my disposal by a gentleman[2] whose name should ever be associated with the good work done in this Expedition, and for three days passed up the big river, looking out upon the life of the land—the mud village, the pigeons in the Coptic towers, the shadouf water-lift, the sakeeyeh-wheel, the fringe of date-palms rustling in the north breeze, the groups of naked children racing along the banks, the fields of waving dhurra, the goats that are half sheep and the sheep that look whole goats, and the toil of water-lifting from the full-fed river to the thirsty shores that goes

[2] M. Rustovitch.

on, by bent back of fellah and ceaseless circle of oxen, night and day.

Hay is not made on the Nile while the sun shines, but while the river flows, and early and late this lift of water by "shadouf" and "sakeeyeh" must be continued, for in another month the now high-running flood will be fast sinking from its upper level, and the labour of the lifter will be doubled.

The Nile below the Second Cataract has probably had more people to tell its story than any other river in the world, and there is scarce a bookstall in England which would not be found to supply the most exact information on the height and number of the pillars at Denderah, equally with the price of chickens at Girgeh. It might be said indeed that the literature of a considerable portion of Nile travel consists of equal divisions of antiquity and aliment. These, with a general sense of unspoken but continually implied superiority of the modern Briton over anything the world has yet seen, not excluding Sesostris, Cambyses, Cæsar, and Alexander from the parallel, have done a good deal towards what is called bringing the subject of the Nile down to the level of the masses. No portion of the great river has undergone this lowering process more completely than this part between Assiout and Assouan, over which the little launch *Iris* is now speeding.

So low indeed would the stream appear to have been brought, that more than once the *Iris* and her companions managed to get aground upon the top of some submerged sand-bank; and as this event generally occurred in the late night, when the Reis had fallen at his post, asleep, one was often roused from rest by a sudden shock, to find the boat tilted over on its side at an angle that was bound to suggest ideas of probable immersion in the quick-running river.

Despite the popularization process and its inconveniences, there came moments on this upward journey to be long remembered—one scene in particular. It was the night of the 4th October. We were running up the centre of that long reach of river where the desert hills, retreating from the shores, leave a wide space of level land on either side of the "sea-like stream" which here once washed the walls of Thebes.

The night was worthy of the scene. A full moon rode in the zenith; to the south, Canopus burned above the desert rim. All the poverty and wretched ruin of Egypt were hidden; moonlight had wrapped its cloth of gold around the misery of the fellah, and left us only the river, the stars, and the outline of the hills. The Nile poured down its mighty volume, no longer turbid, as in daylight, but flowing blue and silvered in the glory of the Egyptian night.

The night breeze, blowing cool and gentle after
the heat of day, and the measured stroke of the
engine, brought rest to every sense, and I was
soon asleep on the little deck. A shout from the
Reis roused me. What had happened? All the
light was gone, and a dull, dead colour overspread
land and water. Our sister launch, the *Maud*,
was steering down upon us across stream at full
speed Her Reis had gone fast asleep, and with
his helm anyhow was now about to ram us.
Shouts and imprecations roused him, and between
our efforts and his own the collision was brought
to a striking angle that did not smash anything.
But, meantime, what had become of the moon?
I looked from underneath the awning, and the
darkness was soon explained. The full moon was
reduced to little more than a new moon. It was
an eclipse, soon to be a total one. Gradually the
shadow deepened, a thin edge of light lay around
the disc of the moon, and then the fringe of light
grew broader on the further side. While yet the
dull light of the eclipse overlay river and shore, a
great wall rose amid palm-trees on the right bank.
It was the front pylon of the Temple at Karnak.
Twenty minutes later we put in to the east bank
at Luxor. The moon was now clear of shadow,
and in all its light two long lines of gigantic
columns rose above mounds of clay; from capital
to capital stretched enormous single blocks of red

stone ; above this vast entablature a sharp-pointed obelisk rose against the sky. If the eye was inclined to doubt the reality of the size of these columns and pediments, the moonlight was there to bring their great shadows within reach of measurement. Vast and dark upon the moonlit dust, lay the shadow of a reality which was itself only a shadow—the ruins of the great Temple of Luxor.

A mile from Luxor, in low ground, where the life of the fellah is lived in mud hovel and bean-patch, where the wind moans through the dry leaves of scattered dom-palms, stands the ruined Temple of Karnak. We know all about it now. Belzoni has dragged to light from their cunningly devised hiding-places, over yonder in the Theban hills, the dust of the dead builders of this gigantic pile. Mariette has read the stone-cut beetles, the little birds, and the whole array of hieroglyphics that cover the columns of the great hall. We know who built the sanctuary, who reared the various pylons, what king set up the sphinxes, who quarried and carried those wonderful obelisks. We know the campaigns that one king fought on the Orontes, and the expeditions which another king made beyond the Cataracts. We know the names of the sculptors who cut the images, of the painters who coloured the frescoes, the quarries whence the great blocks were hewn, and of the years

that went by in the building of the mighty mass;
and we know all the grandeur they wished to tell
us, and a good deal of the littleness they wished
to hide from us. We know that Rameses rubbed
out the cartouch of Sethi, and Thothmes tried
to obliterate the name of Rameses; and that a
modern official is not more anxious to write his
signature below the labour of his prototype than
was an Egyptian king 3000 years ago desirous of
cutting his sign-manual upon the pylon of his
predecessor. And yet with all our knowledge we
are much where we were before. To go to Karnak
with the guide-book is something like lying on
your face in the middle of the desert at midnight,
with a farthing candle in one hand, and the outlines of astronomy in the other, imagining you
were watching the night-march of the starry host
across the wilderness. No; dates and measurements won't do at Karnak. In this forest of pillars,
this cataclysm of monolith, statue, sphinx, and
column, the story-teller and the compiler have no
place. Abbas Pacha couldn't knock down with
his artillery these two red granite needles, and
Murray and Baedeker, with their host of lesser
measurers, have been just as powerless to bring
this wide wilderness of ruin within the canons of
the tourist's bible.

I have read somewhere of one bit of testimony
given to ruined Thebes which seemed to be for

once in keeping with the grandeur of the scene. When the French army, under Dessaix, in the last year of the last century, came in sight of these vast temples, an instantaneous emotion spread through the ranks. Chiefs and soldiers halted by a common impulse, and with uplifted swords and presented arms, the whole army saluted Thebes. Such was the homage paid by the young army of Napoleon before the relics of Sesostris. It remained for our own time to out-Abbas Abbas. On board the *Iris* I had an official guide-book, printed in London, for the better navigation of the Nile and the clearer comprehension of its shores. This is an extract from that report :— " At Karnak there are some old ruins to the westward, on slightly raised ground, from which heliographic communication could take place with the minarets at Kench." That the Temple of the Sun would be a fitting spot for heliographic signals no one would be disposed to deny, but that the Theban temples should be described as " some old ruins to the westward" is sufficient to make the mummy of the great Rameses moan in the museum of Boulak. Let us get away while we may.

When we got back to the *Iris*, confusion reigned on board that tiny craft. The engineer was absent ; the Reis had declared war against the Reis of the *Maud*, and the black stoker appeared to be the only reliable person in the united crews. Appealed to through the interpreter as to the whereabouts of the Maltese engineer, this stoker appealed in turn to a crowd of naked Arab boys, who combined an incessant demand for " backsheesh " with an intermittent tendency to throw mud at us. More than one of these infant Mahdists now declared that the where-abouts of the missing Louis was a secret known only to himself, and that for a consideration he was willing to divulge the knowledge. Prolonged use of the steam whistle at the hands of the negro stoker having produced no other result than partial deafness to ourselves, and complete delight to the small boys, we determined to issue to a police functionary, who was standing near, a commission to arrest and deliver the body of the missing Maltese. This was followed by a rush of small Arabs and old policemen in various directions among the mud huts, all equally anxious to have some hand in the work of conveying a recalcitrant European to justice.

Finally, from behind the pillars of the great temple appeared our engineer ; he was surrounded by a posse of police sufficient to have formed the escort of a first-class murderer. An officer of gendarmerie held Louis by the arm ; three other policemen and several small boys carried large water-melons as though those ponderous fruits had been unmistakable evidences against the prisoner of some deep-laid crime.

When the rival Reises saw that the onus of delay could no longer be laid upon the shoulders of the Maltese, and that there was now a prospect of an immediate start, their hostility towards each other became more bitter. Finally, the whole crowd appeared before me to settle the dispute. As my interpreter laboured under the difficulty of having about one English equivalent for every 200 Arabic words in his vocabulary, my knowledge of the cause of dispute was vague, and I therefore contented myself with declaring that there was nothing for it but to refer the whole question to the Board of Trade, with a view to the suspension of the sailing certificates of the three Reises. Although the efforts of the interpreter to explain this decision to the crowd were painful in the amount of physical exertion they involved, it was still gratifying to observe the respect paid to an important department of English life by the mixed inhabitants of Luxor. A magic silence fell upon the principals, their seconds, and upon the crowd, and we steamed away from the wharf as though Somerset House had changed places with the Temple of Luxor.

This was on the afternoon of the 5th October, and at daylight on the 7th we were at anchor at Assouan.

CHAPTER VI.

IN WHICH WE PASS THE FIRST AND SECOND CATARACTS.

T Assouan would begin the first real test of our boats, for here the Nile flows for some six miles amid granite islands, and through many rock-encumbered channels, and a difference of sixteen or eighteen feet between the water-levels at Elephantine and Philæ, causes what is called the First Cataract. Here then at this First Cataract our much-abused craft were to make their first essay in Nile navigation, the starting-point being the old Tower of

Syene, the winning-post the famous temple at
Philæ. I had not long to wait for the trial.

At noon on October 7th the first steamer
arrived, carrying thirty-two boats; by the same
evening they were all afloat off Elephantine Island,
and early next morning the ascent of the cataract
began.

A dozen boats were taken in tow of the launch
Iris, and brought up through the lower "gate"
to the village of Mahatta, where the first rough
water begins. They were here handed over to
Sheikh Keiralla of the cataract, who with about
100 of his "Shillal" Arabs stood waiting for
them.

Then began a curious sight. In the twinkling
of an eye the naked Arabs were on board, and
the boats were out in the rushing stream. If
there had ever been a doubt on my mind as to
the practicability of our craft to cope with a
Nile rapid, that doubt would have been soon dispelled, for the Arabs, utterly disdaining ordinary
methods of hauling from the shore, began to shove
the boats forward, sometimes in them and often
out of them, swimming, poling, and diving as
easily as a lot of laughing children would slide
straws along an English brook.

Accustomed to the labour of dragging heavy
native vessels up this cataract, the "Shillal" men
now made nothing of our light and buoyant

boats. They paddled, poled, swam and splashed, shouting all the while. Sheikh Keiralla appeared to be much shocked at the want of gravity displayed by his people, and as long as any of them were within reach, he and a couple of his particular henchmen, running along the bank, continued to pelt his servitors with dry Nile mud; but the ascent was too rapid to allow this mode of dissatisfaction to be long indulged in, and a few minutes sufficed to carry all out of our sight. Three hours later the entire twelve boats were lying safely at anchor opposite the Temple of Philæ, and the cataract was seeing again repeated, with succeeding convoys, the antics of the morning.

As the sun set that evening, I stood on the east bank of the river watching the last of our thirty-two vessels coming in to their anchorage, some of them arriving in charge of old men and small boys, all of them having passed the First Cataract without the smallest accident or difficulty.

Across the sky-coloured bay in which the fleet was anchored rose the palms and columns of the sacred island, Philæ the Beautiful; beyond the ruins, the wild rocks that keep sentinel around this famous spot were topped by the distant wastes of the western desert; and beyond all, boats, ruins, rocks, and desert, the saffron afterglow was in its glory.

Having seen the start and finish, I wished to see the cataract throughout its course, and accordingly on the morning of the 9th of October I embarked in No. 69 with five Arabs. My crew worked away much in the same fashion as that of yesterday, dipping the oars anyhow, splashing, diving, and poling, but moving up the rapids all the same. We had gained a point about midway in the ascent, when suddenly around an island point swept a large vessel running down the main channel of the cataract with all the rapidity which crew and current could give it.

This craft carried a high English Minister, and as I stood up in my little boat to salute him it was impossible not to feel a sense of deep satisfaction at the coincidence which had made the First Lord of the Admiralty the first spectator of our success in the First Cataract of the Nile.

By the 14th of October more than 200 boats had passed the First Cataract, and 130 of these had gone on to Wadi Halfa. It was time for me, too, to go forward to the more formidable obstacle of the Second Cataract, which had always been looked upon as the *crux* of our difficulties.

Accordingly on the 15th I left Philæ for Wadi Halfa. Above the former place the Nile lies in an unbroken water-way of 220 miles. Deep and broad the river rolls for the greater portion of that distance between two bordering lines of desert hills, which are frequently impending rocks rising sheer from the water; intervals of palm-trees and spots of vegetation occur, and between the arid hills and the river a narrow fringe of cultivation sometimes runs for a long distance; but so thin is this margin between water and desert, that for scores of miles there is not space for the living to find room for a hut, or for the dead to find a grave in.

But with all its desolation this Nubian Nile is in every way grander than the Egyptian river. In the length and beauty of its reaches, in the grandeur of its deserts, in the colour and outline of its rugged hills, in the unending sense of space which the mind here first begins to grasp when the sun goes down beyond the sands of the western desert; in all but its temples, and even in one of these, the river is more striking above the First Cataract than below it.

We steamed slowly along, towing two dahabiehs and fourteen of our boats; the days were still intensely hot, the thermometer going up to 96 degrees in the afternoon, in the coolest part of the vessel. Somewhere about midday, between Philæ and Wadi Halfa a flight of swallows passed, going south; but with a temperature in the nineties, it could not be said they had brought winter with them from the north they had so lately quitted.

I

It is only when the traveller enters Nubia that he is able at a glance to realize the complete helplessness of the Egyptian to escape from the clutches of any ruler who plants himself in the Delta.

There is no escape from Egypt—the man who holds the Delta holds by the throat this long line of river; hence it has happened that a conquering race, or ruler seated at Cairo, has been ever able to skim the cream of the eight million slaves who toil along the shores of the river. The bordering deserts are impassable walls keeping in the slaves, keeping out the light that might enfranchise them.

I have said that only in its temples is the Nile in Nubia inferior to the Nile in Egypt, but there are temples enough above the First Cataract to satisfy the most fastidious Egyptologist; with one exception, however, they lack the colossal character of the great ruins on the lower river. They are chiefly, too, of later periods, many being of Greek and Roman days. Why are they all upon the west side of the river? It cannot be because of larger area of arable land on that side, since, as a matter of fact, the east shore possesses quite as large a margin of soil, and is less exposed to the endless drift of desert sand. The reason must be sought for in the security from Ethiopian assault enjoyed by the

west over the eastern side. If this reason be the
right one, and I believe no other can be found,
then a curious change must have taken place in
the character of the desert lying east of the Nile
above the First Cataract, in the last 2000 years.
That desert is to-day the most hopeless one in the
whole of North-Eastern Africa; only small and
well-appointed Arab caravans can attempt to cross
it. It is, in fact, Egypt's best barrier against
attack from the south. Even among the Arabs
it bears the name of the Waterless Sea. If then
this Waterless Sea was passable to the Ethiopians
in Greek and Roman days, it must have possessed
water which has since disappeared.

The chief Roman fortress in Nubia was at Ibrim,
where still the Eagle's Nest is plainly visible. This
fortress must have closed the route along the east
bank to any force coming from the south; therefore if the east shore north of Ibrim was open to
attack, it must have been from across this Waterless Sea. But to suppose that the conditions of
life in the desert have changed for the worse since
the beginning of the Christian era is only to apply
to the desert what we know for certain has taken
place along the river shores. These numerous
temples above the First Cataract, all these vestiges
of forts, towns, and fortresses tell of a production
of the necessaries of life ten times more abundant
than now. Was there then some secret of making

the same area of soil produce fourfold its present yield? or has the drift of the western desert covered vast tracts of cultivation? or again did the mineral wealth of Nubia enable a large population to live on these arid shores supported by the gold they washed or mined, and fed with food imported from Egypt? Many other questions might we ask and enter upon if time permitted, but the road is long before us, and we can only glance at these things as we go by.

For five days we steamed slowly along—yellow desert to the west, dark rock desert to the east, at times sharp or table-topped masses of cindery hills cut the clear sky, and catch, when evening comes, wonderful tints of purple, and level sunlight that is shining from beyond vast horizons.

Out in the western desert stand the lonely temples—Gertassie, Kalabsheh, Dendoor, Dakka, Maharagga, Sabooah, Amada—sometimes built on sandstone ridge, with blue sky for background —often lying half buried in the sea of sand that has left only the lofty pylon still visible above its waves.

There is an inscription cut on a pillar in one of these temples, which I have seen translated in an old book of travel, that gives a glimpse of these old temple times better than pages of description could do. Here is what a pilgrim wrote on a column at Kalabsheh Temple, 1800 years ago,—

" Be it prosperous, oh Lord. This is the homage of Vulsilius Cassius Celer, knight of the 1st Theban Cohort, that finest troop of horse, for himself, his son, and his brothers, may they be safe from envy, also for all that belong to him, and for his horse."

It was not from the outside enemy, the Nubæ, or Blemyes, that Vulsilius prayed for protection, but from the envy of his Roman friends; nor was this honest soldier beyond asking a benediction upon his horse. Why not? It was only a few years before that men in Judea were listening to these words, " Are not two sparrows sold for a farthing? and one of them shall not fall on the ground without your Father."

At a point about 170 miles from Philæ, a ridge of sandstone hills touches the river on the western side, and is continued upon the east bank until it is lost in a maze of rugged region upon that side. The Nile flows in a deep stream close at the foot of the western ridge, which at one point descends in an abrupt wall of rock to the river. Both above and below this sandstone ridge the western desert spreads out again to the horizon.

It was this spot which Rameses II. selected for his most wonderful work. Here, about 3400 years ago, he caused to be cut out of the sandstone cliff overhanging the river, the Temple of Abu Simbul. The temple itself is but a dark and lofty hall, running deep into the hill-side, with its gloomy roof upheld by twelve colossal figures, and the walls of its inner chambers covered with the pictures of old Egyptian wars; but the façade can never be forgotten by those who ever pass this spot. Cut out of the face of the rock, four gigantic figures sit looking across the river, with the expression of that vast immovable calm which seems to have been the essence of Egyptian art. The guide-books will long ago have told you the length and breadth of these colossi; how the ears on the great heads are six feet in length, and are still in proportion to the size of the figures; but nothing of measurement and nothing of art can ever realize the desolate majesty which rock, river, and desert have cast around that wonderful façade.

There will, perhaps, come a time when all the great temples of Thebes, Edfou, and Philæ will have gradually worn away into desert dust, and become the prey of earthquake or inundation; but while the hills are left Abu Simbul will stand, and if it alone remains when all the rest have perished, enough will still be there to tell the latest future the majesty and mystery of the old story of the Nile.

On the evening of the 19th of October I reached Wadi Halfa. One hundred and twenty of our boats were lying either there or six miles further

up river, at the very foot of the Second
Cataract, and so far we were still nine days ahead
of our estimate of time.

Wadi Halfa was a curious place in the month
of October, 1884. Its shore was covered with
the vast preparation of the coming campaign;
under a sun which still blazed fiercely overhead,
soldiers, sailors, black men and yellow men, horses,
camels, steam-engines, heads of departments, piles
of food and forage, newspaper correspondents,
sick men, Arabs and generals, seemed to be all
thrown together as though the goods station of a
London terminus, a couple of battalions of infantry, the War Office, and a considerable portion
of Woolwich Arsenal had been all thoroughly
shaken together, and then cast forth upon the
desert. Had such a conglomerative catastrophe
really taken place, the last item to pick itself
together would have been the goods station, and
this was what had actually happened at Halfa
during the last half of October. The infantry,
the War Office, the stores, and the supplies had
got into some shape and working order, but the
goods station was still hopelessly congested. I
do not know the number of trains that succeeded
in leaving Halfa and reaching Sarras in these
last days of October, but of this I am certain, that
so far as our boat expedition (which really meant
the whole expedition) was concerned, the Soudan

railway, which began at Wadi Halfa, and ended thirty-three miles away, at Sarras, might just as well not have existed during those October days. Nor was this a matter for surprise when the nature of this railway was considered. It had been built at prodigious cost a few years earlier by order of the Khedive Ismail, with the ambitious object of reaching Khartoum. It had been completed to its thirty-third mile at a cost so enormous as to put a stop to further progress. Although fully half of the track lay through open desert, where the sand had been just scraped together to form a permanent way, four millions sterling had gone in construction. How much had really been spent upon the line it would be impossible to say. When the financial crash came in Egypt, the Soudan railway collapsed. A vast quantity of material and rolling stock had been collected at Wadi Halfa to await, or assist, in the completion of the line. This, under the altered circumstances, became soon a sand-drifted wreck; engines on wheels and off wheels, tanks and tenders, bolts and boilers, lay around, while the walls and chimneys of buildings that were to have formed the terminus and storehouses of the railway stood unfinished in the desert. A very limited portion of rolling stock had been kept in semi-repair up to the summer which was just closing; and, more with a view to keep the line open and free from sand than to meet any traffic requirements, a weekly train had been run to Sarras.

It was little wonder then that this wrecked railway, suddenly called upon to perform the functions of a military line of communications, should have collapsed, and that at the time of my arrival at Wadi Halfa the energies of the single good locomotive should have been barely sufficient to supply with the necessaries of life the Egyptian troops who were already stationed at many places in the cataracts to the south.

Everything now depended upon the success of our boats to pass the Second Cataract. This long and intricate obstacle was admitted to combine in its ten miles' maze of rapid and waterfall as many impediments to navigation as the whole of the cataracts between it and Dongola could muster between them. It will be remembered that in our original scheme the passage of this cataract by water was not included, as it was supposed that the railway from Wady Halfa to Sarras would be able to carry the boats.

On the night of my arrival I heard, at the Commander-in-Chief's table, a full account of the difficulties of the Second Cataract. One of our boats had already navigated it in safety, but the route taken had been what is called the western channel, and ·t was only in the hands of the most experienced cataract-swimmers on this part of the Nile—the Sheikh Koko and his kinsmen Daoud and Suliman—that the attempt could at all be made. As I have already said, the boat had safely surmounted all the rapids of the Second Cataract, but the labour had been so great and the time taken so long, that the Chief of the Staff, who with Colonel Alleyne had gone as passengers, were both of opinion that the western channel could not be used for the 800 boats we proposed to carry through.

There still remained the eastern channel, a route which culminated at a spot about twelve miles from Wadi Halfa in a tremendous rush of water known as the "Bab-el-Kebir," or the Great Gate of the Cataract.

On the day preceding my arrival, the Commander-in-Chief had visited this *crux* of the cataract, and both he and those with him who in former years had been familiar with the rapids of the Winnipeg river in America, were obliged to acknowledge that they had not remembered a more formidable obstacle in the Red River Expedition. At this particular time the Bab-el-Kebir was a busy scene of toil. A number of native boats, kyassas, and merkebs, of from four to ten tons' burthen, were being hauled through the Gate by the efforts of several hundred Dongola natives, brought hither for the purpose. These native vessels were meant to work on the different short reaches of open water lying between the various cataracts above the Second and below the Third. The success of these large and strongly-built craft in passing the Bab had been far from satisfactory; about ten out of sixty had been totally lost in the rapid, and the injuries sustained by many of the others had been considerable. What then, it was asked, will be the fate of these light and fragile English boats in this fierce rush and whirl of waters?

Listening to these views and forecasts, I was naturally anxious to see for myself this "Great Gate," which, according to all accounts, was barred against us. That it was a very ugly bit of water there could not be a doubt, but I had seen too many instances of lightness proving the best source of strength in dangerous water, to believe there was any cataract on the Nile which, some way or other, could not be conquered by our craft.

On the evening of the 21st I reached the Bab-el-Kebir, in company with the second in command of the Expedition, a general officer whose name will often appear in the later pages of this narrative.[1]

We had ridden hard, covering the distance of about fourteen miles in less than two hours. Dismounting at the foot of a group of black

[1] Major-General Earle.

rocks we climbed to the summit, and were at once in sight of a busy scene. Right below us lay the Bab; on the surrounding rocks men of the Naval Brigade stood as guides and signalmen to hundreds of natives who, at certain moments, were to haul upon the large hawsers which lay in every direction over the shores. So various were these hawsers, and so numerous were the gangs of natives employed, that united action could only be obtained by means of an elaborate system of flag signals. Just as we reached the top of the rock, which commanded a full view of every part of the Great Gate, a kyassa was ready to attempt the ascent, and the signal was being given to all the native haulers to "stand by." Below the last plunge of the rapid the kyassa was visible in comparatively smooth water. The word was now given by the officer in charge, the lines were drawn "taut," and the boat was soon in the flood. Full in her bows stood the figure of the Cataract Reis Koko. With voice that was quite inaudible in the roar of the torrent, but with gesture easily to be followed, Koko directed a crowd of his own immediate followers who covered the lower rocks at the edge of the rapid. As the boat gradually was drawn on into more tumultuous water, the shouting and gesticulation became more intense. Suddenly something went wrong, the boat veered to one side, gave a convulsive lurch, and seemed to plunge head foremost into the flood. The last thing I saw was Koko waving and shouting wilder and louder than ever, as he disappeared amid a tangle of lines, ropes, and hawsers beneath the boiling torrent. The natives near the scene of disaster dropped their lines, rushed to the rescue of their chief, and just as the last vestige of the kyassa vanished out of sight, Koko was dragged triumphant but exhausted to the shore.

This misadventure closed the day's proceedings.

I had now time to take a good look at the "Gate." It was a very ugly-looking, deep, and steep chasm, between black rocks, through which poured an enormous mass of water with a fall of many feet in a distance of some sixty or eighty yards. A circular bay at the head of the Gate, fed by two arms of the river, collected a great body of water immediately above, and made the pressure through the narrow gorge one of immense force. It was evident from the exceedingly broken nature of the water rushing through the "Bab" that the bottom of the slant was impeded by huge rocks.

Bad as the place looked, I felt assured that our boats could be taken in safety through it by the ordinary method of tracking used in the American wilderness, nor did the broken and mangled remains of some dozen Nile craft strewing the shores of the river below the Bab, all victims of the last few days, shake the opinion now hastily formed as I looked down upon the scene. Then we remounted, and riding hard while the light lasted, reached Wadi Halfa at seven o'clock.

Immediately upon arrival I sent a note to the Commander-in-Chief to say I had seen the Bab-el-Kebir, and that with the assistance of six bluejackets and about 100 natives, I would guarantee to take from thirty to fifty of our boats daily through it, without any more elaborate preparation than the provision of ordinary two-inch ropes. Next day, the 22nd, I received an intimation from the Chief of the Staff that it was not intended to attempt the Bab-el-Kebir until all the native vessels had been put through it, which would take about two more days, that it was also thought desirable not to change the existing organization for working the cataract, but that it would be within the scope of my duties to interfere with that organization in the event of actual loss or damage being occasioned to our boats through the adoption of methods other than those I advocated. Of one thing I felt assured, namely, that if the same method of hauling with *long* hawsers was pursued towards our small boats as that which I had observed used towards the large Nile craft, loss as great as had

occurred to these Nile vessels must at least happen
to ours. Now this would have been a very serious
misfortune to the Expedition. Too many doctors
had too loudly proclaimed their belief in the
feebleness of constitution possessed by our English
craft to allow us to hope that a loss of fifteen to
twenty per cent. among them, suffered in the
earliest stages of our attempt, would not have
been regarded on all sides as fatal to their success,
and as fully justifying all the criticism passed
upon them. It is true that the Nile merkebs
and kyassas had already suffered this loss at the
Bab-el-Kebir, but that was a fact that would have
borne little weight in the scale.

Weighing all these things I determined that
the only course to pursue was to take up my
residence at once at the Bab-el-Kebir and watch
the development of the arrangements for hauling
up our boats through the " Gate." Accordingly
on the 23rd of October I quitted Wadi Halfa on a
very rough camel, and took the road to the Bab.
There is a spot on this track, about ten miles
from Halfa, named Gebel —— by the Arabs,
since it is said to mark the extreme limit reached
by the engineer who designed and built the Soudan railway. Here, the Arabs say, this Effendi
Kebir tumbled off his donkey, and having been
reinstated upon that animal turned back again
to Halfa, civilization, and well-earned reward.

At this place the line of railway runs through a
cutting between rock and river, and the traveller
looks down upon many rapids and narrow passages
in the Second Cataract. The news which met
me at this point was not cheering. About an
hour earlier, four of our boats which were being
dragged by a party of Egyptian soldiers up these
rapids had been all allowed to go adrift; three
had been recovered lower down stream, but one
had struck some of the numerous rocks, and had
been lost.

The rapid in which this accident had occurred
was only an ordinary piece of stiff water; the boats
had been let go through utter carelessness, three
or four men only being on the track-line at the
time.

I rode on to the Bab-el-Kebir, dismounted,
and sent a short report of the occurrence back to
Wadi Halfa. The sun by this time had set, and
soon the black rocks and the rushing water were
hidden in the night; but the dull roar of the
Great Gate seemed to grow louder as all the
stillness of the starlight lay outspread above it.

As soon as it was daylight next morning I
went down along the rapid and had a good study
of its worst spots. All around lay the heavy lines
by which it was proposed to haul up our little
craft; and, judging from the masts, spars, and
ribs that could be seen at the foot of the fall,

relics of previous disaster with heavier craft, it might well seem that these hawsers and " whips " were destined to become the ropes and nooses for the coming execution of our boats.

The camp of the sailors lay six miles distant : the Dongola natives dispersed every evening into the hills, and as they did not reappear until the morning was well advanced, I had the whole place to myself.

Having fully confirmed the previous views I had formed upon the practicability of taking our boats through the " Gate" by ordinary methods of " tracking," I set up my tent at the other side of the round bay above the Bab, and awaited the development of operations.

About nine o'clock the sailors and natives arrived, and the work of laying lines and stretching hawsers went forward. During the day scores of natives were perched about on the black rocks, or listlessly pulling hawsers, but no attempt was made to take any vessel through the " Gate." The Egyptian soldiers were at work, however, on the 2000 yards portage, and had already carried across that long distance about a dozen of our boats. Shortly before sunset, the whole party, sailors and natives, disappeared, and I was again alone with the Bab.

During the day I had seen two English boats enter the reach of smooth water below the fall.

K

With these it was intended to test the various appliances for hauling when they should be completed, but these appliances seemed to be yet in an unfinished state.

It was now the night of the 24th of October; five days had passed since my arrival in Wadi Halfa. More than 200 boats had reached that place, and as yet only one had passed this Second Cataract by the western channel.

The Big Gate was now clear of the native craft for whose passage we had stood aside, and for whose benefit four of the days we had saved in the original estimate of time had slipped away.

Left alone with the Big Gate, and taking stock of these and other things, it suddenly occurred to me that I might, during the interval, before sailors or natives again made their appearance, get one of the two boats I had seen in the day at the far end of the reach, over the Bab. It was such a taking thought that I could not resist it.

I got Koko—the head Cataract Sheikh—our acquaintance of a few days earlier, and took him and a few of his kinsmen down to the edge of the rapid. He was still suffering from his accident, though not, I suspected, to the degree he would have the outside world believe, and he used a stick to lean on. It was already growing dusk, but light enough remained to show us the white-tipped torrent plunging wildly between its black shores.

I explained to Koko and his confederates what I thought was necessary to success, and I showed them where boat No. 3 was lying in a quiet nook below the falls.

At daylight next morning they were to take this boat, and with a two-inch line in the stem, and another in the stern to act as a steadying guy-rope, they were to track up the rapid, keeping along this shore. If Koko would do this work to-morrow morning, "backsheesh" to the amount of two hundred piastres would be given him. But the work must all be completed, and No. 3 must be lying in the smooth water at my tent before any one would arrive from outside.

For the rest, the fame of Chief Cataract Reis Koko was known far up and far down the Nile, and I felt sure that when this exploit was accomplished, even a wider area of distinction would belong to him.

All this was presented to Koko through my interpreter, the Syrian, with some difficulty, but Koko was thoroughly acquainted with the values of money and of rapids, and was quick to catch what was required of him. If I would write a letter to the Sheikh of the Dongola natives, who dwelt in a hut some little distance away, asking for the assistance of thirty of his men at the Bab early to-morrow morning, he (Koko) would guarantee to take boat No. 3 from the foot of the Bab-el-Kebir to the smooth water below my tent, and to do this before a sailor had reached the ground.

A letter to Hassan Effendi was forthwith despatched, asking for the required assistance, a present of vaseline to Koko for his injured leg closed the proceedings, and I went back to my tent to await the result of the negotiations. Before lying down for the night, I sent the interpreter again to Koko to ascertain if all was right for the morrow. The reply brought back was eminently satisfactory. "He thought I was a Turk," said the Syrian, "and therefore he spoke his mind to me, and this is what he said: 'I will bring the boat safely up the Bab-el-Kebir to-morrow morning if no Christian comes near me while I am at work;' he added," continued the interpreter "that whenever a Christian came behind him he could do nothing right." The die was now cast, and, sink or swim, the boat must try the Big Gate.

At daybreak I was up; no figure could be seen on the black rocks, all was deserted and silent, save for the roar of the pent waters pouring through the narrow passages. Sunrise came, but still no figures showed upon the rocks, which now glistened like newly-mined coal in the level rays of the morning sun. It was close to seven o'clock

when the first native appeared ; dots of white
began to show about the black rocks, then after
a pause I saw the boat in the reach below the
rapid coming up towards the Bab. Many halts
and delays now took place to adjust lines ; and I
could see that a figure perched upon a commanding rock was gesticulating with great vehemence.
It was Koko. So much time had been lost, and
the hour was now so late, that I think if I could,
I would have stopped the attempt ; but my tent
was pitched, as I have said, at the far side of the
smooth bay from the Bab, and while I could see
right down the torrent, I could only reach the
spot by a détour. And it was better that it should
have been so, for had not Koko pledged himself
to succeed " if no Christian came behind him ? "

By this time the craft had reached the foot of
the rapid, where she was hidden from my view by
the descent of the cataract ; but I could tell by
the shouting and increased gesticulation among
the figures upon the rocks, that the tug of
war had begun ; and with glasses fixed on the
rim of the descending flood, I watched anxiously
for the reappearance of the ascending bows. It
was only a short interval before the boat came
in view, but it seemed to me a very long time.
Daoud Koko, nephew to Koko the Great, stood
in the bows, naked in case of disaster, alternately
waving his arms to incite the men on the shore to

fresh exertions, and using with extraordinary dexterity and rapidity a long pole to keep the boat from the rocks.

The Big Gate had three very bad lifts in its total distance of eighty yards. When the first of those jumps had been passed there came a brief pause to take breath and rearrange the lines for the next ascent. Then came a second series of shouts and waving of arms, and again the white bows rode up the slanting flood, and Daoud's black figure stood triumphant in the stem. At the foot of the third and last step there was again a pause, and then the final struggle began. It was the steepest ledge in all the Big Gate—so steep indeed that the boat and Daoud's figure disappeared altogether from my sight, and for a moment I thought all was over. But it was not so. Up out of space came the bows again, showing as though the boat was being lifted perpendicularly out of the whirl of waters. In this position the little craft hung for a moment, and then, with one great pull, her centre passed the edge of the fall, and she struck down in her entire length upon the smooth surface of the bay, safe and sound over the Bab-el-Kebir.

All this, long as it seemed to me, had only occupied about fifteen minutes of time, and now, when success had been achieved, and No. 3 came skimming lightly across the waveless water of the basin to the foot of my camp, I felt that I could show myself upon the scene without danger of drawing upon Koko the misfortunes he had feared; indeed, now that the hour of reward had struck, Koko and his brethren were not slow to seek the companionship they had before deprecated—and soon at my tent were gathered Koko the chief, Daoud the muscular, Suliman the supple, Hassan Effendi the venerable, besides many other able representatives of the great institution of " backsheesh." But the work had been admirably done; and had they been twice as numerous they would all have been welcome. When the " backsheesh " had been distributed, and a short despatch sent to Wadi Halfa announcing the successful passage of the Big Gate by the ordinary method of native navigation, it was not yet eight o'clock—the outside world might now come when it pleased.

It is no easy task to write these pages so as to make them exactly reflect the picture of the scenes which day by day, a year ago, passed before me. Almost in spite of one, memory will run on in advance and take its stand upon some future vantage-ground to add together the broken day-bits which each night then severed. Looking back on that morning's work at the Bab-el-Kebir from a standpoint of even three months later, it is difficult to recall the feelings of satisfaction with which this success filled one. And yet it was something more than the success of one individual opinion over another, for behind the easy passage of this pioneer boat through the worst water in Nile's enormous cataracts lay the justification of our past proposals, and before it might well seem to open out through all the long vista of obstacles yet to be overcome, the fair prospect of ultimate triumph.

CHAPTER VII.

IN WHICH WE MUSTER AT THE STARTING-POINT AND BEGIN THE GREAT RACE.

HE road being now clear, and a lead given over this formidable fence of the "Bab," the work of passing the boats from the foot to the head of the Second Cataract went on with alacrity. To Koko was given the exclusive working of the Big Gate. A battalion of Egyptian soldiers

were employed in carrying from a point about
a mile below the Bab to the village of Amkah,
at the head of the cataract, a distance of over
2000 yards ; other Egyptian soldiers, and later
on the Canadian voyageurs, were at work in the
lower portion of the cataract nearer Wadi Halfa
thus a force was brought to bear upon this formidable obstacle which very soon had the effect
of placing 200 of our boats above the cataract.

But this work was not really set in thorough
motion until the 27th of October, or ten days after
the date upon which 100 of our boats had reached
Wadi Halfa. As I have already stated, this
delay of ten days was occasioned through the
decision of the transport chiefs to give the native
craft the right of preference through the Bab.
That such preference was unfortunate in the long
run I am absolutely convinced of, nor was my
opinion in that respect only arrived at after
catastrophe and mishap had multiplied the wrecks
of these native vessels along the river shores.

Nevertheless, much as I was opposed to a
proposal which necessitated a delay in our movement, I cannot now, reviewing all the circumstances of the time, say that those who took
the line of adherence to the old methods of
navigation which the Nile had known through
all its history could have been expected to have
done otherwise. They preferred what seemed to

them the certainty of those old ways and means
of movement to our newer schemes of craft and
carriage,—schemes brought from a distant continent, and as yet unproven by actual test under
the altered circumstances of this strange land ;
and if that preference for these older methods
condemned our English boats to a long week's
inaction at Wadi Halfa, and lost us the saved
moments hitherto gained in the rapid execution
of labour, the logic of time and the opinion of
experience were alike in keeping with such a
preference. Let us pass on from this unfortunate
period of our enforced inaction to busier days.

Among all Life's favours to man, few are greater
than the veil which hangs between the present
and the future,—that veil which is just lifted
enough to show us the nearer hills, the sunlit
pathway in the foreground, but shuts out the
black mountain-tops beyond, and hides those icy
summits where so often the road of life is destined
to die out in an unaccomplished purpose. So is it
with the progress of that collective life which we
call a campaign. Once committed to the venture,
the actor sees only the immediate foreground of
labour that lies before him. He hews away at
the particular impediment of the moment, and
passes on to ultimate victory or defeat with light
heart and pleasant smile.

It was thus that we began on the 31st of October

at Gemai, four miles above the Second Cataract, the work of refitting our craft for their final work. The passage through the Great Gate was now open, the portage was in full swing, and boats were arriving at our refitting dockyard at the rate of fifty a day. Thus, although the railway upon which we had counted for transport past the Second Cataract had hopelessly failed us, and that failure had compelled recourse being had to the cataract itself for passage, that passage was being effected at the rate of fifty boats each day, and without a single wreck save the one we have already told.

It was curious to look back from the realization of this state of things to the prophecies and vaticinations of only a few days earlier. I have now before me an estimate of the probable English boat losses in the passage of the Second Cataract made by the officers whose acquaintance with the Second Cataract had begun more than two months previous to our arrival. The lowest estimate of loss is four per cent., the highest is twenty per cent. ; so far our actual loss was not one-half per cent., and even that was the result of manifest carelessness.

Nor was the condition in which the boats arrived at Gemai less satisfactory than the rapidity with which they came. Although they had changed hands three times in the passage through the long rapids of the Second Cataract, the damage sustained by them was so trivial that all repairs could be executed in a few hours. We were, in fact, repairing, painting, equipping, and completing boats at the rate of twenty-five and thirty a day, and within a week after setting to work, our dockyard presented a long double line of craft with masts set, sails, sheets, oars, poles, rudders, and rollers fixed, and everything in perfect readiness for the start. A company of infantry, a small party of Engineer carpenters, and about a dozen bluejackets formed our dockyard hands, and despite of hot sun, we managed by early and late hours to quickly accumulate a reserve of completed boats in excess of possible demands.

One day, the 4th of November, I was engaged in the daily work of the dockyard, when across the river a strange object caught my sight—strange only in this Nile land, for in other lands it had been a well-known friend, but one now so far off in memory, and so distant in the scenes of river and shore which were connected with it, that it might well have seemed a shadow called up from the past—a mirage of pine-cliff and canoe, destined to vanish again into the dead world from which it had arisen.

There, hugging the back eddy of the muddy Nile, a small American birch-bark canoe, driven by those quick down-strokes that seem to be the birthright of the Indian *voyageur* alone, was moving up the further shore. When this strange craft had got well abreast of our dockyard, it steered across the swift river and was soon underneath my tent. Out of the canoe, with all the slow gravity of his race, stepped a well-remembered figure—William Prince, Chief of Swampy Indians, from Lake Winnipeg in North America. After him came seven other Indian and half-breed *voyageurs*, all from the same distant land—they were the pioneers of the 400 Canadian *voyageurs* whose services we have already seen secured in the preceding August; but personally to me there was something more in this visit of these Indians than the advent of the pioneers from the North-West who were to aid the Expedition in its fight with the rocks and rapids of the Nile.

Fourteen years earlier this same William Prince had been the best Indian in my canoe when we forced our way up the rapids of the Winnipeg to meet the advance of the Red River Expedition through the wilderness of the North-West. And here to-day, on the Nile above the Second Cataract, stood William Prince, now chief of his tribe, grown more massive of frame and less agile of gait, but still keen of eye and steady of hand as when I last saw him standing bowman in a bark canoe among the whirling waters whose echoes were lost in the endless pine-woods of the Great Lone Land.

Seated in my tent in old Indian fashion, cross-legged on the ground, Prince and his companions soon found themselves at home in this strange land, for dry and arid as these deserts were, there were drops of whisky and plugs of tobacco to be found in them, and these are keys to unlock the tongue of a Redman just as potent in the sands of Nubia as in the pine-islands or prairies of the North.

"How many Indians had come from Winnipeg?"

"About a dozen; but had longer time and fuller notice been given, fifty or even a hundred would have come."

"Were the *royageurs*, taking them all together, up to the old North-West mark?"

"No; but there were a good proportion among them able boatmen. The Iroquois and French Canadians were nearly all first-class men; there were also several excellent boatmen from the Ottawa, but there were some 'dead-beats' who knew nothing of the work."

Then it was their turn to ask questions.

"How long would it take to reach Khartoum?"

"From two to three months."

"Were there many rapids?"

"Yes; but no rapid longer or more difficult than this Second Cataract they had just passed."

"Well, if that was the case and they were to start at once they could get there by Christmas."

Then we talked about old times and friends.

Their world had changed, they said, towns had grown up along the silent river-shores, farms and fences covered the far-stretching prairies, the buffalo were all gone, the lonely lakes had steamboats on them. People said the new times were better, but for themselves they liked the old days, the old days of the log-house along the river, the wilderness lying out to the west with its free life, its herds and hunts, its trading and its trapping. "People were friendly towards each other then," was their final summing up of the case of old *versus* new.

They went back in the evening to the foot of the Second Cataract, and on the following day Prince and a Cree half-breed, named Cochrane, again appeared with a batch of *voyageurs* who were to act as guides and pilots to the 38th or Stafford Regiment, which was about to embark for the ascent of the river. Our fleet lying ready for service at the foot of the steep clay-bank at Gemai was daily growing in number. On the morning of November 1st, five boats carrying a pioneer party of Engineers started for Dongola, and a few days later the embarkation of the first infantry battalion began. It did not take long to accomplish; thirty-two boats carried

the half-battalion which was the first to start.
The embarkation commenced at 7.30 a.m. and
at 8, the last boat was under weigh. It was a
very simple business: the men were marched
down to the shore, told off in tens, put into the
boats; arms and packs were soon stored, and
then in succession from the front, or upstream
side, the fleet moved off. A light breeze blew
from the north; the lug-sails were loosened, and
with oars pulled in many fashions, the white
flotilla moved up the broad river, and was soon
out of sight. It was the 5th of November; just
thirty years had passed since this same battalion
of the 38th Regiment was engaged in stemming
the strong tide of the Russian hosts up the slopes
of Inkermann. It was a soldiers' fight then, and
in the coming months it was to be a soldiers'
fight too.

The following morning saw the second wing of
the Stafford battalion start from Gemai, with
similar ease and rapidity.

Seventy boats had now been despatched, and as
many more stood ready for service, but there were
only scattered companies of the Essex and Cornwall battalions to put in them. The supply of
coal at Assouan had run short, and the steamers
between the First and Second Cataracts were
delayed for want of fuel. It was a serious want
at such a time, for the links in the chain of this

L

great enterprise still stretched back to the Mediterranean, and to cut one link in any spot was to affect the line of effort through its entire length.

I remember in the old days of Mississippi steamboat story, thinking that captain who burnt his cargo of live hogs rather than lose a race for want of fuel a very savage fellow; but circumstances alter judgments as well as cases, and with the later experience of this old-time and Turk-dulled Nile, I have come to regard that Yankee skipper as only the right man on the wrong river.

The Staffords being started on their journey, and our dockyard ready to meet all possible drafts upon it for many days, I determined to run up the river as far as the Semneh Cataract and see for myself the passage of that famous obstacle by an infantry battalion loaded with its fullest load.

Semneh was the first water-jump in this great steeple-chase. If the boats got safely over with their immense freights, then there could remain little doubt about subsequent success.

So, taking boat on the morning of 6th November, I pulled away for Sarras—Prince at helm, Cochrane in the bow, four strong and willing men of the Stafford at the oars. A light breeze blew as usual from the north; but better than wind or oar

was the steering of the Indian chief, and so closely
did we cut the rocky points, and hug the backwater along the shore, and take the advantage of
some current-breaking rock in quick-running
stream, that we reached Sarras—eighteen miles
from Gemai—more than an hour in advance of
any other boat, although ours had been the last
to leave the shore at Gemai.

But this eighteen-mile run to Sarras was only
a preliminary canter to the big race, for at Sarras
the food supplies for four months had to be
taken on board—the 5000 lbs. weight of meat,
biscuit, tea, sugar, and preserved sustenance of
sorts had here to be stowed away under the
thwarts and up to the gunwales. It was a prodigious load, but as the little boat had eaten it
up two and a half months earlier at the Gun
Wharf in Portsmouth, so here on the wide desert
shores of Sarras it was swallowed again.

It wanted but an hour of sunset when the
last load was stowed; deep in the water lay the
thirty-two hulls, each carrying fully four tons'
burthen. Outside the little bay which held the
boats the big river was pouring down its red
flood between the high sandhills and rocks
which stand sentinel around Sarras; looking up
the river one saw, about a mile distant, three
island rocks, steep and ruin-crowned, which
marked the end of the smooth reach and the be-

ginning of troubled waters that extended to the foot of Semneh Cataract.

Would these deep-freighted boats be able to make head against that full-flooded, impetuous current? The load of boxes rose in stem and stern well above the gunwale; the men at the oars were half hidden behind the high piled cargoes. Portsmouth's trial had been in still waters, here the central stream was racing along at four and five miles the hour.

All was ready for the first start and for the final test. It had blown a light breeze all day, and for the last hour or two it had been almost calm. As I stood on the top of the high bank overlooking the river, a few cool puffs of wind came up the deep river valley from the north, and looking back one saw the faint ruffle on the water that told of steadier breezes behind. Moving off in succession from the shore, the boats put out into the stream; for a moment there was a pause ere oars had got good hold of the water, and sails were set, and sheets made fast; and then, slowly but steadily, the white-winged flotilla began to move up the great river.

It was a very beautiful evening; across the western wastes of sand the level sunlight flashed full upon the wild rocky hills which stretch away from Sarras into the steeper mountains of the Batn-el-Hager. Along the reach of river the

START OF THE FIRST BOATS FROM SAWWAS.

Page 148.

white sails were glowing in rifts of sunlight that
sometimes streamed upon them through western
valleys, and were sometimes reflected from the
vivid light of the eastern hills. Over the nearer
slopes of the desert ridges on the west side, the
soft cream colours were lying, growing softer and
richer as the sun went down ; beyond all rose the
rocky isles, closing the long river reach, the
ruined church still in sunlight, a lone relic of
days before the Arab had carried his creed into
these distant wilds.

But already the leading boats have got close
to the foot of the rocky isles, and we must overtake them ere camping-time has come. If the
toiler in the wilds would carry away with him
for future sight those wonderful bits of sky and
earth, sun and shade, which so often pass before
him, he must accustom himself to catch quickly—
even in the excitement of some toil-filled moment
—the essence of the scene that lies around him.
One thing he may be sure of : if thus he catches
in the cup of his labour, and amid the hardship
of his life, those golden drops, they will give him.
many a rich recompense later on ; and it may be
that in far-off memory, the labour, the hardship,
and even the failure will wear no other light.

No time for longer survey now. Taking boat
again, we, too, pulled out from shore, and running
quickly up with sail and oar, passed the fleet as

it rounded the island bend of the river, and were soon at the foot of the troubled waters beyond. On the east shore a wide curving bay promised anchorage and level camping-ground above it. We would halt here for the night, and attack the rapid on the morrow. The whole fleet was soon at anchor, the men bivouacked along the shore, and the fires for supper began to glow in the lessening light.

To the south of the camp a wall of rock rose sheer from the water; over the river the western horizon was flaming with red, and the serrated rocks stood dark against the after-glow. From beyond the impending cliff that shut out the stream to the south, the voices of many rapids reached us; and as the night deepened around the bivouac, voice of rapid and outline of rock seemed to grow in sound and steepness.

I got a level shelf in the southern rock, spread my blankets, and sat down. Close by an old friend of Red River[1] days had also made his camp, and between memories of bygone scenes amid the American wilderness, and forecasts of coming toil in the cataracts before us, the early night passed quickly away.

The morning found us at work, and the sun was not well over the eastern rocks before we had entered the first rapid of the Batn-el-Hager.

[1] Lieut.-Col. F. Dennison, Canadian Militia.

Many of the boats were able to pull and sail through this bit of quick water, but many others had to track up it, and for the first time the coils of track-line were laid out. One or two of the boats in charging the rapid had come into collision with others, but no serious damage had happened, and by nine o'clock the entire flotilla was safely at anchor at the foot of the last long rapid, which, with little intermission, extends to the "Big Gate" of Semneh.

Breakfast was over, and the men were taking their places again, when a large native kyassa came in sight below our halting-place, with her great triangular sail outspread in the breeze, which had now freshened to its normal daily strength. There was an impression firmly set in the minds of nearly all the officers and men engaged in this Expedition, that the native craft of the Nile were better suited for the work we had to do than were our English-built boats. The soldier's mind is not a far-seeing one; it is prone to live in its present moment, and the fact that there was a time rapidly approaching when a falling Nile would leave high and dry every native vessel that might attempt to navigate the cataracts of this Batn-el-Hager was lost sight of in the apparent ease with which these boats could now, at high water, force up against the strength of the current before a strong north wind.

As the soldiers stood on the shore watching the approach of this large kyassa, with sail well filled, and white surges driving before her bows while she forced her way through the troubled waters, it occurred to me that this was a good opportunity of proving that our little English craft could beat all native rivals even under circumstances the most favourable to the native. We accordingly took our places, and shoved out into the stream just as the kyassa was abreast of us. The crew on the native boat were not slow to realize the intention, and with sheets hauled "tauter," and another hand put on the long helm, they made ready for the trial. Before us lay a troubled mass of water, growing gradually stiffer until at the head of the rapid a large rock stood full in the centre of the stream. Round this rock the current broke furiously, and between the two severed rushes lay the usual interval of seething and whirling, but comparatively quiet water. The art of forcing up a rapid consists in running up this lane of easier water, clinging to it as long as possible, and leaving it only at the very edge of the rock which has formed it. Then, with all the strength of oar and paddle, the effort is made to lift the boat over and through the neck of the rush, by the right or left of the rock. It is at this point that the art of steering tells. If the sheltering eddy be held to one instant too long, collision with the rock is certain. If the eddy be quitted too soon, the bow, caught in the gathered volume of the descending water, is whirled back, and the boat is borne broadside down stream. In his birch-bark canoe, the Indian can effect this last lift over the shortest part of the rapid with wonderful dexterity, for the canoe is without keel, and the bow as it leaves the shelter of the rock, projects slightly out of the water, and being above the current, may be said to slide up the incline.

Up this lane of water Prince now steered, keeping ahead of the native vessel, which was following close in our wake. Arrived at the edge of the rock, he turned his helm a-port and shot out into the rapid; but either he had not grown accustomed to the full strength of the flooded Nile, or the stem of the boat offered too wide an angle to the stream, but the quickly reversed rudder was powerless to hold her head up-stream, and we fell off into the rapid. At the same instant a sudden freshening of the breeze took our sails aback and threw the boat over on one side, knocking the men off the thwarts.

For a moment things looked bad; the wind and the rapid had the boat between them, both intent as it seemed upon turning her over, one acting above, the other pressing below; but our seven feet beam was too much for their combined efforts, and, despite of wind and water, the good craft kept her keel until sheets were let go and we were able to bring her head to the stream and put her again at the jump. This time there was no mistake; the breeze held well, and up we went into the good water above the rock, walking clear away from the kyassa, whose utmost efforts were at this time powerless to pass the rapid.

The next bend of the river brought us in sight of a strange scene. Between us and the steep rock of Semneh, the shores were lined in many places with the wrecks of native kyassas and nuggers, all of which had been lost in the last few days in endeavouring to pass the lower "gate" of Semneh Cataract. If any doubt about the relative merits of English *versus* native craft for these wild waters yet lingered in the minds of the Stafford half-battalion, this wreck-encumbered reach below Semneh must have dispelled it for ever. As we drew nearer to the middle of the rapid, the full harm which these wrecks caused became apparent to us. Many of them had been run on shore, after striking some rock in the rapid; some of them had sunk as they reached the shore; some had been drawn partly out of the water, while the sterns remained sunken in the stream. Thus in every case they formed obstacles to our upward progress, greater even than the rapids that were foaming beyond them; for, as they occupied the

rocky shores of the rapids, we could only pass
them by the slow and difficult work of stretching
our track-lines outside these half-submerged
hulls, and as the river was here running fully
eight and nine miles an hour, the labour of
dragging our heavily-laden boats through the full
force of the cataract, outside these stranded
vessels, became very great. Track-lines were
constantly fouling some sunken mast or broken
rudder; and the lengths of line which had to be
let out in order to clear the wrecks made the
control of the craft in this dangerous water a
most difficult matter. The men worked well, the
voyageurs were skilful and untiring, and one by
one the thirty-two boats were taken safely past
the wreck-encumbered rapids to the foot of the
Great Gate at Semneh. The afternoon sun had
beaten down upon the sharp rocks and giant
boulders that line the shores between Sarras and
Semneh, and the desert ridges beyond the shores
had added their fiery breath to make the men
realize to the utmost the toil that lay before them;
doubtless many among them thought that all the
long miles they had to travel were as bad as these,
that the shores were all as flinty, and that the
Nile was everywhere as it was here at this door-
way to the Batn-el-Hager—a huge slant of yellow
water.

When I lay down that night on the sandy

shore below the rock, which still holds aloft the ruins of the old castle that 3000 years ago was Egypt's frontier fortress, I could not prevent my mind from running back over our past. It was three months to a day since in the Portsmouth Dockyard we had tried the whale-gig in the basin, and had settled the shape, size, and design of our future Nile boats; and now this day had seen the final test. From early morning to late evening these thirty-two boats had been passing through water than which there was none more difficult on the river; water, whose difficulties had been doubled by the wrecks and ruins of the craft which we had been told a thousand times were the sole, safe, and certain transport for the Nile. Our loads were at their heaviest; our crews were at the most unpractised moment of their work; the heat had still in its strength the fierceness of the slowly dying summer. Yet not a soldier had been hurt, not a pound of the heavy freights had been damaged, not a boat had been lost or even injured; and 300 soldiers had passed in a single day over ten miles of the worst water in the Nile, carrying with them four months' food, 300 rounds of ammunition, and all the *impedimenta* of clothing, stores, and tentage necessary for a long and distant campaign. Truly, there were false prophets in other lands besides the Soudan.

There is an episode of that day in the Semneh

rapids which comes to my memory as my mind
now goes back over the scene. We had reached
one of the many spots where the boats had to be
hauled up a rapid outside the stranded wreck of
a native kyassa. The men in double or treble
crews were toiling over the rocks, a couple of
voyageurs in the boat were keeping her out from
the wrecks, and half a dozen men were employed
in running along the shore, climbing in and out
of the sunken vessels to free the track-line when
it fouled. At one spot the line had got fast in
the bottom, and we could not cast it loose.
Most of us were in the water, but the line still
baffled us. On the shore, behind where we were
thus employed, a group of native officials of minor
degree sat watching us. They were the late
passengers in this very kyassa whose recent
wreck was giving us all this trouble, and now,
as they sat amid a salvage of beans and boxes,
they seemed perfectly content to spend the remainder of their existence on this particular sand-
bank. Unfortunately, it struck me that beneath
this aspect of profound resignation with wreck,
ruin, and delay, I could distinguish a half-concealed
expression of pity for the deplorable condition of
persons who could be wicked enough to work
as we were working. I may have been totally
wrong in this impression; but at such moments,
and under such a sun, we are prone to act without

a quiet consideration of the case. The thought that we were toiling up to our middles in water to free a line which had got foul because of the bungling of the very vessel which had carried these people, who were now regarding us with, to say the least of it, the most placid indifference, was sufficient to accentuate the effect of the sun upon the brain. In a moment I was out of the water and in the middle of the seated group. "Into the river and help us!" I cried. They knew not a word of English. Arabic to me was an unknown tongue, but I have ever found, in moments of this sort, language of little use, and the sight of an Irish blackthorn a more potent medium for conveying thought than the knowledge of a Max Müller. In another instant the solemn-looking orientals were running down to the Nile as though they had been young crocodiles just bursting from the parent eggs. Aided by these new recruits, our line was soon set free, and our upward course resumed. Among these Egyptians there was one whose appearance impressed me. I asked his name, and was told he was a Syrian medical officer belonging to an Egyptian regiment higher up the river. Many months afterwards I chanced to meet this official again. All connection with the rope incident near Semneh had completely faded from my memory, but there was a friendliness in his recognition that recalled his features to my

recollection. "Surely we had met?" "Yes, in
the water below Semneh—did I not remember the
day?" He was my fast friend.

Semneh is a wild and lonely spot. Standing
upon the summit of the lofty rock, which projects
from the east shore far into the river, the traveller
sees only the serrated ridges and calcined peaks
of a savage solitude. Beneath him the river
pours its pent waters through three passages,
separated from each other by rocky islets which
some writers think once formed the piers of a
great bridge across the river. Both on the east
shore and on the west, in a line with the three
rocky isles, rise steep impending cliffs, bearing
upon their wind-swept summits two ruined
temples; the massive but crumbling walls of a
fortress crowns the whole crest of the cliff on
the east side, enclosing the more perfect ruins of
the temple.

From this ruin-crowned cliff on the east bank
the Nile is seen coming out of the desert to the
south, vanishing into the desert to the north between shores that always present the opposite
aspect of sand and rock—bright yellow sand on
the west side, dark burnt rock on the east: the
wide channel of the river has, in fact, stopped the
drift of the Lybian desert, and hence the western
shore is golden, and the east is ashen-grey.
Below the cliff the river pours with hoarse tumult

through the narrow passages which form the upper gate of Semneh's cataract, and as the whole volume of the Nile is held in these three confined channels, the rush of water through them is of great strength and swiftness. Beyond Semneh to the south lies the Batn-el-Hager, the " womb of rocks." In this region, which extends along the east side of the Nile for eighty miles, the extreme of rugged desolation has been reached ; everywhere black burnt rocks are confusedly grouped together in masses varying in elevation from 100 to 1000 feet; numerous valleys, or " wadis," intersect these hills, but viewed from a distance nothing except a maze of cindery mountain can be seen.

There is in old editions of Moore's "Epicurean " a vignette illustration by Turner which has caught with singular power the wild character of the scene at Semneh. Upon a high cliff overhanging the Nile the columns of a temple are falling, in the shock of an earthquake, into the deep river chasm beneath. He who has seen the Nile only to the Second Cataract might well fancy the picture to be an extravagant rendering of the river of Egypt, but whoever will take the trouble to penetrate as far as the cliff where Thothmes placed his frontier fortress and built his Temple of the Sun, must acknowledge how faithfully the great painter's fancy had caught the spirit of a scene he had never looked on.

Early on the morning of November 8th, the Staffords began their portage at Semneh; the boats were unloaded, the loads carried by the men across the steep ridge, and the empty boats then hauled through the east passage of the " gate." This done they were reloaded on the south side of the portage. The work was excessively severe, but it was done with a good will, and by three in the afternoon the two leading companies were again under weigh. The morning of the 9th saw the second wing of the Stafford safely arrived at Semneh, without damage to boat or man. The day was spent in the heavy work of the portage, and by midday on the 10th the last of the battalion was away from the cataract. When all had left, I ascended the ruin-crowned cliff to have a final look at the scene, and take stock of our prospects. At the end of the wild reach to the south the last white sails of the Stafford fleet were disappearing into the maze of mountains. From the foot of the cliff the ring of many hammers told that the work of riveting together the 700 pieces of the Yarrow stern-wheel steamer was going on. A fortnight earlier these pieces had been brought to the north side of the portage in eight native vessels, and from thence carried across the ridge

M

.

to a level spot at the south side, where they were now being put together. One of the vessels, carrying portions of this steamer, had gone down in the rapids between Sarras and Semneh, but fortunately in a place where it had been possible to recover her cargo. In another three weeks' time the Yarrow steamer should be ready for launching. It was not yet three months since those white-winged boats, vanishing in the desert distance, and that steamer's hull building at the base of this rock, had been ordered in the building-yards of the Thames, and here, to-day, the first were bearing their crews and stores past the wild shores of the Batn-el-Hager, and the last was being put together beyond the cataract of Semneh, 1050 miles from the sea at Alexandria.

It all seems easy enough as one writes it down, now when the toil and heat are hidden in that veil which memory ever flings over the burthen of the past, but it would be difficult to put into words the measure of the labour, mental and physical, which had achieved these results. To us, who had our eyes fixed on the distant goal of our effort, toil and thought were only the looked-for incidents on the way that led us to a glorious achievement; but with the "man in the ranks" it was different. His is the burthen unrelieved by the reward; his the certainty of the toil, and almost a similar assurance that if his name is to find its way into the home paper it will be in the record of his death.

It was the evening before this day that, re-crossing the portage at Semneh after dark, I happened to come upon a soldier down on the ground, with his heavy load lying beside him in the sand. He was dead-beat. "If they are putting down for anything new," I heard him mutter as I went past, "they had better put down for new soldiers."

CHAPTER VIII.

THE CATARACTS OF THE " WOMB OF ROCKS."

HEN the last white sail of the Stafford boats had vanished into the rock labyrinth of the Batn-el-Hager, I descended from the ruin-crowned cliff, and taking ten *voyageurs*, whose services were to be utilized with succeeding battalions over this rough water, we ran down the rapids to Sarras (ten miles) in one hour and five minutes. At Sarras I found a train for Halfa, and by midnight was able to report personally to the administrative chiefs the success which had attended the passage of the first boats of the expedition across the cataract of Semneh.

The experience gained in these three days had shown me upon what articles of boat and man equipment the labour of Nile navigation most heavily told, and fresh supplies of these articles were now demanded from the base to meet such losses as might be looked for in the future. On the following morning I was again at Gemai, where the work of boat-refitting was still in full swing.

During the ensuing six days our fleet grew rapidly in number, and by the 16th of November 200 boats stood equipped, waiting at the dock-yard, while 200 more had already been des-patched up river. Of these last, however, only about half carried troops. The failure of the coal supply at Assouan had cut the flow of sol-diers up the Nile, and during the ten days follow-ing the departure of the Stafford there were only six mixed companies of Essex and Cornwall battalions ready to be sent off. In order, how-ever, to utilize the interval before other troops could arrive from Assouan, some seventy or eighty boats were despatched from Gemai with extra store of supplies. These boats were manned by a mixed combination of Egyptian soldiers, Don-golese boatmen, and West African Krooboys. The stores they carried were destined to supply the deficiency caused by the numerous wrecks and losses of the native vessels, and were also meant to enable the English craft to fill in at Dal the amount of food which had been consumed in the passage up to that point. Thus the middle of November came to find our dockyard supply standing far in advance of possible demands upon it. We had sent off 200 boats. Two hundred more stood ready for instant service, and we were adding to this last number at the rate of thirty a day.

While here we stand with fleet ready at Gemai, and food supplies waiting at Sarras, let us take advantage of the delay in the coming of the troops to glance along the entire length of the enterprise as it now stood throughout the 475 miles of river which lie between Dongola and Assouan.

At Dongola stood the Sussex battalion and a small body of mounted infantry, the whole under the command of Brigadier-General Sir Herbert Stewart.

At Dongola the Commander-in-Chief had also fixed his headquarters early in November, not because he permitted himself to hope in the possibility of making an early forward movement towards Khartoum, but in order to superintend on the spot the negotiations with the Arab tribes of the deserts lying contiguous to that part of the Nile, and also to control with greater effect the action of the Egyptian authorities in Dongola, of whose sincerity and loyalty to our Expedition there was but too much cause for suspicion.

On the river between Dongola and Wadi Halfa there was only the single battalion of the Stafford Regiment, and six companies of mixed Essex and Cornwall. Below Wadi Halfa the remainder of the Essex and Cornwall battalions and portions of the "Black Watch" and Gordon Highlander battalions were moving up from Assouan. At Assouan portions of the "Black Watch" and Gordon Highlanders, and all the Royal Irish and West Kent battalions were still either in camp, or *en route* from Assiout.

Along the right bank of the Nile from Dongola to Assouan, a mounted force, numbering about 2000 men, cavalry, artillery, mounted infantry, and Camel Corps, were moving south in many detachments, the first of which had already reached Dongola, the last being still at Assouan.

At Wadi Halfa the administrative staffs of the Expedition, and of the line of communications, had still their quarters. Along the cataracts between the Third and Second, small bodies of Egyptian soldiers were stationed, while the Canadian *voyageurs*, Kroomen, and Dongolese boatmen were chiefly camped about the Second Cataract, or employed in the 200 boats which had already taken their departure from Gemai.   Such, on this middle day of November, was the disposition of the relieving force along the 500 miles from its front to its rear.

To us, who, working daily at our allotted tasks, saw only the immediate foreground before us, the immense "beyond" that lay outside our advanced post at Dongola was then hidden in utter darkness.   All the cloud that overshadowed Khartoum has since been lifted, and now we know the daily life that was going on, 500 miles beyond Dongola, where the Arab leaguer was drawing closer around the doomed city, and day by day the solitary figure stood on the palace roof looking out over the desert horizon to catch the smoke of the long-expected steamers.

It was at this very time, in mid-November, that the Arab attack was being pressed with its first real determination.   The fort of Omderman was cut off, one of the two little steamers remaining after the other four had left to await our coming at Shendy, had been sunk, the food supply was lessening, desertion to the Arabs was increasing, the spirit of the miserable garrison was sinking lower, and, day by day, the proof was gathering that the long-talked-of Expedition was still afar off beyond the deserts of Dongola.

Curious were these stray gleams of information which, sometimes by accident, oftener by design, came through the dense cloud of surrounding Arabs to gladden with false hopes, or to damp by their part-told truth, the hearts of the beleaguered.

"A report has come in," writes Gordon on November 23rd, "that the Expedition had arrived at Metemma, and had encountered the Arabs twice; that a steamer had been sent up to inform me, but the Arab guns had forced her to return." Two months later the Expedition did reach Metemma, having encountered the Arabs twice, and a steamer was sent up, and the Arab guns did force her to return, but all was then over by thirty-two hours.

On the night of the 16th November the General-in-Chief passed Gemai on his way from Dongola to Wadi Halfa. He had travelled with the utmost rapidity from the head of the Third Cataract, covering the distance by camel to Sarras in four days. It was two o'clock in the morning when the train reached Gemai; but neither the hour nor the long and rapid ride which had preceded this short respite on the railway had made the traveller think of rest. I had been waiting since midnight for the coming of the train, and when it stopped to take water I stepped up on the carriage door-step and looked in. In two corners of a third-class compartment two aides-de-camp were lying in postures that bespoke much discomfort of body—the result of four days' incessant camel-bumping; but there was a third figure at the nearer side, wakeful, watchful, and erect. His eye caught sight of my face at the window, and I was soon in the carriage.

"What was the cause of the delay?" "Why were the troops not moving up?" "Why had not the Stafford battalion yet reached Dal?" These and many other questions were rapidly asked. I could only speak of our own part in this enterprise. We had sent off 200 boats. We had 200 more ready within a stone's throw of where he spoke. As for the progress of those which had already started, I had seen their course up to and over Semneh, and it had been excellent in all respects. For myself, as my dockyard work was now far in advance of all possible demands upon it, and as the equipment of the remainder of the boats had only to follow the lines already existing, I proposed to embark and start up river on the following day, and do my best to hurry on the troops already *en route.* I would thus see the cataracts through their entire length, and be in a position to telegraph back instructions or recommendations for the benefit of succeeding battalions.

The General-in-Chief passed on to Wadi Halfa, remained twelve hours at that place, then took train back to Sarras, and mounting camel again, reached Dongola in five days.

On the morning following this short interview
I quitted Gemai for the head of the Third Cataract, Prince at the helm, six Krooboys and an
Indian at the oars, one Arab guide, one Syrian
interpreter, and one English servant—a crew of
eleven all told. The boat that carried this strange
mixture of races—representatives from the four
quarters of the world—bore the number 387. We
carried an extra store of supplies and tools for the
benefit of boats in distress. It was my intention
to push on with all speed to the head of the Third
Cataract—200 miles. I would then know exactly
the nature of every obstacle on the river, and I
would be able to judge the time which boats
should take to complete the passage to Dongola.
That it was possible to pass these Nile cataracts
with celerity I never for a moment doubted; and
if I counted upon the effect which a rapid passage
would have in inducing succeeding crews to ac-
celerate their rate of progress, whatever element of
vanity might lie in the attempt might surely be
excused in the general advantage that would
thereby result to this great enterprise.

The day of our start from Gemai was hot and
sultry, there was little or no wind; nevertheless
five hours' pulling brought us to Sarras, and
taking on board fifteen days' food supply, we
pushed on to the foot of the ruin-crowned island
in the cool of evening.

On a sandy margin, between rock and river, on the right shore, we made our first camp. In all its long history it was scarcely possible that the Nile had ever seen upon its shores a group so strangely composed. Red Indian, yellow Asiatic, jet-black Negro, brown Arab, and white Englishmen, all lay in peaceful slumber under the Nubian starlight; and if, during the day just past, the common brotherhood of man on earth should have appeared doubtful to a listener who had heard the guttural sounds of the Indian Cree, the soft accents of the Arabic, the ceaseless jabber of the West African, and the curt command of the Anglo-Saxon tongues, all spoken in the narrow compass of our little boat, these doubts would have for ever vanished before the similarity of the long-drawn snore which Cree and Kroo, Arab, Syrian, and Saxon poured out alike from their blankets spread upon the Soudan sands.

On again at daylight—sunrise found us in the rapids. The ten days that had gone since our last ascent had lowered the river, and tracking round the wrecked native craft was no longer difficult; but as now we had no wind, the oar and the track-line had alone to be depended upon. Despite a sun that made the rocks glow as though they had been furnace-heated, we reached Semneh at 10.30 a.m., and by noon had left behind that famous cataract.

While the Krooboys were carrying a portion of our load across the portage, and Prince was steering up the straight rush of the east "gate," as the Egyptian soldiers hauled the line from the high rocks above, I stood beside the officer whose report on the Nile between Dongola and Wadi Halfa had been by far the ablest contribution to our knowledge of the cataracts.

This boat of mine, now going through the gate at Semneh, made about the two hundredth that had passed with perfect safety this dangerous spot.

As we stood overlooking the scene, I could not help asking my companion how it had come about that his opinion had been recorded against the possibility of our light English craft being able to stem these waters. The reply was suggestive of many thoughts : " I did not think the boats would not carry the Expedition," he said; "but I did think that the Expedition would not be able to carry the boats." Beneath that tersely put sentence there lay a good deal of meaning. Twenty years before no man would have ever doubted the capacity of British soldiers for any labour that land or water could call forth. Was it a long cry to Khartoum ? Yes; but so had it been a long cry to Delhi, Cabul, Ava, and a score of other distant capitals. Was the Soudan sun hot, and the Soudan sands blinding ? Yes ; but sun and sands as hot and as blinding had been braved

a hundred times in causes which had not one-
tenth of the real glory which this Nile effort
possessed.

Poor modern Tommy Atkins! What wonder
that your capacity for this wild work of cataract
navigation should seem doubtful to outside eye!
Three years ago you were shuffling along the slums
of Whitechapel, almost an outcast among even that
terrible "two million of human beings who never
smile;" and here to-day you are doing, or trying
to do, hero's work. It is no fault of yours, my
poor fellow, if your chest is not deeper and your
shoulders are not broader. Long years ago, your
forefathers, then honest cottiers in Sussex weald
or on Yorkshire wold, dealt many a stout blow of
battle-axe, drew many a feathered arrow to its
steel head, thrust many an iron-headed pike
against the ranks of England's enemies. Nay,
not so far off as that iron age; 'tis but a half or
three-quarter century ago since your grandfathers,
stout of body, as well as true of heart and spirit,
won us dominion under sun as strong and against
odds as long as this and these, and if to-day you
are not of your forefather's bulk and build, if your
chest is hollow, and your body gives out under the
strain of sun and service, 'tis through no fault of
yours, but of those who in their lust of gold and
greed of possession forced you from open country
life to join that herded multitude of four million

beings, of whom half never smile and the other half know not how to fight.

On from Semneh, through a long, calm, fiery afternoon, evening found us passing the small rapid of **Wady Attireh**; a range of wild, serrated mountains ended a reach of the Nile, far-stretching between grey deserts and golden rocks. "Grand! grand!" I heard Prince mutter as, sitting behind me at the helm, he steered along the river which lay before us, opening like a mighty pathway into the heart of this immense wilderness. At dusk we drew in to the east shore, and made camp upon a ledge of rock until daylight again came stealing over the eastern hills.

Next noon found us in the cataract of Ambigole, one of the wildest scenes of rock and water in all this waste of the Batn-el-Hager. The mountains had receded from the shores, and yellow sand, in high-piled ridges, touched the water on the west, while on the east side black and burnt rocks cumbered the desert. Through many islands the Nile poured down its troubled flood. No chance for vessel of any kind in the central rush of waters; but along the edges of projecting points, and through channels soon to be made dry shore by the action of the falling river, our boats were poled and dragged.

At this cataract I found many of the boats that

had started with troops from Gemai eight days earlier. The past four days of calm had told upon the spirits of the men. The work was still new to them; all the hardships of sun, rock, and rapid were at their worst, and the comparative ease which continued habit brings to the heaviest labour had not yet had time to show itself.

The load carried by each boat was an enormous one, and was in excess, so far as the proportion between it and the crew was concerned, of the original estimated cargo; thus, ten men in every boat were carrying over this cataract portion of the Nile 1210 rations of food, or 121 days' food for each man; whereas our London estimate had not exceeded 100 days per man. This extra twenty-one days' load per man was ordered because the number of mounted troops had been doubled since the Expedition had first been conceived, and provision must necessarily be made for the carriage of rations to feed these thousand men, who could not carry their own food.

At first it was hoped that the native craft would have been able to convey to the Nile shore above Dongola this additional load of food, but the increasing number of wrecks and the ever-lessening area of river navigable by these native vessels dispelled that hope, and forced upon our English boats the added burthens.

So long as the boats were sailing or working

through the ordinary rapid water of the Nile, these heavy burthens made little matter; but in the cataracts they told terribly against progress. All sailors know that with sea-going vessels it is the last foot of load that reduces speed, so now with our little craft it was the last inch or two of immersion that gave the trouble. Keels touched rocks or sand-bars at twenty or twenty-two inches, that would have floated lightly on an eighteen or nineteen inch draught, and when the full force of a rapid had to be stemmed, the extra 100 pounds' load which every man had to pull or drive, became a powerful factor against speed.

Of course the individual soldiers knew nothing about these nice proportions between weight and motive power; they only knew that the strain on the track-line was very great, that in rapids the boats seemed suddenly endowed with the strength of twenty runaway horses, and that the toil of this cataract navigation was often excessive.

Working these heavy loads through rapids such as these of Ambigole, brought out in glaring contrast the difference between the real and so-called *voyageurs*.

While the craft that was in charge of some French-Canadian Indian or Winnipeg half-breed passed safely through a maze of rock and whirl-pool, the one that carried some rough lumberman would be seen often wedged between rocks, or

N

aground on some projecting point.   Here strength would endeavour to atone for the absence of skill by efforts which the real expert would never have used.   "Double the gang on the track-line, and haul away," would too frequently be the sole remedy, the only possible result being damage to boat and cargo, amid the innumerable tooth-like rocks that lay above and below the yellow surface.

The attitude of one huge tree-cutter from the backwoods I well remember in this Ambigole Cataract.   He had got his boat fast aground at stem and stern.   Recklessly and with unskilful strength he laboured at his pole, shouting to the men on the track-line to haul away, while he relieved his over-burthened feelings by repeatedly kicking the ribs of his boat with heavy hob-nailed boots.   All his efforts were useless, he was trying to drag the keel with its three-ton load straight over a ledge of rock.   It would seem as though he had exhausted the upper portion of his body in fruitless curses and imprecations upon cataracts in general and Ambigole in particular, which for the most part the roar of Ambigole mercifully drowned; but that the lower man—and there was a good deal of that—had still sufficient vitality left to viciously kick at the unoffending boat-timbers.

Passing quickly through the lower rapids of

Ambigole and their varied scenes of toil and effort, we soon reached the upper " gate " of the cataract. Here a steam-launch, No. 79, had become a hopeless wreck ; a couple of hundred Egyptian soldiers were hauling at long and powerful hawsers in a vain effort to move the launch from the rock upon which the rapids had cast her. It was very fortunate that their united strength was not a match for the force of water which held the wreck in its place, for any movement of the steamer from the rock must inevitably have been followed by her swinging over across the only narrow channel by which our boats could, on this side of the river, pass the spot. A sudden snapping of the hawser put a stop, however, to this danger, and left No. 79 securely fixed until the falling Nile would add her rocky resting-place to the main shore of the river. Then I passed on my upward way to the next big water-jump, the great cataract of Tangour.

We camped at dusk, some four miles from the foot of Tangour, and the next sunrise found us at the rapid.

A large island here breaks the Nile into two channels, both being as full of rock, whirlpool, and breaking billow as earth and water can evolve out of an incline of perhaps twenty feet in a mile. At the entrance to the proper right chan-nel—the left as we looked up stream—the over-tilted hull of a large steamer seemed as though it had been hung out upon the rocks as a warning to all succeeding navigators not to attempt the eastern passage. This ill-fated vessel was the *Gizeh*, a steamer which had been put through the cataracts above Wadi Halfa a couple of months earlier, only now to lie here, a further example of the hopelessness of attempting to navigate these waters with the large craft of the Nile.

It would take long to tell the incidents of our morning's work in the rapids of Tangour—how, with no wind to aid us, we forced up the lower sheet of smooth-running but furious-flowing water, zigzagging from one dark ripple to another, as Prince's quick eye caught the difference in surface-colour that told where amid this wild waste of water there lay some sunken rock whose hidden presence broke the full fury of the stream; how deftly he shot from eddy to eddy; how at moments we hung suspended in some gathered volume of water, unable to make head, until a fresh move of the rudder or a quicker stroke of oar prevailed, and we won our way into an eddy where the panting Krooboys could take breath for other efforts.

There was not a puff of wind, the oars had to do it all, and well they did it; but twice their freely-given effort would not have conquered those rushing waters if the steering had been in the

least at fault. By this time the book of the Nile
was an easy volume to the eye of the American,
and the life-long craft of canoe, the knowledge
gained in hundreds of wild scenes of rapid and
whirlpool in far Winnipeg waters, opened at first
sight all the secrets of Tangour to this Salteaux
Indian chief.

An hour's work, impossible to recall in any
shape, brought us to the foot of the "big gate"
of the cataract, where the rear wing of the
Stafford battalion was struggling with the last
but most formidable obstacle of Tangour. One
by one the boats were being dragged through a
tremendous rush of water which here poured
down the western channel in high-running and
thundering billows. On the rocks overhanging
the "gate," the soldiers clustered thickly, slowly
tugging at the track-lines, as bit by bit the upward way was won. It was eleven days since
this half-battalion had left Sarras ; three cataracts
and about thirty-eight miles of river had been
passed in that time, a slow rate of progress, but
the river was at its worst in that distance, there
had been little or no wind, and the loads were
heavy to haul in these still and fiery afternoons.

Nevertheless, allowing for all these drawbacks,
the rate of progress had been slower than it
should have been. This was the middle of my
third day from Sarras, and although my load was

only a fifth of what the troops carried, the difference of time was too great between us.

Arrived at the foot of the big gate, we prepared to track it up with only the assistance of our own crew: the two Indians remained in the boat to steer and guide with pole; the Krooboys, myself, servant, and interpreter were on the track-line; the Arab, Achmet, skirmished along the shore, now freeing the line from some sunken rock, now diving through the rushing flood to lift it over a projecting boulder. Below the upper or first leap of the rapid there was a very powerful back eddy, which, catching the boat, caused it to move faster up stream than we on the track-line could move along the rock-impeded shore, thus making the boat overshoot the tow-rope. These back eddies always circle into the rapid at its most impetuous point, consequently when our boat met the descending flood there was nothing to hold her head straight to stream. In vain Prince shouted to haul in the slack, and thereby save the sheering of the boat. The pressure of the vast torrent, suddenly multiplied to twenty times the original strain, gave to her the power of a runaway team, and although all stuck to the line gamely enough, it was torn from our hands as a hurricane would sweep a feather before it, and away went No. 387 down the cataract of Tangour, riding the big billows like a sea-bird.

The two Indians got quickly to the oars, and had the boat into shore again, then we dragged her up to the "gate," and with a dozen men of the Stafford to assist, we were over the last step of the cataract before the sun had passed the meridian.

On again into smooth waters, where the shores of Okmé rose into lofty hills of black granite, and between them the river lay tranquil as a mountain loch. Up these rugged shores a breeze came from the north, freshening as evening drew near. It was the first wind we had had since leaving Sarras, and with well-filled sails we sped rapidly along, sailing and pulling up the sharp rapid of Okmé without laying out the track-line.

Beyond Okmé another long reach of good water opened out, and as the sun sank behind the western hills we were at the foot of the short rapid of Akasha. All around rugged mountains lifted their splintered peaks, and held high into a brighter light than reached us, gigantic masses of coloured granite, strange-shapen boulders that stood poised upon narrower pedestals as though they would topple from their lofty heights into the valley beneath. The sun had set, but the afterglow was red over the western waste, and by its light we passed the rapid which marks the Arab tomb, and old mimosa group, where the twelve prophets of Mahomet are said to sleep their last sleep, and then, steering into the east shore, we found a sheltered spot for the night.

There are men who hold that our dreams are memories from a life which the soul lived in some long-vanished age, and that even in our waking hours the mind often catches faint echoes of a by-gone existence, whose threads are lost in distance; so, as I look back upon these lone camping-spots by the Nile shore, of the Batn-el-Hager, it seems to me that they lie altogether in some other world, that the sun which went down beyond the silent desert was not the sun we daily look upon now, that the glow long lingering over the Western horizon, and colouring with weird light the gigantic rocks and deep reaches of the great river, came from infinite remoteness, and that the slowly darkening desert was itself only the shadow of some ruined world.

CHAPTER IX.

GOING back over these long days of labour on this great river of the desert, the shifting scenes that daily passed before us must have stamped themselves with strange distinctness upon the brain, so vividly are their pictures still seen in memory.

The early start from the bivouac, in the blue light between dawn and sunrise; the ring of the oars beneath some overhanging wall of rock; the moving shadow of mast or sail travelling along

the west shore, when the sun first looked over the
eastern hills ; the struggle to pass some projecting
point where the current ran smooth and swift
with the flood strength of the river ; the glare and
heat of noon ; the midday halt under the group of
palms ; the hours of tracking along the boulder-
lined shores ; the rush and roar of cataracts ; the
strong breeze that carried us at times through
rapid and whirlpool ; the mountain, red in the
afterglow—all these come back without effort
of recollection, as though the absence of human
existence had given to these lonely shores a life
which time and distance could not kill.

Above the old tomb of Akasha there opens
out a smooth reach of the Nile, held between
rugged hills whose ruin-crowned summits rise
in many places almost perpendicularly over the
water.   This long reach of silent, rock-shadowed
river, its crumbling castles, and utter loneliness,
might well seem a bit of Rhineland—rainless and
dead.   It was yet early morning on November
21st when, leaving this beautiful reach, we
rounded a sudden bend from west to south, and
came face to face with the cataract of Dal.

It looked a wild scene.   Through a width of
fully a mile from shore to shore, the river poured
down its troubled flood, foaming and flashing in
the morning sun ; a waste of yellow sand, drifted
into endless ridges, spread away to westward ; on

the east shore, rose cliffs that looked hopeless of
foothold; the centre of the cataract held bare
rounded granite rocks whose smooth red sides
were beaten by furious currents. At the upper
end of this waste of waters, a maze of islands
closed the southward river view, but over the
isles, the flat tops or sharp peaks of distant desert
mountains still carried the imagination into space
beyond. Such was Dal as we rounded the pro-
montory which marks its northern end, and ran
out into its whirling eddies.

" Dal," or " the place where the child can live."
Why? Of all the hopeless wastes in this wide
realm of wilderness, Dal was surely the most
hopeless. Not even if mimosa-thorns yielded
grapes, and thistles gave figs, could man's
sustenance be found on these desert shores. No,
Dal had other claims in the old days for the
truth of its title. It was a good place for a
child to be born in, because these bare rocks and
furious rapids gave in the distant times, when
even this part of the Nile held traffic, many a
wreck to feed the hungry shores, and on the
scattered date or dhurra cargo the Arab " child
could live." Prince made a rapid survey of the
cataract, and decided upon attempting its ascent
on the west, or desert side; we therefore crossed
the foot of the first rapid, and working up the
west shore, halted for breakfast, for the work

before us promised to be long and difficult. About
a mile above our halting-place, a white tent was
visible on the desert, this was the military
telegraph hut, the first office above Sarras.
Rightly or wrongly, I had formed during my
journey many opinions upon matters of moment
to our enterprise, and these opinions now went
back by telegraph to Wadi Halfa. Breakfast
over, we set to work at the cataract. Coasting up
the west bank, we crossed to a small island,
crossed again to a larger one, and made our way
along the outer shore until we gained a point
from which advance seemed to be no longer
possible—rocks, rapids, whirlpools everywhere
barred the way. Prince had taken this west
shore passage because the Reis Achmet had so
advised. Achmet now appealed to, could give no
clue to the labyrinth of obstacles that confronted
us. He could only vaguely point to the boiling outside sea that lay between our island and the far
east shore, and tell us that it was necessary to cross
from here, and seek a passage along the opposite
side; but in the face of such a torrent, and without wind to help us in the struggle from rock
eddy to rock eddy, the passage across the wide
river appeared hopeless of success. While we
thus stood looking out from our point of rock at
this blank prospect, an old Arab came out of a
mimosa thicket on the island close by; he was

closely followed by a very small naked boy. They
had evidently been watching us for some time,
and guessing our dilemma, saw in it a good chance
for "backsheesh;" the old man was installed as
guide. Soon a little passage, hidden by islands,
was revealed to us; this opened into wider waters,
and following them, we found ourselves by noon
at the foot of a great rapid—a rush of water more
formidable than anything we had yet faced on the
river. That the boat could live through this
torrent was certain enough, but had we the
strength requisite to haul her up? The two
Indians must remain on board; would our crew
of nine, with the addition of the old Arab and the
two small boys (a second had joined us *en route*),
be sufficient to drag the boat over this cataract?
Tangour had already shown us the strength of
the Nile. However, it had to be done, it was too
late now to think of going back.

We laid out the line to the fullest length we
could control, and were soon ready for the great
tug. Going along the track-line to see that every-
one was in his proper place, I noticed that the
end of the line just reached beyond the stump of
an old sont-wood tree which here jutted from the
shore. Round this tree we put a turn of the
rope, and at the end of the rope stood Ben
Johnson, the stoutest Krooboy of the crew; then
we began to haul. The boat came straight to

the foot of the rush, then with tighter strain we drew her on into the slope of water, until midway up the slant she hung; the least tendency to sheer would now have been fatal, but the rope round the old tree-stump never slackened an inch, and the line of the keel was held straight with the fall. The descending wave of the torrent, forced asunder by the wedge-like stem, curled over the gunwales in two great wings of water, as though they would meet in the centre and swamp the craft, but they glanced off again like gigantic shavings flying from a rapidly, worked plane. For a moment it seemed as if the river must win, but every instant was a gain to us—the force of the rapid never varied, we could improve ours; one Krooboy dug his heels deeper into sand, another got his foot at a better angle upon a rock. Ben Johnson, with one foot against the tree, took in every inch of line we won from the river; for bit by bit we were winning. Then with a pull whose united effort was doubled by the sense of approaching victory, we drew the boat out of the descending surge into smooth water. Again the great brotherhood was clear enough—the four quarters of the world, *plus* a sont-wood stump, had vanquished the Nile at Dal, and while red man and black, yellow, brown, and white, straightened stiffened fingers, or wrung glistening foreheads, their variously-

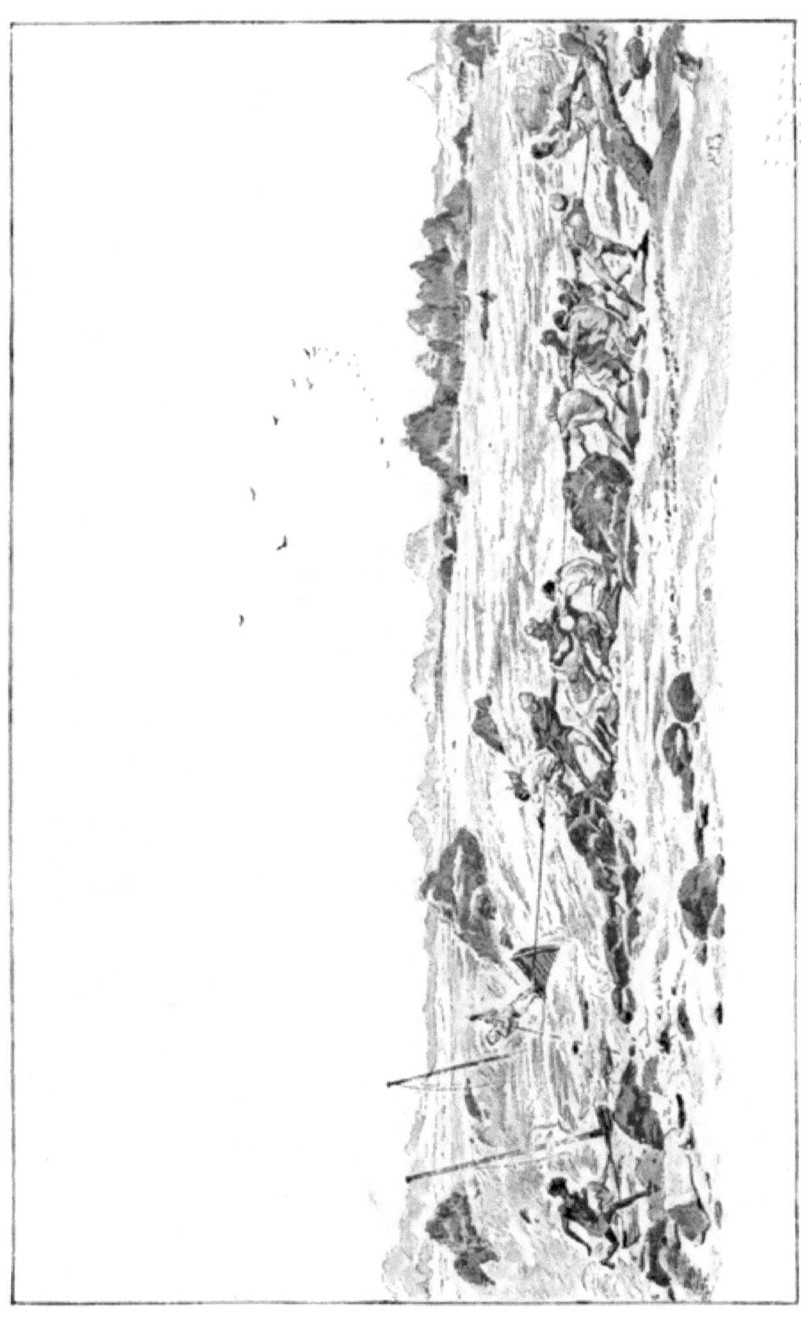

THE TUG AT DAL.

Page 210.

uttered words of mutual praise and approval
showed how keenly the scattered children of the
earth will join hands to fight the Great Mother
in her angry moods.

But this victory did not end our battle with
Dal; there yet lay full two miles of bad water
before the last of the cataract was passed. With
a wind there would have been no difficulty in
surmounting what still remained before us, but
the day was now hot and calm. Still keeping
the old Arab as guide, we held on through the
glowing afternoon, until evening found us at the
foot of the last rapid. We had worked from
eddy to eddy by the oar alone, and were now
almost in the centre of the river, below the
islands which mark the beginning of the cataract.
Twice we had tried to force up this last rapid,
and twice had been driven back. The Krooboys
sat glistening like liquid tar, and nearly done.
Resting a bit in a backwater below the rapid we
had time to survey the scene.

To the east, and about 500 yards below us,
the boats of the leading wing of the Staffords
were working slowly along the shore. We could
see groups of men on the rocks watching our
fight with the centre of the big river.

"They are looking at us," I said. "Surely
you will not let them see us beaten at this last
rapid." Setting again to the oars, we ran up

the eddy and shot out once more into the stream. With every effort freely given, we could not gain an inch upon the rapid; defeat seemed again inevitable. Just then there came a puff of wind. I held the sheet of the main-sail in my hand, the sail filled and flapped, then filled again. " Pull, pull! if the breeze holds for a minute we are over Dal." It was only a passing puff which was eddying up the broad bosom of the cataract, but it lasted long enough to give us victory—the top of Dal was won.

We rested awhile amid the green isles which here lie thickly upon the wide river. It was sunset; the mimosa-trees fringing quiet sandy bays, and growing amid cliffs of coloured rock, were rich with yellow blossom, and the evening air was deep-scented with their perfume. Above these odorous trees the rocky isles were crowned with many ruins—ruins of tower and town and rampart, built by long-forgotten hands—ruins of whose ruin there is not even a story lingering in the Arab mind to tell us of those bygone times when Dal could give its children other sustenance than the chance salvage of the cataract. For that there must have been such a time these crumbling dwellings of a vanished race plainly tell, standing above the present world of desolation, the ruined reminders of a forgotten past.

We rowed slowly through this mimic archi-
pelago as the evening shadows deepened over the
river; perhaps it was the strong contrast between
the long day of struggle just ended and the quiet
of these numerous isles resting amid tranquil
waters, that gave such beauty to the scene. In
the uncertain twilight the outlines of the ruined
bastions looked the massive mason-work of early
Norman times. Whenever channels opened between islets to westward, glimpses of orange and
crimson skies were seen behind tufted palm
or broken battlement; and, outlined in the
smooth surface, rock, tree, and ruin lay in waveless
water, that continued up to the ripple of our oar-
stroke the gold and purple of the afterglow. Night
had long fallen when we reached the post of Sarkamatto, and made bivouac, as best we could,
under palm-trees on the east shore.

South of the cataract of Dal, the Nile for one
hundred miles is clear of any formidable obstacle;
the small rapids of Amara become difficult when
the river is at very low level, but there is no real
obstruction to navigation during seven months
of the year, from the top of Dal to the foot of
the steep ledge at Kaibar.

Up this great stretch of open river we had now
to hold our way, a pleasant prospect after the
closely-set cataracts of the Batn-el-Hager, whose
final limit we had passed at Dal.

o

It was near noon on the 22nd November when
we left Sarkamatto; the puff of wind which
came so opportunely to our aid on the previous
evening seemed to have been a prelude to the
end of the long calm, and now a strong north
wind carried us before it, through the rapids of
Amara, past the large island of Say, and far into
that river oasis of fertile shore and palm-lined
bank, which bears the name of Dar-Sukkôte.

On the afternoon of the 22nd we passed the
leading boats of the Stafford battalion off the
little village of Ginnis, and made our bivouac at
Atab, a short distance below the Amara rapid.
How far off seemed the Arab enemy that night!
Here at Atab my mixed unarmed crew were as
secure against the soldiers of the Mahdi as
though the palm-trees beneath which we lay had
been an oak-copse on the Thames' shore; and
yet only one short year had to pass before the
Arab enemy would be here on this spot, and I
was to find myself leading a brigade of troops to
drive from this very village, and the neighbouring one of Ginnis, nine thousand of these same
soldiers of the Mahdi, whose camps at Berber
and Khartoum seemed to-night so distant
from us.

Three days of mingled sail and oar carried us
far along our way. The wide river that flows
through the palm-groves of Dar-Sukkôte was

RUINS OF THE TEMPLE AT AGOULAI.

Page 195.

curling with high waves, and the palm-trees rustled loud their lofty tops as we sped through the water.

The Nile in this portion of its course is a glorious river; broad and deep it flows past fertile shores and ruined temples, in width and volume more striking than elsewhere in Nubia or in Egypt.

There is a ruined temple on the west bank at Agoulai, which seems left to tell what this region of Sukkôte must once have been. It stands 400 yards back from the river, the centre of a desert point which ends a long reach from the north, and is in sight, from the south, miles after the traveller has left it. There are no squalid hovels, as in Egypt, built among the ruins, or standing near them. Alone in sand-swept space, ten or twelve lofty columns of red sandstone stand out against a sky whose blue is deepened by the clear atmosphere of this lofty desert. Pylon and pillar, shaft and capital, lie around; the Nile, here 1200 miles from the sea, rolls its vast volume, visible throughout a great distance; the desert spreads its sands to a remote horizon, above whose far-off but clear-cut rim a few lone mountain-tops raise their heads to make imagination better realize the vast 3000 miles of yellow sand that sleep beyond that sky-line.

Nowhere else in this old land of time and space

have I seen age and distance deeper marked than here. A hundred temples stand upon the shores of the great river, broader and loftier than these lone columns and their shattered surroundings, but no temple rises amid such majesty of river and plain, and not in all those 1200 miles of Nile is there to be found a spot where the desert wind, rustling through ruins, finds deeper voice to tell the story of ended time and endless solitude.

The north wind partly held through the 25th November, and evening found us a few miles below the cataract of Kaibar, camped upon a fertile island; the harvest had just been gathered, and our beds were made comfortable with bundles of dhurra-straw. Close by stood the usual island village of mat hut, with its talking but busy women, its naked children, roving goats, restless dogs, and quiet sakeeyeh-cattle munching their evening forage in straw lean-to's.

For an hour after dark these little centres of human life on the river-shore are, at this time of year at least, noisy with talk and laughter, for dhurra-cakes are plenty, and the merissa[1] and bilbul pots are full, and although the prophet has no more bigoted followers than the Nubian islanders of the Nile, they by no means make his law of abstinence from fermented drink their rule of life.

[1] Fermented liquor made from dates and dhurra.

I was lying on my dhurra bed, listening to the village sounds gradually growing fainter, until at last they were confined to an angry altercation between two Barabara dames who continued with much animation to discuss the question of goat trespass in a tone and with exclamations that would have puzzled a supporter of the primordial ape theory to explain their close relationship with Billingsgate. At length these, too, were silent. The moon rose over the opposite shore, and only the long-drawn howl of the hyena broke the stillness. About midnight I heard the sound of a single shot some distance up the river. I had half forgotten it when morning came, but the wakeful ear of the Indians had heard it too, and Prince spoke of it as we took our places in the boat.

Two hours later we reached Kaibar. Under palm-trees on the east shore a few tents were visible, and in one of them lay the body of the commandant, shot through the head. Men sleeping close to this tent had heard no sound, and the sun was sometime risen before the deed was discovered. At first there were suspicions of foul play on the part of Arab or Egyptian, but further examination dispelled these, and showed that life had been self-taken. There are many English dead lying along the Nubian Nile, some under palm-trees, as here at Kaibar, others with the sand of the desert drifting over them ; but in all that long line of graves from Kirbekan to Assouan, I know no sadder resting-place than that which marks where this young life was laid.

It took us but little time to pass the cataract of Kaibar, and evening found us camped amid a very beautiful circle of hills, close to an old castle of massive build. From a hut near by, an Arab came to hear the news and share our fire.

As I had now passed every English boat, except the five which had started from Gemai on November 1st, carrying a party of Engineers, my boat was an object of interest to native eyes. Only the day before he had seen five of these strange craft pass this old castle; now another lay at anchor here, it would be a good opportunity to gather news.

The Arab and the Indian, or for that matter all untaught races, will never allow their curiosity to conquer their sense of good breeding. It is only in civilization that you find the absolute rudeness of inquisitiveness. This Barabara had doubtless heard the wildest stories of the strange men and boats who were ascending his river, but he was careful to let our conversation lead up to his anxiety.

" When had he seen the five boats pass ? "

" Yesterday, one hour after sunrise."

"Had he heard anything about the Expedition?"

" Yes, a good deal. He had heard that there were many boats coming up the river. Was it true ? "

It was. The boats covered the Nile for many hundreds of miles. He would soon see them passing this place.

" He had heard, too," he said, " that in the bow of every boat there was a man standing whose work it was to dip his hands into a bag of money and throw it out upon the shore. Was that also true ? "

" No, not exactly."

And yet wild as seemed this idea, it was not in one respect so much at fault. If half the millions which this Expedition was to cost had been put in sacks and cast out upon the sands and rocks, as the sower at seedtime scatters grain, it would have amply sufficed to sow with piastre-coin all the Nile shores of the Soudan.

From coming events our conversation turned to past history. The old fortress on the rock above us was built by the Turks in Sultan Selim's time; before that day he had heard the country held many towns, as the ruins everywhere showed. When the Turks came again in Mehemet Ali Pacha's time, his father was alive. He had often heard old men speak of those days, and of the wars of the Arab Sheikhs among themselves, and how the desert Arabs used to raid upon the river villages. It was on that account that so many castles and forts had been built on shore and island, so that the people might sleep in safety.

" Was not all that wild life of raid and ravage stopped when Ismail Pacha came up with his troops to conquer Dongola and Sennar ? " I asked.

" Yes, it was. But had I heard the final fate of Ismail Pacha ? "

I had often heard and read the story of Ismail's end at Shendy, but I asked for the particulars again. The Arab needed little asking, nor did I, the listener, require to wait for the interpreter's version in order to follow the narrative, for gesture kept pace with words, and the story-teller's eye glittered in the firelight as he told the final vengeance of the Nim'r. Gathering the dry halfa-grass around his seat he broke the stalks into miniature bundles to show how the dhurra-straw had been piled around the sleeping Pacha. Then he cast the grass upon the fire, and as the flame sprung up I could mark the flushed face that told of a heart all in sympathy with the avenging Tiger. Truly the plant we call Freedom dies hard in these deserts.

Another day's work went by, and evening found us at the foot of the Third Cataract. A long series of rapids extends twelve miles below this cataract, which for some strange reason is named the Third. It should in reality be called the

Eighth. In a short rapid near the foot of the isle of Zimmet we had overtaken and passed the five Engineer boats, and when, an hour later, we made our camp under an old mimosa-tree, by the solitary straw hut of Mahomet Hassan of Sardak, No. 387 was the most advanced boat of the Nile Expedition.

Next morning we rowed up between many islets, where sand-grouse and wild geese were numerous, and where the tracks of many crocodiles lay fresh in the soft sand of willow-fringed bays, and were soon amid the troubled waters of the Third Cataract. For some days Prince had suffered from fever, the result of exposure to the sun.

To-day, however, he was again at the helm, and as this cataract was intricate from its innumerable number of islands, it was fortunate he was able to be at his post. I will not stop to tell the incidents of our ascent, they had now become the everyday events of our lives, and although the excitement of forcing up or running down a rapid are things that never become stale to the man who has to do them, their repeated relation might soon become wearisome. Through all the island channels Prince had taken during our ten days' journey, I do not remember having once had to retrace our steps; he had only to look at the water coming out at the end of some long channel to know whether it would prove practicable through its entire length.

A hot sun was beating down upon the red granite rocks and green isles that mark the head of the Third Cataract as we pulled out from the last ripple, and ran up under sail to the post of Abu Fatmeh.

All the cataracts between Wadi Halfa and Dongola now lay behind us.

In the space of ten days we had carried No. 387 over 200 miles of the Nile, which the Father of History had described as " being so impeded with rocks as to render passage in a vessel impossible," and which, 2500 years later, was said, by the highest authority in naval matters, to be " quite unsuitable to passage by small boats." Nor had we come slowly over this 200 miles of river. Seven days out of the ten had been calm, yet, cataracts and all included, we had made a daily average of twenty miles.

At Abu Fatmeh I found an order from the General-in-Chief, directing me to proceed without loss of time to the nearest telegraph-station at Hafir, as he wished to converse with me over the wire.

Hafir was still some nine miles distant, and on the opposite shore of the river. As the ferry-boat that plied between the two shores sometimes took hours to effect the crossing, I sent on my own boat to the point of passage, and proceeded thither on a camel myself. If the ferry-boat was at the east side I would use it, if not, I had my own boat to fall back upon. A fresh breeze was now blowing; the boat made nearly as good progress on the water as my camel did over the sand, and it was still more than an hour from sunset when I reached Hafir. I sent two telegrams, one to Dongola announcing my arrival, the other to Wadi Halfa conveying all the information gleaned since I had left Dal. Then I sat down to await orders. Night fell, midnight came, and still I waited. My position was a curious one. Ever before me one fact had been growing stronger in my mind since I had quitted the cataract of Semneh : it was the fact that our boats were carrying a load under which it was impossible they could travel fast.

I have already said that not only were the boats carrying over the cataracts of the Batn-el-Hager 100 days' food for every man on board, but they were also carrying 100 days' food for the mounted troops. And there was no eating out going on. At Dal they filled in again the quantity that had been consumed up to that point, so that when they came to fight the stiff rapids that lie between Kaibar and Abu Fatmeh they were as deep in the water as they had been at Ambigole.

Here, as I sat at Hafir, the full sense of what I

had seen at all these cataracts was more than
ever present to my mind. To-day was the 28th
November,—not one boat except my own had yet
passed the Third Cataract. It was the eleventh
hour of our effort, but even yet it was not too
late. Cast only on the shore from every boat
this extra twenty-six days' food, reduce the big
load by even 1000 lbs. weight, and that long line
of slow-moving, hard-labouring little vessels will
fly forward over this great stretch of rock-encumbered river. It is the last straw that breaks
the camel's back,—the last straw that was breaking the back of our progress was one thousand
pounds in every boat. To say that I felt anxious
on the subject of this delay would be to give very
feeble expression to the emotions that filled my
thoughts as I sat awake waiting for the message
which I hoped would summon me to Dongola. I
believed that if I could put exactly before the
General-in-Chief all I had seen and heard on my
upward journey, I would do the greatest service
that at that moment it was possible for any one
man to render to the Expedition.

At last there was no use in waiting up any longer.
I went to the telegraph-office, left word that if a
message came it was to be brought to me at once,
and then going back to the boat, lay down in some
green corn for a couple of hours' rest.

Shortly after daylight I was again at the telegraph tent,—still no message. A strong north

wind had sprung up, and the river, as far as the
eye could reach, was running high with waves.
With such a wind I could reach Dongola in eight
hours. True, my orders told me to await here at
Hafir a message from Dongola, but I had now
been here fourteen hours without result, and I
felt convinced that whatever might be the object
which the General-in-Chief had in view in desiring
to speak with me through the wire, the im-
portance of reaching his ear was sufficient to
outweigh every other consideration. I resolved
to start at once for Dongola.

We embarked. The wind was blowing almost
a gale, and before it we swept along the great
water-way which, above the Third Cataract, opens,
in immense reaches, bordered by green cultivated
shores, and holding large and fertile islands
scattered through them. As our boat kept the
slack water near shore, crowds of men, women,
and children ran along the banks, shouting with
astonishment at the sight of the first English
boat they had ever seen.

Throughout the morning the high wind held,
and before it we sped on, the great island of Argo
to our left, the isles of Binneh and Bonarti on the
right. But midday brought a change; the wind
lulled, and the sun came out in all his tropic
strength.

Above the isle of Binneh there opens out a
great reach of river, at the end of which the eye

catches the yellow sheen of the desert sands which from the east shore look across at Dongola. Suddenly in the far end of this long river reach a small speck became visible; above this white dot we soon saw a puff of smoke. The speck was easy of identification. It was a toy steam-dingy which had been given by the Admiral at Malta to the General of the Expedition.

Whatever may have been the value of the experience which I had gained on my rapid journey over the cataracts, and whatever hopes I might have entertained of being able, before the close of day, to put the results of that experience, orally, in possession of the centre and source of authority, this toy steamer carried the final end of such hope and expectation. It brought an order directing me to return to Dal. There was nothing more to be done. I wrote down as rapidly as I could the leading points which seemed to me to require change, handed the letter to the boatswain of the dingy, and gave the word to turn down stream.

"It is not for men to upset the decisions of Providence; we must only follow what we are powerless to avoid." So spoke a Persian soldier in the ranks of another great expedition, 2500 years ago, and so, doubtless, in the far future many another subordinate toiler in some mighty effort will speak again.

CHAPTER X.

IN WHICH WE HEAR AND SEE A GOOD DEAL OF THE NILE.

I WENT back down the big river, over the Third Cataract, through swift-running Shaban, down the *chute* of Kaibar, past the lonely columns of Seseh and Agoulai, by the date-groves of Soarda, and through the isles of Amara, until the afternoon of December 4th found us again at Dal.

No boats in all that one hundred and fifty miles of river save those that carried the Stafford battalion and a single company of the Essex. During these four days a strong north wind swept the river; the twenty days' November calm which a Nile proverb asserts is as certain as the month, had apparently ceased, and henceforward we might look for those strong breezes which for ten months of the year blow with little intermission from the north.

At Dal I found the boats belonging to the leading companies of the Essex and Cornwall battalions arriving. These boats were averaging about twenty-two days in passage from Gemai, the same distance which had taken my light-boat five days to accomplish. Many boats had suffered damage from mishap in cataracts, chiefly caused by rough or unskilful handling. The real *voyageurs* were bringing in their boats with scarcely any damage; the imitation ones were easily to be discovered in the amount of repair their craft required. In no case, however, was the damage more serious than a few hours' labour sufficed to repair; but even these few hours meant delay, and delay was the single item in the long catalogue of our possessions which we could not spare.

On the 7th December an order reached me from Wadi Halfa to ascend the river again to the Third Cataract, and remain on that portion of the Nile until the Expedition should be further developed. So, on the morning of the 8th, I put out again upon the river for the south, this time without that prince of pilots, Chief Prince. Fever still clung to him, and I was obliged to leave him in hospital at Dal.

Evening found us again in the Amara rapid. Sixteen days had passed since we had last camped at this spot, and the islands and rocks showed how much the river had fallen in that time. Opposite our bivouac, on this evening, a few rocks covered with willows stood about fifty yards from the shore. The crew were still engaged near the boat when a loud bellowing noise apparently from the willows caused them no small astonishment. I was on a higher bank some little distance away, and at first I thought the bellowing proceeded from one of the Krooboys who in his period of service as a sailor on board a sea-going vessel had managed to purloin, or possess himself of a nautical speaking-trumpet, for the noise seemed exactly to resemble the human voice through such an instrument ; but another instant brought a second roar, and then I perceived the real cause. Between two rocks the large black head of a hippopotamus was protruding above water, look-ing straight at the boat. Presently another roar in a lesser key came from a spot slightly further away. Madame was evidently as little pleased

P

with our appearance as was her lord and master. It was soon too dark to see them, but they still continued for some time to protest against our presence. When Reis Achmet returned from a neighbouring village to which he had gone, I questioned him about hippopotami. "Yes, there were now a good many of them in this part of the river. Some few years ago, during a very high Nile, seven came down from Khartoum; they had established themselves chiefly here in the islands of Amara, and had increased in numbers. The natives of his village at Soarda had killed a very large one last year." Here was a curious testimony to decay in population and general retrogression towards savagery, of the truth of which there could be no doubt. The wild beasts of the Soudan were coming again into these regions from which they had long ago been driven. It was an ominous advent.

Next morning, as we rowed through the Amara islands, the soft mudbanks in many places were ploughed up with the big tracks of the river-horses where they had been foraging in the night among the bean-patches along the shores.

A wild storm blew during the 10th December, and evening fell upon us far upon our way. It was "the first day of winter," Achmet had declared in the morning, as with his head enveloped in all the spare cottons and woollens he possessed, he surveyed a most desolate scene of sandstorm, high-running billow, and palm-tops swaying in the howling blast. If this indeed was the beginning of winter, nobody could say it had come too soon, but " better late than never." The Soudan sun teaches thankfulness for small mercies, and if there is any spot on earth where man could realize without regret, Byron's terrible dream of a day when the sun did not rise, that spot is surely to be found among the deserts of the Upper Nile.

It was in a gale such as this of 10th December that the sailing qualities of our boats became so apparent.

Despite heavy cargoes, and billows large enough for a large lake, the boats of the Essex and Cornwall battalions were making splendid progress over the long and deep river-reaches of Sukkôte and Mahass. The seven-feet beam, broad keel, and " whaler" bows, were now proving their use, and these deep-laden boats were making their thirty miles a day through water that would have proved fatal to narrower craft.

Again we passed the rocky *chute* of Kaibar, and currying a steady breeze on the 12th, ran up that beautiful reach of the Nile where the river flows around the large island of Faretti in a curve so great that in a distance of twenty miles its course follows three of the four cardinal points of the compass.

In no part of its great length is the scenery of
the Nile finer than in this place. Nowhere are
the ruined fortresses so close together; nowhere
do the near and distant hills stand in stranger
outline of peak and table-top; and nowhere are
the evidences of a past history of warfare more
apparent than here at the southern end of Dar
Mahass; for this was once the frontier. It was
here, at the Third Cataract, that old Egypt ended.
Here stood the golden stone of the empire of
Ramses the Great; and here, too, the legions of
Selim the First halted in 1517, when that savage
Sultan set his face again for Constantinople.

As now we sped along the broad river before
a breeze that came laden with the perfume of the
sont blossom, it was impossible for human spirits
not to feel the freshness and exhilaration of such
a scene. The storms of the past few days had
been followed by an extraordinary brightness of
atmosphere; the sun no longer burned like a
globe of molten copper, but felt pleasant, although
the afternoon was still early. The desert air had
in it a wonderful sense of freshness. Mellowed
by distance, the sound of the " sakeeych " water-
wheels came across the broad reaches of river
from the green palm-lined shores, and far or near,
the conical peaks or rugged outlines of many
mountains stood out in singular distinctness in
this clear desert air.

Man over the earth has, generally speaking, only one method of showing sorrow; his satisfaction he demonstrates in many ways. To-day, as we sailed along through this wild and beautiful scene, lying in all the glory of the Nubian winter, my Krooboys showed their satisfaction by lying along the thwarts and oars fast asleep, with their round black heads on the gunwale, and the broad, light-coloured soles of their flat feet upturned to the sun. Hitherto I have said little about these strange helpers in our labours. Eleven years before the date of this Expedition, I happened to be a passenger in a steamship bound for the West Coast of Africa, which called at several of the larger Kroo villages between Sierra Leone and Cape Coast Castle. Before our vessel would be many minutes at anchor crowds of Kroos would be on deck, it being apparently a matter of perfect indifference to them whether they came from the low sandy shore, swimming through a boiling surf, or paddling long mahogany canoes with great ease and dexterity. Indeed, on one occasion when a sudden alarm had spread through a couple of hundred of them on the deck of the steamer, that they were about to be carried away for service on the Gold Coast, the whole crowd effected an instantaneous retreat in the twinkling of an eyelid, by the simple process of vaulting over the bulwarks into the sea.

Remembering their dexterity in paddling, rowing, diving, and swimming, it had occurred to me, in the preceding month of August, when the question had been discussed in England of how we were to overcome the almost certain difficulty of finding the Arabs of the cataracts either disinclined to assist us in any shape, or to give us a half-hearted help, which would have been always subject to desertion, that valuable assistance might be obtained by sending a steamer to West Africa to engage Kroos for boat service on the Nile. In the preceding April I had suggested the employment of Canadian *voyageurs*. Both these suggestions were, as we have already seen, approved; but not, however, without considerable reluctance, so far as the *voyageurs* were concerned. In putting forward the proposal, I had unfortunately laid stress upon the great desirability of obtaining as many Indians as possible. I say "unfortunately," for the name Indian conjured up in the mind of a Cabinet Minister visions of the scalping-knife, the tomahawk, the war-whoop, and as one hundred years earlier Chatham had protested against the employment of the Redman in the War of Independence, so now it was thought necessary to safeguard the Arab of the Soudan against the savage proclivities of the French-Canadian and half-breed *voyageur*. That was one view of the Indian question; but there was also another, which is perhaps as good an illustration of the difficulties that beset any attempt at the rapid organization of such an enterprise as this we were now engaged upon. When it was announced in the London papers that the Government had decided upon engaging the services of Canadian *voyageurs*—Indian, half-breed and white —a prominent member of the Opposition rushed simultaneously into print and to Canada, for the purpose, as he expressed it, of saving the poor, harmless natives of the Dominion from the certain death which a reckless and unscrupulous Government were preparing for them in the deserts of the Soudan. I have already said that out of the 300 or 400 men who responded to the invitation which was telegraphed to Canada in August, 1884, about four-fifths were good hard-working boatmen; half of the entire number were expert *voyageurs*, the best of these last being French-Canadians, Iroquois from Lachine, and Swampy Indians and half-breeds from Winnipeg. Could we have obtained a couple of hundred more of this class of real *voyageurs*, our gain in time would have been very great—so great indeed that the saving of an entire week might easily have been effected in the concentration of the fighting force at the rendezvous at Korti.

I know not how many Canadian Indians and half-breeds were deterred from throwing in their lot with our Nile effort, by the speeches, letters, and denunciations of this Opposition Member of the Imperial Parliament. Indeed it is not unlikely that these far-away Colonial cousins understood far better than he did, the strength, both of their own constitutions, and of real loyalty to the mother-land; but this I know, that had the most determined foreign enemy of Gordon's succour, and of England's success, been bent upon preventing the first and striking a blow against the second, no fitter method of effecting his purpose could have been devised than the task which this prominent politician imposed upon himself.

Despite, however, opposition from opposite quarters, and the lateness of date at which we were permitted to seek such wide-apart fields for our boatmen, both American and African contingents were assembled at Wadi Halfa in the last week of October—in little more than two months from the date upon which the first conception of their enlistment had been submitted to the Government in London.

Steam and electricity are powerful agents to real power. If ever there should be born into the world another Napoleon, it is not improbable men will find that, in girding the earth with iron roads and lines of wire, they have also been forging chains.

Meanwhile, let us return to our own particular Krooboys, who all this time have been toasting the soles of their feet over the gunwale "strake" of No. 387. They had curious names—Jack Everyday, Jack Sunday, Tom William, Screw Bolt, John Bull, Ben Johnson. All were pure black—short, well-built, very muscular, of immense appetite, great good-humour, strong to work, but loving idleness all the same.

It was curious to watch the intercourse of life between the members of the widely-differing races who formed the crew of my boat. That the Arab and the Negro should have little friendship for one another was natural enough. For centuries they have held towards each other the relative positions of slave and master; but the close intimacy that soon sprang up between Arab and Red Indian was a thing I was not prepared for. Chief Prince and Achmet were good friends from the first, and three weeks sufficed to make the Indians understand and speak a good deal of Arabic. At night the Kroos camped together, while the Arab, the Indians, and my servant lay down beside each other.

The Indians and the Kroos were never friendly companions. The Negro habit of incessant chatter was not in keeping with the cold and slow method of conversation which is characteristic of the Redman.

A very taciturn and ugly-looking Kroo, named Tom William, from the town of Jack Jack, seemed to be the only one of the six who was looked upon by the Indians with the least respect. I have reason to fear that the exception made towards Tom William was not on account of any moral superiority possessed by that negro, for one day Prince remarked to me *en passant*,—

"That fellow," pointing to the native of Jack Jack, " he have two wives at home."

But with all their chatter and love of eating, the Krooboys, after a little management, were excellent fellows, and when a month later than the time I speak of I wanted a crew to man my boat about to enter the wilds of the Fourth Cataract, when the Monassir and Robitab Arabs had assembled to fight us, my six black oarsmen volunteered to a man.

On the 13th of December we entered, for the second time, the Third Cataract, but it was late in the afternoon when we began the ascent, and night compelled us to halt upon an island, almost in the centre of the big " gate," for every large cataract on the Nile has its " Bab-el-Kebir." Our island resting-place had been formed by an enormous boulder of red granite, which had gathered behind it in the course of time the drift of the great river, which in turn had given birth to sont-trees and halfa-grass, whose roots held fast the soft alluvial clay. From the top of the big boulder the cataract was seen on all sides, its troubled waters pouring through a hundred passages, every passage sending forth its wild music to join the deep, thundering, bass note of the Bab-el-Kebir. Our island gave good store of dry wood. The night fell cold, and soon a large fire sent its glare far over the wild scene of troubled waters, and the red rocks stood in fantastic outline around us. At sunrise next morning we passed the remainder of the cataract, and having arranged with the commandant of Abu Fatmeh[1] for the passage of the large numbers of boats soon to be expected from below, I returned to the foot of the cataract, where, upon an island little more than a rock, which commanded a long view down stream, I made a temporary camp.

A line of rocks, covered at higher water, afforded communication between the island and the east shore. At the land end of this causeway I kept my camel. My boat lay in a sheltered cove on the outer side of the islet. As the nights had now become cold, I pitched a tent for the Krooboys, and a thick-leaved mimosa-tree gave excellent shelter for myself from sun and wind. I was thus in a position to work the river by boat, or to cross the desert to Kaibar by

---

[1] Colonel Frederick Maurice, R.A.

camel, and as now a few days must bring to these
waters a very large number of our boats, whatever guidance or assistance could be rendered to
them over the six-and-thirty miles of difficult
Nile between Kaibar and the Third Cataract,
could be easiest given from this point. Had
there been time to think of other matters there
was much in the surroundings of my island camp
to afford occupation to geologist, antiquarian, or
sportsman.

At the opposite side of the river lay a labyrinth
of rocky isles, where wild geese were numerous.
Three hundred yards below the island, a long
tongue of black sand, daily lengthening as the
water fell, formed the basking-ground for a
couple of crocodiles, whose glistening backs were
usually visible in the early sunlight. Only a
short distance to the east, amid some granite
rocks, lay the colossal figure of an Egyptian god,
or king, hewn from the quarry long ages ago,
when the frontier of the Pharaoh was drawn at
this Third Cataract, but probably left lying where
it was worked when some wave of Ethiopian war
sent the frontier again back to Semneh, or Syene.
Close by this prostrate statue stood the old
" Golden Stone," with its defaced double inscription, looking north and south, so long regarded
as the southern landmark of the empire, which
Sultan Selim in the sixteenth century established

on the Nile. Still further away to eastward rose
the lofty double-topped Jebel Arambu, or Rambia,
" the Chameleon," so called because its rugged
sides, veined and seamed with many-hued rock
strata, show ever-changing colours as the sunlight moves from east to west across its solitary
summits. At the foot of the Chameleon the
desert lies in even surface for many miles,
covered with cornelians, agates, and coloured
pebbles, as though a sea, once receding from its
bed, had left these stones stranded in groups
amid wider expanses of sand.

Yes, there was ample material to fill the vacant
moments of a stranger's stay at this Third
Cataract. But life held no vacant moments
now, and if all the art wonders of old Egypt,
and the mineral treasures of a new California
had been lying within a mile of my island camp,
there would have been little time to seek them.

I gave the crew a short holiday at the island,
and set out on the 14th of December for a
camel-ride to Kaibar. While the river route
was some six-and-thirty miles, that across the
desert was only twenty-one; but as I had not
travelled it before, and the track led at first
through very broken ground, I determined to
take the camel-driver along with me. This man
was a Darfourian, named Farag, a strong and
powerfully-built black of the true Darfourian type,

than which Africa does not hold a darker, stronger, or more formidable race.

Farag had managed to possess himself of a donkey altogether out of proportion to his own colossal size; but the Nile donkey is a very wonderful animal, and it would be rash to say what manner of man or load he cannot carry.

On this occasion, however, the forecast of the eye was correct, for scarcely had we started before the donkey's legs seemed to close up like the joints of a telescope.

I stopped a moment to see if there was hope of resuscitation, but the animal looked such a complete wreck, and the Darfourian biped appeared so big as he stood over the prostrate quadruped, that I gave up all hope of salvage, and turned off alone to the north-east.

In the deep angle which the Nile makes between Kaibar and the Third Cataract, lie hidden away some of the wildest spots in the whole river's length. Enormous single blocks of granite, smooth and polished with age, are set up on end, as though in some bygone day a legion of giants had been here at work building monoliths over the desert. Often these singular blocks stand opposite each other at the mouth of some pass or valley, giving still more the idea of human agency by their relative positions.

In some long-distant age the whole of this

portion of the desert has been subject to violent denudations. Whenever the change from granite to sandstone takes place, in these water-worn regions the traveller soon sees what, in all probability, was the origin of the Sphinx of Egypt. Some rock of pink or white sandstone will stand alone in a level desert, with impending frontlet and narrower neck, and often, in peculiar shades of light, or seen against sunset or afterglow, the rude lineaments of a human face can be traced in these solitary masses.

Riding for four hours through this wild land, I came in sight of the two great conical rocks of " Light " and " Darkness," which stand on the right bank of the Nile, about seven miles above Kaibar. A few miles beyond this point the path touched the river. Looking down towards the cataract the eye caught sight of white sails through the green palm-trees, and below the *chute* the tops of other sails were visible in the long reach of water, where Seseh's lonely columns stand in a wide circle of desert hills.

It would take too long to tell the doings of the next ten days, full of labour though they were. The strong north winds, now blowing with little intermission, swept our boats quickly over the 100 miles of open water lying above Dal, and each day brought the white-winged fleet in scores to Kaibar.

During the ten days preceding Christmas I traversed the river between the Third Cataract and Kaibar many times. The rapid at Shaban, ten miles below the Third Cataract, had now become one of the most dangerous cataracts on the Nile. This rapid was not marked on any map, nor had it been noticed in any report until my first ascent of the river, when I spoke of it as being worse than many of the obstacles the names of which were well known.

Unfortunately, it was now to prove the truth of that description by the victims which its hungry waters claimed from us. Out of the dozen soldiers who were lost in the whole length of the Nile cataracts from Wadi Halfa to Dar-Robatab, Shaban was answerable for about one-fourth of that number. As the boats were now coming on in numbers, it became necessary to live on this twenty miles of bad water in order to be of use to them. The river changed so rapidly—places that were safe this week, became dangerous the next, new channels opened, or old ones closed—that the information gained one day would prove quite useless a few days later. Often have I found no bottom with a ten-foot pole, where a couple of weeks earlier our light-draught boat had grounded. As the Nile falls the current changes its direction, and will sometimes scoop out a sandbank, or cast one up, in the space of a few hours.

The swift stream carries with it such a quantity of sand in suspension that its action in sharpening and polishing hard rocks is very marked; everywhere throughout the cataracts one sees constant evidence of the wearing away and leveling down of these granite barriers. When the river is at its lowest level, a vast number of the rocks are laid bare; the great alteration of temperature between day and night then causes even the most metallic-looking boulder to chip its surface. With the rising flood the wearing away goes on with greater effect, and as diamonds cut diamonds, so the sand of the Nile itself, so largely granitic, files year by year these enormous masses. Thus day by day, living from dawn to dark on the water, sleeping from dark to dawn on the rock shores, one came to learn the secrets of the great river.

The histories of Tomb and Temple, Sphinx and Monolith, have long been given to the world, and he who runs may read the story of old Egypt; but the daily, nightly secrets of the Nile, the life of the river as it is to-day, its cataract voice in the desert silence, its soft heaving murmur under the moonlight, its blue-grey surface in the purple morning, its reflected sunsets, its steep shores suffused in light, or lying dark against lustrous afterglows,—these must be lived with day by day, and night by night, ere their infinite

Q

gradations of voice and colour can be understood.

There is no other river upon earth which centres on its shores the entire human, animal, and vegetable life of an immense region. Behind in the desert, five miles to east or west there are a thousand spots whereon the foot of man has never pressed, but wherever the desert drift, or the close encroaching rocks, will allow a tree to take root,—wherever a level spot can carry the wheel-lifted water along its little winding channel,—there man has built his home and dug his grave since human life began on earth. Take away this river for one entire year, and man, beast, bird, fish—even the hyenas in the rugged hills—all must disappear.

Many names have been given by different nations to this River of the Desert. It has been called the "Sea," "Gihon," "Ægyptus," "Noym;" the Greeks called it the "Niger," the Hindoos the "Cali," and an old Arab writer tells us that the present name is derived from "Nal," to give liberally; but the single name "Life" would have been its fittest title.

Behind every village throughout 2000 miles of river-shore there lies the denser-filled resting-place of the dead. Often where the village has disappeared, the line of snow-white pebbles still marks, in the desert, the long-disused burial-place.

The vast generations of atoms which the river called to life, and fed and nourished during their brief span of existence, have gone back again into desert dust, and the mighty stream rolls on its unchanging course, unheeding whether the human mite it had given life to, built the lordliest temple or filled the lowliest tomb upon its shores.

CHAPTER XI.

CHRISTMAS came. It found me again at Kaibar. The boats were coming on hand over hand; all the reaches of the river were white with sails. Three hundred boats had passed Kaibar, 200 were over the Third Cataract, the Naval Brigade and some companies of battalions were running from Sarras to Abu Fatmeh in twenty days. A reduction of 500 lbs. weight in every boat had been ordered, and the whole Expedition with this lightened load was now averaging ten miles a day over the worst water on the Nile. But for all that it was Christmas Day: had this average been made a month ago, we would now have been assembled at Korti, with the vanguard of the army within touch of Metemma.

I set out in the afternoon for the Third Cataract; eight or ten first-class Indian and Canadian *voyageurs* had arrived from Dal, and I was desirous of bringing these men as quickly as possible to the assistance of the many boats which were now in the difficult waters between Shaban and Abu Fatmeh. So, declining the allurements of a Christmas dinner at Kaibar, we set out to make what way we could while daylight lasted. The outlook for our Christmas fare was not enticing. We carried only the now well-known tinned beef ration of Chicago; but I still had in my possession one last remaining bottle of Irish whisky, and I was well aware from old experience that a single gleam of this "fire-water" would suffice to light the heart of Indian, half-breed, or Canadian in the darkest hour of misfortune. There was still a chance, too, that I might be able to add a wild goose to our bill of fare. There were some sand-islands on our road that were favourite haunts for these shy and wary birds.

Sunset found us in that fine reach of river which has the twin rocks of "Light" and "Darkness" marking its western end. Night was coming on, and there was no goose. The time-tired tinned meat of America must again give us dinner.

In the centre of the river a patch of green bank had lately become visible with the falling water. As we drew nearer to this patch, a few black spots were discernible upon it. They were wild geese; but cover there was none, and there seemed small hope of getting within gunshot of them. As we drew still closer things looked more hopeful, for we could hear a good deal of angry cackling going on, and some of the birds were flying at each other as though a grave family or matrimonial dispute was going on among them, which withdrew their attention from our approach. When we had got within one hundred yards of the group, I tried a bullet at them as a last chance. The ball splashed right among some seven or eight birds. They all rose from the bank, but one tumbled back again into the water. The bullet had found its billet, and we had got our Christmas goose.

It was now nearly dark. We put in to the left shore, made camp and fire. The night fell cold. Wood was scarce, but there was enough to cook the goose and boil two kettles of water; and when the whisky had been mixed hot and sweet, the toughness of the goose or the tinness of the beef were soon forgotten by Kroo, Canadian, and Swampy Indian.

There was an old white-haired French-Canadian among the *voyageurs* whose typical face and figure had often attracted my notice in the lower cataracts during the earlier days of our work. Coteau—for such was his name—was one of that hardy race of *voyageur* now all but extinct, who, in the bygone days of the fur trade, had been wont to carry the canoes of the Hudson's Bay Company through the wilds of the North-West. Coteau was now sixty-eight years of age. That at that time of life he should have been ready to leave his little frame-house on the St. Lawrence and come all this long way to fight the battle of this Expedition with the cataracts of the tropic Nile, was a striking instance of the pluck and hardy spirit of his race. He had taken the boats of the Stafford up the lower cataracts, had gone down again, and here he was now on his way to the upper portion of the river, still ready for work, but showing, in his old weather-worn face, tanned by the sun and snow of nigh seventy years, many traces of the toil and hardship of life in this strange land.

I gave this old veteran of a thousand cataracts an extra issue of grog, and began to question him about his old life. For forty years he had set out from Montreal in the spring, said his prayers in the little church of St. Anne, where the great Ottawa River falls into the still mightier St. Lawrence, and then held his way for months into the wilderness, through pine-forest, over rapid, up rivers and down rivers, across lakes, over a hundred portages, until at last the broad waters of Lake Winnipeg opened before the laden canoes.

"Ah! those were good days, monsieur, and those were fine rivers—not like this river—this Nile."

"Why, Coteau, what is there in this river that is different from others?"

"Different, monsieur—everything is different. Here you can see no rock until you strike it; then you put the pole down on one side and you find twenty inches of water, then you change it to the other side, and, lo! there is no bottom at ten feet. Ah! it is a bad, bad river!"

It grew late. The moon had risen, and the desert was a flood of yellow light. I left the sleeping camp, and made my way some distance to a ridge of hills inland from the river. Through the intensely-clear atmosphere of this elevated region the greater stars shone with extraordinary brilliancy. Sirius, Canopus—all that southern starry host, whose night-march across the desert is, of all sights on earth or in the heavens, the most sublime—were out in all their splendour.

Over the desert lay a vast stillness. There was no breeze to find echo in the distant line of whispering palms or amid the nearer crannies of the old grey rocks. No cry of bird or beast broke the immense silence, and, as the moon rose higher in the heavens, all the weary look of sorrow, the dead anguish of the years that know neither rain nor dewdrop seemed to vanish from the parched face of the desert, leaving it as though "the brightness" which had shone upon Judean shepherds on that first Christmas-night was falling again upon these lonely hills.

Next day we ran up through many boats, and, narrowly escaping disaster in the worst bit of Shaban, reached early on the morning of the 27th my island camp at the foot of the Third Cataract. I found here a telegram just arrived from Korti, summoning me to that place—a welcome message; for as two-thirds of the troops and all the general officers had long passed my island, I began to think I was to be the Moses of the Expedition, destined never to enter the promised land.

Passing for the last time this Third Cataract, and taking on board at Abu Fatmeh a heavy cargo of food supplies, we set out, on the morning of the 28th of December, for Korti. It was just forty days since I had left Sarras. In that time we had passed and repassed the cataracts, had traversed a total distance of close upon 800 miles, and during the whole period No. 387 had been but twice out of the water for repairs.

What the ultimate route of the Expedition would be beyond Korti, no one could yet tell for certain. At Korti began that singular bend of the river which carries it, for a distance of 160 miles, in an opposite direction to its proper north course. Not only did this change of direction double the distance by river from Korti to Berber, but some sixty miles beyond Korti a second series of rapids began, neither the nature nor extent of which were known to the modern world. These cataracts were variously called the "Fourth Cataracts," the Shagghieh Cataracts, and the Cataracts of Dar-Djuma. Men on the Lower Nile shook their heads when these wild rapids were spoken of. The few experts in Nile travel whose opinion could be asked in London had taken even a gloomier view of them.

"You will get over the cataracts of the Batn-el-Hager and of Dar-Mahass," said a traveller who had visited Dongola and the Bayuda Desert, to me, when we were building our boats; "but you will never pass with these boats the cataracts of Shagghieh."

Between us now and these terrible rapids of Shagghieh lay a perfectly open waterway of 240 miles. Korti was about 175 miles distant along

that open river. Once at that point, the choice
would lie between crossing the desert to Metemma,
or moving by the long détour of the river, taking
the cataracts as they came.

Four days of varying wind and calm, and
always of unvarying sun, carried us far to the
south, past the great island of Argo and all the
isles that lie on Nile's broad bosom below New
Dongola,—past Handak, with its crumbling castle
and high-perched houses, until the last night of
the old year finds us camped in the yellow sand
of the east shore, a short distance below the
ruined city of Old Dongola, and 110 miles above
the Third Cataract.

Although it was the last day of the year, it had
been intensely hot. We seemed to have caught
up the summer again on its slow retreat to the
Equator, and one could not help feeling anxious
for the success of prolonged operations if already
we seemed to have reached a latitude to which
winter never came; but in truth this Soudan
climate has to be lived in for an entire season to
understand its strange inconsistencies. These
fiery hot days are common even in the depth of
winter, as sometimes in the other extreme of
April heat a comparatively cool day will be
found.

A night of perfect temperature, and of a beauty
which can never be fully recalled even in thought,

had succeeded to this fervid day, and the vast expanse of yellow sand now lay glistening like a sea of amber in moonlight that made it visible to a remote horizon. Men often speak of the wonderful moonlight on the Nile. It is little wonder that the moon should there be brilliant; it looks down upon a vast shield of burnished gold, which in turn sends back through undimmed atmosphere a redoubled moonlight. I believe the desert sends as much light to the moon as the moon sends to the desert.

Old Dongola, whose high outline could be discerned from our camping-place, had been a famous Christian centre in times not so far remote from our own day. All deserted now, it lies with drifted streets and ruined houses, sand-choked and silent, bats and owls for citizens, and the hyena at night to call its watches.

As here we sit on the moonlit sands near the ruins of this half-buried city, it will be well to leave for a time the thread of personal narrative, and glance back into the bygone of Old Dongola.

When Amrou-Ebn-Aisai, the great Arab conqueror of Egypt, gladdened the heart of Omar with the flames of the famous library of the Ptolemies, after his second capture of Alexandria, he had been recalled, the Arab historians tell us, from an expedition into Nubia.

How far this renowned champion of infant

Islam penetrated above the First Cataract will never be known, but it is certain that all the region above the Second Cataract remained Christian many centuries after the first great wave of Mahometan conquest had swept over the Eastern world.

Seven hundred years after the death of Mahomet, a Christian king was still ruling over a Christian kingdom between the Third and Fourth Cataracts, holding his court on this rocky ridge where now the sand lies deep above Old Dongola.

That this Christian kingdom should have remained so near the centre and source of Islam through all the years that saw the Saracenic hordes, obedient to the command of the first Caliph, spreading themselves to the Loire, to the Jaxartes, to the Caspian, to Cape Comorin, everywhere smiting the "infidel" and offering the triple choice of death, tribute, or the Koran to the vanquished, is perhaps the greatest proof of the power of resistance against an invader which the Nile cataracts and rocks of the Batn-el-Hager possessed. For at that time the desert had not all its own way as it now has above these cataracts, and Dongola was then a land worth fighting for. Great plains which are now desolate deserts were then rich in cultivation, irrigated and fertilized by canals and inland wells, whose ruins can still be traced, and that this Christian king and his people were foes worthy of Arab steel may be gathered from the assertion of the Coptic Patriarch in the eighth century, who declared that 100,000 horsemen and the same number of camel-riders answered the call of the rulers of Nubia and Ethiopia; nor is this alone the boast of a partial or prejudiced authority, for an Arab historian of old times speaks of the 1300 elephants, each carrying ten fighting-men, and of 50,000 horse and foot-men, who opposed the army which Amru—the first Arab conqueror of Egypt—sent beyond Syene.

We do not know—probably we shall never know—the history of the conquest and conversion to Islam of these kingdoms of the upper cataracts, but we do know that with that conquest, civilization and prosperity vanished from these lands.

In the end of the thirteenth century, three great waves of Moslim war swept over Nubia, submerging for a time the Christian kingdom of Dongola, but breaking in vain against the rocky barrier of the Fourth Cataract. The record of the plunder taken by the soldiers of Sultan Bibar in 674 of the Hegira, is evidence of the wealth and power that then centred in this old sand-heaped city. The Arab writers tell of the gold crosses and silver vessels carried away from the sacked Church of Jesus, and how the army, after selling or killing vast numbers of captives, brought back 10,000 prisoners to Egypt.

Ten years later, another Egyptian army passed the cataracts, and again Old Dongola was sacked by the invaders. Once again, in 688 A.H., the Sultan Seyf Eddyn Kalaoun sent an army of 40,000 men and 500 " harackes," i.e. light boats, to conquer Dongola. In the previous campaign, the Nubian King, Samamoun, had escaped from the wreck of his army into the fastnesses beyond the Fourth Cataract, and the 500 "harackes" were now brought to enable the invaders to follow him into these wild waters. The army and the fleet reached the foot of the Fourth Cataract, but all the strength of 20,000 men on each shore, added to the crews of the 500 vessels, could not force the barriers of the Shagghich cataracts, and King Samamoun remained safe in an island refuge, which, by-and-by, if the narrative should continue, we shall look upon in these pages.

But though the last stronghold of the Nubian king could not be reached, his fair kingdom between the cataracts was ruined. From these waves of Moslim war the land never recovered, and a long night-of desolation settled down upon Old Dongola.

It is probable that had the arms of the earlier Arab dynasties—the Ommiades, the Abbassides,

and the Fatimites—been carried into these distant
Nile regions, there would also have been brought
that civilization and knowledge of the arts which
the Arab conquerers of the eighth, ninth, and tenth
centuries carried to Cairo, Cordova, and Bagdad ;
but when the conquest of Dongola was effected,
the genius of Arab art had for ever disappeared.

The cities of Syria and Egypt whose ruined
tombs and mosques still make the traveller marvel
at the beauty of design and elegance of decorative
art possessed in that early age by the wild
children of the desert, were even then in decay,
and from the "roof of the world," where the
sunrise over Mongolian steppes flooded Oxus and
Indus with the same snow, to where Atlas caught
the last gleam from the Atlantic sunset, the dark
cloud of Tartar domination was closing over the
vast empire of Mahomet.

It is in vain that we attempt to pierce the
darkness of the time that followed the conquest
of Nubia. At long intervals a traveller reached
these distant and jealously-guarded lands, and
from his missionary or merchant notes we glean
a passing glimpse into the state of affairs beyond
the cataracts. From the effects of the Egyptian
invasions of the thirteenth century the country
never recovered. One hundred years later,
Christianity had almost died out in Nubia,
and when in another hundred years an Italian

traveller penetrated to Dongola, he found only the ruined evidences of a former faith.

These still stand. In the drifted sand that now lies deep above the deserted city, a broken column or defaced capital can yet be seen bearing the image of the Cross which some Greek sculptor had engraved before the sword of Amrou had severed Egypt from the lower empire, and islanded the Christians of the cataracts amid the desert sea of Islam.

From many signs observable to-day along the whole length of river from the Second Cataract to the head of the Fourth Cataract, a distance of 600 miles, I am inclined to think that the final conquest of these regions by the Arabs was effected more from the south than from the north.

We know that many migratory tribes crossed the Red Sea from Arabia in the eighth and ninth centuries, founded the kingdom of Sennar, and spread themselves, in the following centuries, across the Blue and White Niles, cutting in two the long line of the Christian kingdom of the upper river, but leaving Abyssinia and Dongola still untouched—one entrenched as now amid impenetrable mountains, the other living for a time behind impassable cataracts.

It was, I believe, the existence of this last-named kingdom that formed the germ of truth underlying the vague stories of the great empire

R

of Prester John which so long vexed the minds of
European kings, and sent missionary travellers to
seek this Christian king reigning over a Christian
people in inland Africa.

They were all too late in their efforts to
reach this mysterious kingdom. The Arab had
triumphed then as 400 years later he was destined
again to triumph, and when in the seventeenth
century French missionaries passed Dongola on
their journey to Sennar, the ruins of cell and
church were numerous along their road.

During 100 years following Poncet's mission an
impenetrable cloud hangs over Dongola. Wasted
by war and invasion from Shagghieh on the south,
and Dar-Mahass on the north, it sank lower and
lower in the scale of civilization—the inland wells
became choked, the canals filled up, and the drift
of the desert blew denser over the land. At last
the cloud begins to clear away. A conqueror
greater than anything the Arab world had seen in
its long history was at work in Egypt, and the
echoes of his conquest were reaching even these
distant regions beyond the cataracts.

At the very close of the last century the shores
of the Nubian Nile above Assouan beheld a
strange sight. The broken squadrons of "the
finest and bravest cavalry in the world" were
moving south towards Dongola. Dessaix had
accomplished the orders of Napoleon to "drive

the Mamelukes beyond the cataracts," and the remnant of that once proud and glittering host was seeking a distant refuge.

The French evacuation of Egypt stopped the exodus of the Mamelukes, and brought them back again to the Delta; but it would perhaps have been better for them if they had persisted in the intention of founding a new kingdom beyond the cataracts, abandoning for ever the scenes of their crimes, their conquests, and their glory. In 1807 a second English expedition invaded Egypt, this time to experience the difference between the Mamelukes as friends and foes. Turk and Mameluke now joined hands against the invaders, and the plain of the Esbekieh in Cairo, where to-day the trees and the fountains of Khedive Ismail's garden refresh the lounger, beheld the ghastly sight of 400 or 500 British heads impaled upon it.

But an enemy more formidable to Mameluke than Frenchman or Briton was even then at hand.

Mehemet, a young Albanian in the Turkish service, determined to free himself alike from Turkish rule and Mameluke power. The first was easier to effect than the second. Three thousand Mamelukes, the flower of their force, were invited to Gizeh under pretence of marching with Mehemet's army to the conquest of Arabia. These were invited to a great feast within the walls of the citadel of Cairo. Fifteen hundred horsemen accepted the invitation. The strength of the party, and the neighbourhood of the other 1500 left at Gizeh, seemed to guarantee the safety of the guests.

They must have made a brave show, these 1500 doomed warriors, as glittering, man and horse, in silver and gilt trapping, burnished steel, and coloured kaftan, they wound up the steep ascent which leads from the great Mosque of Sultan Hassan to the old minaret-topped fortress on the rock above.

Of all the 1500 horsemen that passed beneath the Moorish archway at the head of the winding road, a single rider escaped. The story of the wild leap from the rampart is an old one now, much changed from truth in its descent through time. Nevertheless it is a fact that one chief did ride his horse at the rampart, close by where now the gorgeous mosque of the murderer of the Mamelukes stands, on the very ground which was then reddest with Mameluke blood. The horse was killed, the rider escaped.

It was no common chief who thus hurled himself and his brave steed into space. He was Ibrahim Bey, the partner of the still more famous Murad Bey in the fierce struggle against Napoleon.

Eleven years earlier Ibrahim had escaped from

the disastrous day of the Pyramids to rally his squadrons in the Fayoum, give battle again at Sediman, and finally to retire from that fiercely-contested fight to the cataracts, and Dongola.

These earlier reverses had taught Ibrahim the road to safety, and now after his wild leap for life, he led the remnant of the Mamelukes again to the south. They numbered about 2000 all told. Early in 1812 they reached the Golden Stone we have lately passed, and entered their new home; but only a remnant of the original remnant gained this place of refuge. Four hundred had fallen victims at Esneh to the treachery of the son of Mehemet Ali, to whom they had surrendered under promise and assurance of life and protection. Many others had succumbed to fatigue, privation, and the terrible heats of the Nubian summer, and not more than 500 white Mamelukes, and the same number of black slaves, reached the Third Cataract and entered Dongola. The usual war was being waged at the time between Mahass, Dongola, and Shagghieh; the new-comers took sides with the ruler of Mahass. The Shagghieh were driven from Argo, and the Mamelukes took possession of the west bank of the Nile, and of all its isles and islands from the Third Cataract to nearly opposite this spot, where now we lie camped in the moonlight below the sands of Old Dongola.

At a place called Maharragga on the west

shore they fixed their capital, naming it New Dongola, and here for a few years they enjoyed comparative rest. They armed and disciplined 6000 black soldiers, they were able to cast some rude sort of howitzer that no doubt made noise, if it did little else, and they had among their followers about half a dozen or more English and French deserters who were partly skilled as gunsmiths and armourers, and one or two of whom knew something of surgery.

Under its new government Dongola prospered; commerce with the interior kingdoms increased, and for the first time, at least in its modern history, the smooth water above the Third Cataract was navigated by sailing-boats.

War soon broke out with the restless Shagghieh. Ibrahim led his troops against the enemy, defeated them at Taini and Korti, and pushed them back into the wilds of the Fourth Cataract.

Everything now seemed to promise the establishment of a strong ruling power above the Third Cataract; but a cloud was gathering in the north soon destined to break upon the Mamelukes.

Mehemet Ali had never lost sight of the fugitives, and the news of their growing power only made him more desirous of their final extinction.

I have already sketched the progress of the expedition under Ismail Pacha, which, in the years following 1819, invaded Dongola and Sennar.

When that expedition was about to leave Wadi Halfa, Mehemet Ali sent a message to the Mamelukes offering easy terms if they would submit. Ibrahim Bey, " El Kebir," was now dead, but a leader as brave reigned in his stead. Abdul Rahman Bey sent back this haughty message to the old enemy : " Tell Mehemet Ali we can make no terms with our servant."

But resistance to the Egyptian army was out of the question. War and disease had reduced the fighting strength of the Mamelukes to a remnant of 300 men, and this handful determined to seek their fortunes in the far interior rather than put faith in the promises, or trust the clemency of their now powerful enemy. That they were right in this resolve a sentence in the book of a traveller who for a time accompanied the Pacha's army, plainly shows. On the authority of the principal medical officer in the Egyptian expedition, this writer tells us that it was " resolved to destroy the Mamelukes by poison if they could be prevailed upon by promises to surrender."

Having celebrated the great feast of Ramadan, 1820, with extraordinary ceremony, the last of the Mamelukes, putting their wives and possessions on horseback, turned southwards from Dongola with the intention of following the Nile until they reached a nation that was prepared to fight the

Egyptians. The Shagghieh attempted to oppose the Mameluke march, but a passage was cut through their ambuscade, and quitting the river at Korti, the brave remnant crossed the Bayuda Desert to Metemma, opposite Shendy. It is not unlikely that the character of the Meg (whose deed of midnight murder, two years later, I have already told) gave the fugitives hope of finding him now ready to resist; but the numbers of the Pacha's army had been doubled by rumour, and the conquest of the Shagghieh made the ruler of Shendy—for the time at least—a neutral.

As Ismail drew nearer to Shendy, the Mameluke remnant, under the brave Rahman, turned off again into the desert towards Kordofan and Darfour. Another band, it is said, sought the shores of the Red Sea. Henceforth both are lost to history. Thus ended the last of the Mamelukes, a race that for 600 years had ruled Egypt and Syria. Terrible in onset, cool in action, cruel in conquest, of unequalled skill in all martial exercises; handsome, rapacious, vengeful, prodigal of life and gold,—they had made the name of Mameluke, originally the symbol of slavery, the type of all that was bold and daring in the chivalry of Islam.

There is a story still told in the Soudan of a battle fought in Darfour in which a body of cavalry charged the Egyptian army, captured its

artillery, and changed for a time the fortunes of
the day. Later on the tide of war was turned by
the resolute behaviour of the Turkish and Tunisian
infantry, and the Darfourian army was destroyed.
Perhaps in that gallant charge, so like the onset
at Redania against Selim, and at the Pyramids
against Napoleon, the last of the Mamelukes may
have perished.

Since the date of the Egyptian conquest the
decay which has ever followed the footsteps of
the Turk, has deepened over the kingdoms of the
middle Nile. The ruins that cover the river-
shores above the Second Cataract are, it is true,
relics of a time long anterior to Turkish rule;
but the story of continuous decay is told as surely,
if less loudly, in choked canal and broken sakeeyeh
channel, in crumbling hamlet and deserted village,
in a belt of green ever lessening, and a drift of
desert ever deepening over the land.

Meanwhile, in following the fortunes of Dongola
and its people in former times, I have wandered
a long way from our standpoint in the sands some
distance below the ruins where, on this last night
of 1884, we lie encamped. We must go back to
our boat journey.

Running before a good breeze on the 1st of
January, we reached at sunset the ruined fort of
Debbeh. The Nile here turns sharp to the east,
beginning its great bend towards the north, or, to

speak more correctly and follow the river down stream, ending its long détour to the south.

In olden days this land, where the Nile turned backwards, was known as "Bakou," or "the wonder." As late as the fourteenth century Bakou was a region in which the grape and the olive flourished, and the towns nearly touched each other along the shores ; but the Arab has long ago changed all that, and the " wonder " is now only a wonderful waste of sand far stretching to the horizon.

That the prosperous condition of Bakou in former days had not been exaggerated by the old writers had been abundantly evident to me even during the passage of my boat on this day. Solid walls of stone and burnt brick were often to be seen on the shores of the islands, or the mainland, imbedded in the mud and silt of succeeding ages.

In a glade surrounded by mimosa-trees, during our midday halt I had, on the previous day, come upon the unmarked ruins of a temple. Three granite columns were lying prostrate, and I counted seven capitals amid piles of broken masonry spread around.

Fast as we had travelled thus far—and sometimes we had, when the wind lasted, added a few hours' night sailing to our daily distance—it did not seem, in face of the news that here reached me, that our progress had been fast enough. The vanguard of the Expedition was reported to have already left Korti. One thousand Camel Corps, escorting 2000 baggage-camels, had started for the wells of Gakdul, midway on the desert track to Metemma. The supplies were to be left in charge of a garrison at the wells ; the whole of the camels were to return to Korti for further loads, and the movement of the main body of the mounted troops would then take place.

Of the condition of things in Khartoum nothing was known. This place (Debbeh) was only 250 miles distant from the besieged city, but no echo of news ever came across the desert, and the zone of our information was co-extensive with the area a scout could cover in a day's ride from Debbeh.

These items of information I learned from an officer of the Sussex Regiment who commanded a small detachment of his battalion at this place. In a neighbouring native fort a body of Egyptian Bashi-Bazooks had their quarters. It is needless to say that these worthies were under no discipline whatever ; but if any doubt could have existed in a stranger's mind as to the reasons of revolt against Egyptian authority in the Soudan, the conduct of these Bashi-Bazook soldiery would quickly have dispelled it. It was a common practice of theirs to make a raid upon a defenceless village, and carry the women away on their horses to Debbeh. When the women had been kept in the fort for some days, an envoy would be sent to the village to inform the husbands and brothers of the captives that they could ransom their relatives. Thirty and forty dollars would then be demanded and paid as a ransom for each prisoner. It was a few weeks after this date that the English newspapers informed us her Majesty's Ministers had determined not to abandon the Eastern Soudan until they had established settled government in that region, which would otherwise become a prey to anarchy and disorder. Knowing the exact truth of what " settled government " meant to these wretched natives, one could have laughed if the absurdity of the declaration had not been hidden 'neath the horrible reality of that truth.

Before midnight a light breeze sprung up, and as the moon was bright I determined to get further on my road that night. Rousing the Krooboys from their blankets, we set out from Debbeh ; but the breeze soon died away, and the oars were only languidly worked. After a couple of hours' effort we put in to the right bank, now the north shore, and lay down to sleep in soft yellow sand. The shore was here lined with a dark-green juniper, which grew in thick bushes amid fine sand, and gave out a delicious fragrance on the cool night air. Golden moon-

light, cream-coloured sand, dark-green trees rich
in odours, blue sky, and great river flowing in
silent strength through the wilderness—it is no
wonder that these Nubian nights are long-lived
in the memory.

During the next two days we tracked steadily
along the shores, the course of the river being
still east and west. We had now entered the
country of the Shagghieh Arabs, which extends
from Debbeh to Jebel Kulgaili, a distance of about
100 miles. As this southern portion nearest to
Debbeh has often been the scene of conflict, the
desert, for considerable spaces, has blotted out
former cultivation. Still there are many fertile
spots, and the islands are here, as elsewhere,
gardens of vegetation.

It was here, too, that crocodiles first became
really numerous. One could count three and four
basking on the low sandbanks in a single reach
of river. It is many weeks now since, somewhere about the Temple of Seseh, we saw our
first crocodile, and yet so far that famous denizen
of the Nile has scarcely been noticed in these
pages. If here, as we track along the level
shores towards Korti, we speak a few words
about this last big lizard left on earth, the di-
gression may not be without interest.

During the last fifty years the crocodile of the
Nile has been steadily falling back before the

tourist. Guide books of twenty years ago mark the "northern limit of the crocodile" a long way below Assouan. Now he is rare below Wadi Halfa or Abu Simbul. The travelling "gunning-man" has been his worst enemy. Whenever a dahabieh carried its tourist cargo up the Nile during the past forty years, there was sure to be some "sportsman" on board bent upon "potting a crocodile;" and although the potting process seldom resulted in anything except waste of ammunition and danger to the inhabitants on the shores, still the crocodile has no greater fondness for being shot at than the majority of men. His old compatriot and companion, the hippopotamus, had long since gone southwards, and in view of this pot-hatted, potted-meat-eating potter, it was time for him to do likewise; accordingly he began to take himself off into quieter reaches of his river, above the big rock of Abu Seer, which was the Nile bourne from whence his great enemy the dahabieh traveller invariably returned. It is curious to trace in old books of travel the gradual falling back of this gigantic lizard. A pilgrim bishop from Gaul to the Holy Land saw croco-diles near Damietta in the year 565, where he tells us horses and oxen fall frequent victims to their rapacity. Only 100 years ago they were plentiful from Sohag southwards. The traveller Leigh finds them at Girgeh in 1812, and " very plentiful afterwards." Thirty years ago they were at Luxor, and to-day, as we have already said, it is rare to find them below Abu Simbul. In the cataracts between Wadi Halfa and Dongola, Amara appeared to be the spot most frequented by the crocodile; the islands of the Third Cataract held many, but in point of size and numbers, this part of the river, from Debbeh upwards, far surpassed the regions to the north. Despite the passage of so many boats, and a very general fusilade carried on early and late, with almost inappreciable result, the long-projecting ends of central sandbanks held in almost every river reach the glistening backs of this armour-plated reptile, lying seemingly asleep, but with one eye at least, very wide open.

In these months of winter the natives seem to take small concern as to their proximity to a crocodile, so much so indeed that a traveller passing here at this time would say they could not suffer from the animal's voracity; but in summer it is quite different. Just before the Nile begins to rise, one may see the women at these villages throwing stones and lumps of dry mud into the river while their companions are drawing water from it. It would seem as though the clearness of the water at that season enabled the crocodile to become dangerous to persons even at the edge of the banks. During some

months of the year the crocodile is seldom seen
above the surface of the water.   The natives say
that in order to keep himself from coming to the
top he swallows quantities of stones; and wild as
this theory may appear, I can myself vouch that
the stomach of a crocodile contained a large
number of stones, some of them as large as a
small egg, but whether the period of stone-swal-
lowing precedes the time of seclusion I am unable
to determine.

Early on the morning of January 4th I reached
Korti.   The future course of the Expedition had
already developed itself.   There were to be two
columns operating on two diverging lines.   The
vanguard of the desert column was at Gakdul,
100 miles inland; that of the river column had
reached Hamdab, near the beginning of the
Fourth Cataract.

CHAPTER XII.

IN WHICH TIME WILL NOT WAIT, AND THE SAND IS
RUNNING VERY LOW.

K ORTI, as one looks back upon it during these early days of 1885, presents two widely different aspects. There is the Korti of the moment, full of life, hope, and movement; the boats streaming in, in rapid succession; rearranging crews and cargoes, and passing on again up the long reach that led to the Fourth Cataract; there are the camel convoys also arriving from the north, refitting, loading-up, and starting out in long columns for the desert march to Metemma; there is the news coming in from Gakdul,

s

announcing the easy attainment of that half-way
resting-place in the march across the Bayuda, and
the fair prospect of further success; there is the
coming and going of all the men, whose names
during the past three months had been household
words along the line of scattered posts and cataract stations down to now distant Wadi Halfa;
the busy lines of camels and horses, the rows of
white tents standing in the luminous shade of
palms and mimosas, the broad river flecked with
white boats, the cindery ridge of Gebel Dager
beyond the further shore, and the long, easy
desert slope behind the camp to eastward, where
the camel convoys in their thousands disappeared
on their march, never to come back again.

That is one view. The other is the Korti of
baffled effort and crushed-out hope; the place to
which the tidings of failure were first carried, and
from which they were despatched to bring sorrow
into many homes and cast gloom over the whole
nation.

Looking back, to-day, upon that distant Nile
village, whose unknown existence was so suddenly brought under the world's gaze, it is not
easy to recall through these later scenes of its
short history the earlier rendezvous, so full of life
and hope.

Korti marks the place where the Nile, as we
ascend the stream, first bends from east to north,

a course exactly opposite to its true direction, making the long loop to Metemma, *viâ* Abu Hamad and Berber, which more than doubles the direct distance across the desert—the route by water being 400 miles, that through the Bayuda 180. Here, then, at Korti was the spot at which the choice must be taken between River and Desert, a choice which, but for one sole consideration, could never have presented any difficulty in the minds of those who had to make it. Great as was the disproportion in distance between the two routes, that by the river was unquestionably the right one, and "the longest way round was the surest and the safest way home" to Khartoum. "How can this be?" I hear many readers ask. The reason will be soon shown. A soldier working in hot weather in England will drink in a day three times a greater weight of water than he will eat of food. In the Soudan desert he will drink seven times more weight than he will eat. But that is only half the difficulty. Water in a civilized country seems a very ordinary matter, presenting itself principally to those who may be compelled to drink it in the light of a great grievance; but in war it is a very important element, and in desert war it is by far the most important item in the long list of the soldier's necessities. Now although the carriage of a supply seven times greater than that of food is a very serious matter,

still it by no means represents the whole difficulty. To carry and to store food is comparatively easy work. To carry and to store water
almost impossible. Waste, breakage, leakage,
and evaporation make the daily average loss of
water in the desert almost equal to the quantity
consumed.

There is a fiction pervading the minds of
Western people that the Arab, like his camel, can
almost do without water. It is totally erroneous.
The Arab caravans consume enormous quantities
of water. Burckhardt gives from fifteen to
twenty pounds weight of water as the usual
daily allowance of each Arab, trader, traveller,
and slave; and if an Arab, eating only vegetable
food, and accustomed to restrain his thirst in the
hard school of the desert, will drink so much,
what would be the demand of the English soldier,
fed upon salt provisions under such a sun, and
ever taught to regard thirst as a craving to be
instantly satisfied, not unfrequently by antici-
pating its presence?

"India is a fine country," I once heard a
soldier say, "because you're always thirsty, and
there's so much to drink." But the desert gives
only the thirst—ever-present, never assuaged;
and the water-skin, filled a day or two ago on the
Nile shore, holds already a thick and foul-smelling
residuum, which heat and the "churning" of the

camel is rapidly changing into a black and buttery mud.

No; better, far better, the long road which has water in the desert, than the short one which is without it. I have said that but for one consideration there could have been no hesitation between the routes to be followed from Korti. That consideration was, however, all important. It was time. The New Year had begun; the date to which Khartoum could hold out had been already passed, and if the place was to be succoured and Gordon saved, the attempt, cost what it might, must be made across the 180 miles of desert, and not by the 400 miles of river, to Metemma.

One month earlier at Korti, and there would have been no need of this desert dash. The entire force—horses, camels, and boats moving along the river and its shores—would have reached Metemma by the 10th January, and Khartoum ten days later. The Cataracts of the Shaggieh, which we shall soon see, would have presented half the difficulties of passage they were now destined to oppose to us; and the line of the Nile, taken along its loop, would have cleared every enemy before us. opened up at Abu Hamad the road to Korosko, and at Berber that to Suakim; and meeting Gordon's steamers at Berber would have carried to Khartoum the advanced guard of an army secure in its strength, its resources, and its unmenaced base.

But that was now past. It was no longer a choice of routes. Time had thrown his single weight into the scale, and had overbalanced all other considerations. Across the Bayuda desert 1800 men on camels and 200 on horses must try to get quickest touch with the steamers, even if all the Arabs in the Soudan stood to bar the road between Korti and Metemma. As for the rest of the expedition, it would be divided into two portions. Four battalions of infantry would continue to ascend the river, two would cross the desert, marching on foot to Metemma, one would hold the point at Korti, where the two lines of advance separated. The work of the Desert Column was twofold. First, it was to get touch of the steamers and send a small advanced party to Khartoum. Then it was to take Metemma, and stand ready for one of the two opposite courses— (1) To move on Khartoum if that place was in imminent danger of falling to the Arabs. (2) To move on Berber, and co-operate with the force advancing by river, if Khartoum was able to hold out. In the latter case, the capture of Berber and the junction of the two columns would have preceded the attack upon the Arab army surrounding Khartoum. In the former case, the desert force, moving from Metemma along the river, would have advanced upon Khartoum, leaving Berber to be taken by the River Column. Such was the plan of campaign which had already begun to develop itself from the base at Korti in the last days of the old year.

Early in the New Year the two lines of movement had reached positions well forward on their respective routes. The head of the Desert Column was at the Wells of Gakdul, 90 miles from Korti—the head of the River Column was at Hamdab, 60 miles from the same place.

At this place, Hamdab, the force destined to move by the river threatened the direct desert route to Berber. Its position while it was waiting to complete its concentration, would thus tend to keep at Berber any Arab force which might be destined to attack the Desert Column at or near Metemma. As for the forces opposed to each column, so closely did the Arab keep his counsel, that only the vaguest rumours of his movements and intentions could be gleaned. It was known that he held Metemma despite the presence of Gordon's steamers in the river at that place. It was also known that he had gathered another army to fight the River Column at a place called Birteh, on the Nile, about twenty miles above the Fourth Cataract; but numbers and composition were subject to the wildest variation. As for

Khartoum, closer than ever had become the cordon of silence surrounding it. One little scrap—a postage stamp—on which was written "All right," had come out through the encircling Arabs, but the messenger who bore it had a different story to tell by word of mouth.

"Come quickly—come together—do not leave Berber behind you." These were the message words he carried, and his own spoken testimony was still more pressing—"Famine was in Khartoum; the Arabs knew it; there was not a moment to be lost." This message, the last that ever left the doomed city, was dated the 14th December. It was all that was needed to give to the column which was about to start across the desert the supreme interest of a forlorn hope.

I have already said that the vanguard of this column left Korti in the end of December. Ten days later the main body made its final start. It was a sight not soon to be forgotten. Across the brown ridge to the east long lines of camels trooped slowly into the desert, the evening sun behind them, the lone sands, and distant hill-tops of the Bayuda in their front. Never had any nation confided to her chosen champions a more glorious mission! Nor were the men unworthy of the cause. Bronzed and burnt by the sun of deserts already traversed, these soldiers—the pick

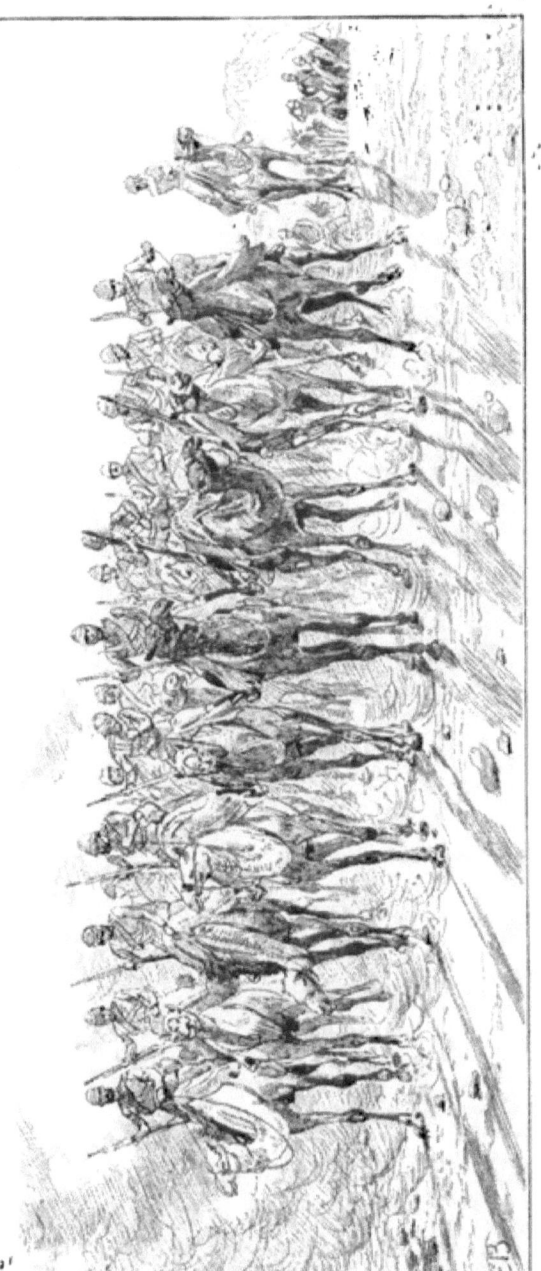

DEPARTURE OF THE DESERT COLUMN FROM KORTI.

Page 264.

and flower of the British Army—looked as hard as the service upon which they were bound.

Well might their gallant leader, as he watched this far-stretching host pass by his stand-point on the Korti ridge, speak the thought that was in his heart that evening—"I could not wish for better fortune than that every Arab in the desert might stand between us and Khartoum."

When the last of the camel columns had vanished beyond the brown ridge, the sunset shadows were following them with rapid steps, lengthening out until they touched the forward sections. Over the line of march the dust still rose into the clear atmosphere, and hung, a cloud of gold, above the moving troops; then the sun went down beyond the river, and darkness coming quickly from the east blotted out the Desert Column.

" Will the Arabs fight?" I asked that day one whose knowledge of Arab nature was deep and wide. " If there were only nine of them left," he answered, "these nine would still fight that column."

And now we must go back to our boats again.

All through this first fortnight in January the boats had been coming in, in great numbers, and the middle of the month saw four battalions of infantry past Korti *en route* for the camp at Hamdab. These four battalions—the 1st Staffordshire, the 1st Royal Highlanders, the 2nd Duke of Cornwall's, and the 2nd Gordon Highlanders—with a small mounted force of eighty Hussars and eighty Egyptian Camel Corps, and an Egyptian Battery of mountain guns, made up the column destined to move by river against Berber and Khartoum, to a strength of about 2900 men.

The 217 boats which carried this column carried also 100 days' supply of food for the four infantry battalions, but as the mounted force and the artillery had also to be fed from the boats, the average supply of food for the entire force was about three months. This was an extraordinary fact.

Not only had the fleet equipped the whole Desert Column, and supplied it with food to last for two months, but it had also brought to Korti three months' food for the River Column; and this result had been achieved in an average time of forty days from start to finish, or at the rate of ten-and-a-half miles per diem, cataracts included. One officer and six men had been drowned, a few boats had been lost, but nine-tenths of the fleet were in as sound condition as on the day they had left the English building-yards. Standing on the high river-bank at Korti, and looking down, day after day, upon scores of boats coming in, closing up their crews and cargoes, and giving out a vast surplus supply to feed the Desert Column, one could not help letting the mind run back to four months earlier, when the prophets of disaster had been loudest in their opposition. How many men were we not to have lost by sunstroke, by disease, by crocodile, and by cataract! How our poor frail craft were to have split asunder in the sun, been dashed to pieces against the rocks, been swallowed up in whirlpool and cataract! What ignorance, what folly, what madness was this scheme of a boat expedition! And here, to-day, were these much-abused boats piling out upon the shore at Korti box upon box of the best English provisions, equipping a desert force of 2000 men for a long campaign, and having still, for the use of another 3000 men, sufficient food supplies to last three entire months.

And the men whose labour under the sun and over the cataracts had achieved this result in these boats—were they the gaunt and sickly skeletons foretold by the wise ones? They were models of strength—pictures of health. Brown, sinewy, and muscular, they sat at the oars or tramped the shore with the track-line in all the ease and freedom of a perfect knowledge of their work.

On the 16th January I left Korti late in the evening for Hamdab. The six Krooboys still sat at the oars, but disease or desertion had caused many changes among the remainder of the old crew. The Syrian interpreter had succumbed to Mahdi fever at the Third Cataract. My English servant had become incapacitated through an injury sustained in one of the rapids. Cochrane, the Cree Indian, had gone down the river suffering from fever; and the Reis Achmet had vanished a day or two after our arrival at Korti. He had, since leaving Dongola, strenuously objected to being brought further south, alleging day after day that we were going among very bad people, whose chief employment in life seemed to be throat-cutting without provocation. In the earlier days of our journey I had given him for his use a soldier's blanket; going to my tent one night at Korti, I found this blanket carefully rolled at the foot of my bed, with some other trifling articles which he had also been given. Next morning he was gone. In the place of the Cree Indian I had now at the helm an Iroquois from the Lake of the Two Mountains, named Leo. Leo had been many things in his day, from canoe boy on a Canadian river to baggage checkman on a Pacific railroad. He was now to prove himself a skilful pilot—a cool hand and quick eye in dangerous waters.

I had been very busily engaged all day at Korti, and night had fallen when I got away for Hamdab. My crew, thinking that I had started on foot in advance along the shore, got under weigh in a hurry, hoping to overtake me ere night quite

closed in, but I was behind instead of before, so
there was nothing for it but a run along the
rough shore. I was soon clear of Korti, getting
along as best I could over Sakeyeeh channels, dry
mud and broken ground. I could hear at times
as I ran, the sound of oars in rowlocks coming
down the wind, and I knew the Krooboys were
pulling their best to catch me up. I shouted,
but the wind was against me, and the noise of
rapid rowing drowned my voice. At last there
came a bit of swifter water, and I gained on my
imaginary pursuers sufficiently to get within hail.
The rowing stopped, and then a shout answering
through the darkness told me the boat had
halted.

At daybreak next morning we pursued our way
up the now southward-running river, many rich
and fertile islands stood in mid-channel, and the
shores held denser groves of palms as we proceeded northwards. We were in the heart of
Dar Shagghieh, the country of the Shagghieh
Arabs, one of the best, and long the most renowned among the old tribes which fixed their
homes along the Nile. For centuries before
the Turkish conquest the Shagghieh had made
their names famous on the upper river. There
can be little doubt that they formed the iron head
of the Arab spear which ended the life of the
Christian kingdom of Nubia 600 years ago, from

the Red Sea side. They are far more Arab than their neighbours the Dongolawis, and they speak no tongue but Arabic. Before the conquest by Mehemet Ali, they could put 8000 spearmen and 2000 cavalry in the field, the latter as expert in all the exercises of sword and lance as were the Mamelukes with whom they had so often crossed weapons. They possessed one art in war which was almost their own, it was the power of swimming their active little horses with perfect safety across the Nile in every state of the water, by day or night. A couple of lances, the long, straight, two-edged sword, and a small oblong shield, cut from the crocodile or hippopotamus skin, formed their weapons of attack and defence. "Peace be yours," was their strange war-cry, as galloping up to an enemy they launched their lances against him. In their battles with the son of Mehemet at Korti, which we have just left, and here by the foot of Gebel Dager, which we are to-day passing, they showed to the full all the old desert valour. Mowed down by the grape of the Pasha's numerous cannon, and shot into by his trained Moggrebin and Albanian troops, the Shagghieh came on time after time, making their little horses spring like the antelope, to distract the aim of their enemies. This curious manœuvre in galloping is peculiar to the horses of the Dongola breed, and although it would speedily unseat riders unaccustomed to its rapid bucking motion, the Shagghieh threw their lances, or dealt their sword-blows with perfect dexterity. But neither trick of horse nor thrust of spear could avail much against the bullets of the Turkish soldiers, or the shells of the Turkish cannon. The "Dogs," as the Shagghieh called their enemies, who had come "from the North, from the East, and from the West," and who had brought "the spirits of hell to fight against them,"[1] triumphed, and Ismail passed on to the Fourth Cataract, to leave the bones of his fleet to bleach upon the rocks of these famous rapids, and to meet his own fate a year or two later in the flaming dhurra straw at Shendy. "I have come to make you a nation of Fellahs instead of a nation of warriors," the Pasha had said to the Arab envoys at the beginning of his invasion. "You may drive us to the gates of the world, but we will not be slaves," was the Shagghieh answer. Since that day sixty years have gone by, and time has brought his usual harvest of revenge—the grandson of Mehemet Ali is to-day the exile, the Shagghieh are now free as their deserts.

To tame a wild bird it is necessary to clip his wings, to tame the Arab it is necessary to kill his

---

[1] It was thus the Shagghieh spoke of the shells which burst among them in their battles with the Turkish troops.—*Wad-dington.*

horse; this the Turks proceeded to do on the upper Nile, and the Dongola horse, so numerous in the time preceding Mehemet's conquest, is now scarcely to be met with above the Cataracts.

Passing up the broad open river, we reached, early on the 18th January, the Egyptian fort of Abu Dom, opposite the town of Merawi, a spot at which I was destined later on to spend some months and to write the opening chapters of this book. Here I parted with my crew of Krooboys, and getting five men of the Cornwall Regiment in their place, set out again for the advanced camp of the River Column at Gerf-Hamdab.

Before leaving Korti it had been intimated to me that my future command would be that of the mounted troops moving with the River Column. As I would therefore, at the camp to which we were now bound, exchange the boat for the saddle, this day was to be my last for many months in No. 387.

For more than two months I had lived on the river, and it was no wonder that, knowing it in its every phase of light and darkness, one had come to feel a good deal of that strange companionship which the Nile has ever exercised over the minds of those who dwell upon its shores or sail its waters. What the secret of that friendship is it would not be easy to define, but its presence has too often been attested to allow even this age, which makes the whole world too small for man, to doubt its reality.

I do not think that secret is to be found in the memory of the bygone glory of the river, nor in the ruins which still stand to verify, even in their desolation, history which without them would read as fable, nor in the contrast between man's misery to-day, and his magnificence in the past. These and more than these memories grow thicker than palm or mimosa on the shores, but they are sad as Nubia's twilight hour, which nowhere sinks upon the earth in light and shadow more intensely mournful. Nor yet do I think that this secret charm is to be looked for in the contrast ever in sight between river and desert, between the extreme of the dry and barren, and the border of green which, though a fringe, is rich with the colour carried from a thousand tropic sources; but those who dwell upon the Nile literally live upon it, it is life—all else, the desert, the cloudless, rainless sky, the pitiless sun, the blighting breath of the Simoom, these are death—death with torment of thirst and hunger; but here, centred in a single stream, is every gift that shower, shade, and sun yield to man on the most favoured regions of the earth. It is this sole principle of life made ever present through every sense that gives the Nile the power of tying to it the hopes, wants, and thoughts of its

T

people, making the river that one central point of home, which in other lands is diffused over many objects. You will find the modern Nubian working on the wharves of Alexandria and in the streets of Cairo, but his toil and his service have only one object—to get back again to that fringe of life amid the sea of death, which is his home. There, until the Turk came, he was probably the happiest peasant on the globe. The brown water was better than the clearest spring to him.[2] The steep shelving bank of clayey sand was his garden, where it rose curving into contours formed by successive water-levels, bright with green-leaved "lubia" and sweet blossoming beans, where the summer flood had softened and fertilized the soil. Higher up, the mimosa, green of leaf and yellow of flower, scented the air with the perfume its deep roots drew from the water. The ring-dove cooed deep amid the branches, and big black and yellow bees were thick around the blossoms. Beyond the mimosa came the palm group, where the north wind rustled cool in the mid-day, and the shade was flecked with sunshine.

[2] Certainly I am of opinion that there are few waters, if any, in Europe that can be compared with that of the Nile It answers all purposes. It has the freshness of spring and the softness of river water. It is excellent to drink, and serves all other purposes.—*Belzoni.*

Beyond the palms the dhurra stood, tall and ripe
in November, or the wheat was green in January, both drawing their life from the "sakeeyeh'
channel, whose rill the oxen in their ceaseless
round kept ever flowing. Beyond all, the grim
face of the desert looked down upon his little
oasis, a wall of rock to him in life—a grave of
sand to him in death. If now memory groups
many scenes into a single picture, it is only
because months of most intimate association find
expression in the recollection of this last day's
boat journey on the reaches that lie within sight
of Gebil Barkal.

We passed the group of pyramids that stand at
the foot of the Sacred Mountain, so frequently
mentioned in the earlier pages of this narrative.
We passed, too, the group that marks the bend of
the river at Bellal, on the opposite shore, and saw
before us the beginning of the hundred isles
where the unbroken current which the Nile has
held for more than 200 miles since the Third
Cataract was left behind—first breaks into rapid
waters.

At this spot the channel bends to the east, a
turn which once more brought the wind favourable to us for a few miles, and with the strong
strokes of the Cornwall men we were soon at the
top of the rapids of Hajar. Then, rowing up

T 2

through many islands, amid strong water, we reached the camp of Gerf-Hamdab a little before sunset. It had often been said of the long distances No. 387 was wont to cover in a single day, that they were achieved because the boat carried only half a load, but now on this, the last and almost the longest day made, we bore the full load of one hundred days' food, and despite of head-wind and rapids, the sun that had lighted our start from Merawi was still above the horizon, when we anchored at Hamdab.

Here ended the river journey, which had begun sixty-five days earlier at Gemai; up and down, backwards and forwards, up cataracts and down cataracts, we had run during that time, but in direct distance traversed, No. 387 had covered 500 miles of river and ten cataracts in twenty-one complete days.

Henceforth my work was to be in the saddle. From many a granite ridge and craggy point in this second " womb of rocks " we were about to enter, I would look down upon the " Toilers of the River " at the old work of rapid and whirlpool; but for the future, the shore, as well as the water, was to be our enemy. Covered by a screen of scouts, far out in front and flank, the daily work must now be done. Whatever might be the nature or number of the obstacles lying in the river in our front, and even their names were unknown to us, one fact was certain—it was that in the wildest portion of the Dar Monassir, a force variously said to number from 3000 to 7000 Arabs had collected to oppose our advance. The campaign of the Cataracts was only beginning.

CHAPTER XIII.

IN WHICH WE GLANCE AT SOME OLD ENEMIES AND SEE A FEW NEW FRIENDS.

CERF-HAM-DAB, like a hundred other villages on the Upper Nile, extended some miles along the shore, but was only a few yards in depth from the river's edge to the bordering desert, which was here composed of sharp rocks piled together in confused masses. At the northern end of the village or district, and about four miles from the camp of the River Column, rose a steep and lofty hill, called Gebil Kulgaili, which marked the limit of our patrols in the direction of the enemy.

Early on the morning following my arrival at the camp, I reached, in company with the officer second in command of the column,[1] the summit of this "Look-out Mountain." As the rugged track which led to the top followed the inner slope of a steep crater-shaped incline, the view that opened before us when the last crag was gained was all the more striking in its immense and naked grandeur. On every side the desert spread its great brown waste into distance, in that endless silence which is more impressive than if the hum of a hundred cities came floating up from its vast circumference. But the view upon which we looked with deepest interest was the forward one along the river to the north. All that waste world of granite, that sea of hill-top, with the thin grey thread of river, lost amid a maze of rocks, held for us the double interest of war and exploration.

Beyond this standpoint of ours the Egyptian writ did not run—the Nile lay an unmapped river, and those grey silent hills hid in their vast and lonely labyrinths all the possibilities of our coming strife. The Nile ran straight in a single stream

[1] Brigadier-General H. Brackenbury, C.B.

from the foot of Gebil Kulgaili for a distance of
six or eight miles, then rocks and islands broke
the channel into many streams, which bent to
west, and then seemed to curve back into the east
until they were lost behind a maze of hill-tops.
There, where the great river broke into these many
channels began the Fourth Cataract—the famous
Rapids, beyond which no Roman soldier had ever
passed; there was the spot where legions of
Augustus Cæsar had turned back, where 1200
years later the 500 " Harakes " of Sultan Kalaoun
had been stopped, and where only sixty-five years
ago the boats of Mehemet Ali had been wrecked
and abandoned.

What were these unknown Cataracts now to
do to these English boats of ours lying below
there, white dots on the blue water at Hamdab ?
Was the fate of Sultan Kalaoun's fleet of " Harakes" and of Mehemet's 150 " Kyassas " and "Cand-
gas," to be repeated on this hitherto impassable
region of the Nile where everything was reversed ;
where the stream flowed from the north, where the
north breeze was a foul one, and where cataract,
wind and current were all leagued with hostile
tribes to bar the road against our progress ?

So far I have spoken of these tribes under their
collective name of Arabs, and now while standing
here on the topmost crags of Gebil Kulgaili, looking down upon this bird's-eye view of the wilder-

ness, it will be well if, letting the mind's eye range beyond the distant horizon, I glance at the wild children of Ishmael who are to oppose our advance through their deserts.

When, a few years after the death of Mahomet, the arms of infant Islam were carrying the white standards to the most distant extremes of Atlas and Hindu Koosh, the tribal feuds that had ceased awhile in the ferment of a new faith, broke out again in Meccah and Medina, and with the triumph of one faction or the other, the migration of the defeated tribe became a necessity. Thus, early in the first century of the Hegira, families, or sections of tribes began to arrive from Jeddah, on the west coast of the Red Sea, where they formed themselves as cadet-branches of the great Arabian families, and soon spread themselves over the deserts lying opposite to their old home. The high parentage of these younger branches has never been forgotten by their children, and to day over all the Nubian wastes, Kabbabish and Abbabdeh, Jaalin, Bisharin and Ghobush, assert their common descent from the " Anzars " of Medina, or the " Mohagerims " of Meccah.

Nor can it be said that the children have degenerated from the stock whose ancestry they thus proudly claim. Despite the intermixture of African blood, no man can say the Arab of Tamai or Abu Klea was one whit a less daring soldier than the devoted men who broke the Greek hosts at Aiznadin, or followed Kaled through a hundred battles. Wherever the sons of Islam have touched and mixed with the Christian races of the North, it would seem that the Arab nature has shown decreasing courage and diminished vitality; but where they have mixed with the Negro, the Moor, or the Tartar the characteristic traits of Arab nature have become quickened and enlarged.

Of the Arab tribes now gathered to oppose the progress of both columns, the principal were the Jaalin, Hassanieh, Robatab, Monassir, Ghobush, together with many roving sons of the Abbabdeh, Bisharin, and Hawawir tribes. These, with the Baggara, or " cattle-owning " tribes from Kordofan and Sennar, formed the bulk of the Arab armies before Khartoum, in front of the Desert Column, and opposed to our advance in the Cataracts; but so far as sympathy with the cause of the Mahdi was concerned, it would be true to say that every man, woman, and child of Arab race, from the Third Cataract to Abyssinia, was either our active or passive enemy.

Among the various tribes I have named, only a select number of men, who had adopted the *rôle* of Dervish, or " Wanderer," were in permanent arms, the majority of the rank and file were liable to be called up to serve upon some great emergency, and like all tribal soldiers they would then disperse to their homes ; but the Dervishes were the regular troops of the revolt, and to their ranks no tribe gave greater numbers or more determined recruits than the Jaalin race, dwelling between Berber and Khartoum.

To the enemies I have named should be added the Bazingas, or soldiers of Negro origin, who had formed the bulk of the irregular troops raised by the Egyptian Government in the Soudan, and who, from inclination or through compulsion, had joined the Arab movement. These men all carried Remington rifles, as did also some of the Dervishes ; but the great body of the Arabs were armed only with the old weapons of lance and sword, such as their ancestors had borne against Greek and Persian 1200 years ago. The spoil of half a dozen Egyptian armies and the capture of many towns had given the better-armed men an ample store of ammunition.

As the "Turk" had succeeded in rendering the horse a very scarce animal along the Upper Nile, cavalry were rare among the Arabs, and only the Emirs, or actual leaders in battle, had horses. But the work of scouting and re-connoitring was done by even surer means—men, mounted on swift and silent dromedaries, which were trained better than horse or dog to all the tricks and habits of watching and hiding, noted every stir we made, and carried with wonderful rapidity the news of our movements to their chiefs.

And now, having looked for a moment at our enemies, and seen all we can see of the rugged land we are about to penetrate, let us descend from our look-out on Gebil Kulgaili and go back again to the camp at Gerf Hamdab. That evening—the 21st January—stirring news came in. A despatch from Korti announced a victory gained by the Desert Column at the wells of Abu Klea, over a large force of the enemy. No details were given, save that the Arabs had charged, and that the charge had been driven home we could read in the loss of officers and men that was recorded. That loss had nearly exclusively fallen upon the Naval Brigade and the Heavy Cavalry. There could be little doubt that the square had been penetrated, but as the telegram spoke of the advance having been resumed on the day following the engagement, the final success of the Desert Column must have been complete.

As the eye ran over the names of the killed, memory went easily back to some wild spot in the lower cataracts, where the figure, now lying at rest in the Bayuda sands, had last been seen ; or the voice, now quiet, had been heard ringing out its command over the rush of waters. But war leaves little time for looking back, and there is in its ever-pressing necessities of the moment and the "glorious uncertainty" of its future, the occupation which stills sorrow, and the possibility which makes the passing of those who are gone seem only the earlier entry into a common home.

That evening, the officer commanding the River Column [2] returned to the camp from Merawi, whither he had gone to communicate with Korti by telegraph, the line not having yet reached Hamdab. During the time the column had been concentrating, he had laboured incessantly to ensure its thorough organization and to make order and exactitude of habit—those twin children of true discipline—the rule and custom of the camp.

Before the first dawn showed above the line of rocks to eastward of Hamdab, each battalion assembled at its post in perfect silence, standing to arms until the sun had risen. Then followed certain exercises and movements, in the broken ground outside the camp, to accustom the troops to form square formation and to move in that order through the rocks. The next two days completed the concentration of the column, and by the evening of January 23rd everything was in readiness to move forward into the fastnesses

[2] Major-General Earle.

of the Fourth Cataract. On the previous day I had explored, with a small cavalry patrol, the country lying beyond Gebil Kulgaili to the middle of the rapids of Owli. All was silent and deserted. The few houses that stood at long intervals by the edge of the river, hidden in some little level nook amid the rocks, were closed and abandoned; the dhurra-plot stood ripe and ready for the sickle, and the two or three palm-trees rustled amid a solitude which seemed the more striking because of the deserted aspect of these lone and far-apart resting-places of man.

At the end of the straight reach which ran from the foot of Kulgaili to the island of Owli, a change took place in river and desert. The rocks came down in denser masses to the shore, many islands filled the river-bed, and the roar of rapids sounded from innumerable channels. From a projecting pile of red granite boulders I got a good look at the Fourth Cataract. It lay before me in the now level light of the declining sun—a mass of rock and rapid, with many a tortuous channel and twisting whirlpool; but nowhere worse than places in the lower cataracts which our boats had already conquered. I found a suitable camping spot at the foot of the last rapid, where the column could halt at the end of its first day's movement, and then, calling in the vedettes, we turned back towards our camp. But,

silent and deserted as the land seemed, it had
many eyes watching our movements. The outer
flankers had come suddenly upon a camel-man,
and though the camel got away, they managed
to secure the rider and his weapons. Whether
the work of bringing the prisoner through the
rocks was too much for his captors and he was
allowed liberty, or whether he achieved freedom
by a sudden flight, I cannot say; but, at all
events, he finally got off, and only the sword and
spear were brought in. No other enemy was
met with, but we could see, at times, on distant
rocks, a spear-man watching us from afar, and
so densely cumbered with crag and broken into
ravine was the whole face of the wilderness that
a thousand men might have lain concealed along
our route with little chance of their discovery.

Night had fallen when I got back to camp,
carrying the assurance that whatever difficulties
might be in store for us beyond the Fourth
Cataract, that obstacle at least would not bar
our road.

Hitherto I have spoken but little of our allies—
the troops of the Egyptian Government in Dongola—known as the Mudir's army. We have
caught a glimpse at Debbeb, on our upward way,
of the art of war as it was practised by the
irregulars, or Bashi-bazouks, of this force; but
as we may occasionally have to come in contact

with the "regular army" itself, in our forward course through the cataracts, it will be well to introduce it here to the reader.

The Mudir's army, which was now stationed at Abu Dom, twenty miles in our rear, numbered about 350 men, two-thirds of whom had been recruited from slave caravans coming to Dongola from the remote interior. A short extract, taken from an official document, giving descriptive particulars of these recruits, may serve to illustrate the type of soldier thus obtained :—

Name of Soldier.	Colour and Qualities.		Remarks.
Fadle-el Mousa Hassan-Abu Gert.	Red.	Indifferent in long	Open in the eyebraws.
Farag-el-Said-Mohomed-el-tap-tawi.	Black.	Do. do.	3 cuts in every cheek.

The above is a literal translation, made by an Egyptian English-speaking official, of the Arabic "attestation" paper of two of the Mudir's soldiers. Another recruit, whose name I did not copy, was described as being "blue" in colour, and "indifferent in long" was the definition of height usually applied to the majority of the soldiers.

During the autumn just passed, this army had fought two battles; one at Debbeh, the other at Korti. In these encounters it had acted behind walls of mud or mimosa thorns, strictly on the defensive, and had repulsed the assault of its

enemies. In these instances the assailants had
been Shagghiehs of this same district through
which we have lately passed. Each assault had
been made under cover of darkness, and had on
the last occasion at least been all but successful.

The enemy had only a few rifles among them,
and as matters turned out, it would have been
better for their chance of success if they had had
no fire-arms at all. The plan and method of the
Shagghieh attack showed that the old spirit which
made them regard "arms as playthings and look
upon war as a sport," had not been killed out by
sixty years of Turkish rule.

The Mudir's soldiers being entrenched up to
their eyes behind a high and dense zeriba of
thorns, it was necessary for the Arabs to cross
this formidable *chevaux de frise* before getting
within spear-thrust of their opponents. A large
number of the Shagghiehs had, therefore, on their
heads the native "angarib," or oblong bedstead,
made of twisted palm-rope stretched over a frame
of wood, with four short legs to it; others carried
the skins of goats sewn together. These were to
be placed or thrown upon the broad thorny fence,
and then the charge was to be made.

In order to distract the attention of the Mudir's
army from the threatened side of attack, a body
of Shagghiehs took up a position on the other
face of the zeriba, and began a loud beating of

U

war-drums, uttering at the same time the shrill war-cry of the Arab—Illa! illa! illa! The garrison, in full expectation of an assault upon this side, thought little of the face which had been selected for the real onslaught, and kept their eyes fixed upon the quarter from which the noise of preparation seemed to proceed. Meanwhile, hidden by the darkness, the Shagghiehs approached rapidly, but without noise, the zeriba; the skins and angaribs were quietly laid over the mimosa fence, and the leading men of the stormers were already creeping across the path thus made, when one of them, who happened to carry a rifle instead of a spear, inadvertently discharged his weapon. This saved the Mudir's army. Turning towards the menaced point, they opened a heavy fire into the mimosa fence; numbers of the Arabs were killed in the very act of crossing the dense obstacle; more fell among the crowd pressing forward to the assault; the principal Emirs fell in the leading ranks, and the attack ceased almost as soon as it had begun.

There could be little doubt that had the Arabs once got fairly into the zeriba, the end of the Mudir's army would have been a question of a few minutes, and descriptive particulars of Farag-el-Said-Mohomed-el-tap-tawi and his brethren would soon have had to reckon more than "three cuts in every cheek."

During the past month or two the army of the Mudir had held the post of Abu Dom, where the memory of their narrow escape from the spears of the surrounding Shagghieh caused them every night to place a cordon of sentinels seated out in the desert around their quarters, making a most unearthly and incessant noise, to prove to their officers, who were within the post, that they were awake. It was now decided to call up the army from Abu Dom, and employ it marching along the right bank of the Nile, parallel with the advance of our boats. An order was consequently sent to the Egyptian officer in command, directing him to " mobilize his force immediately " and move northwards. He replied to the summons by announcing that the mobilization of his force would take one month. As his troops were always in the habit of summarily impressing all the camels and donkeys of any village they came to for transport, and as their food supply was also derived from the grain and goats of the districts through which they passed, the time necessary to complete what was termed their mobilization need not have occupied twenty minutes. The fact was, the word " mobilization " had given the commander of the army the excuse he and his master wanted. The " Vakeel," as the Mudir's lieutenant was called, was a very clever and astute little Circassian, who was by no means in a hurry to take the field; not at all from a personal disinclination to fight, but simply because, to the Egyptians, this Nile Expedition was purely an English matter, in the success of which they had, if the truth were known, the very smallest interest. Now the Vakeel, who was fairly versed in the military history of our times, had no doubt read that the German army required a full fortnight to mobilize—why then should his army not take a month? and, looking to the fact that it had absolutely no transport, and was completely deficient in food, there was indeed no reason, except those already given, why it should not take a year, provided that the two military essentials of food and carriage were to be supplied in the regular course of things—from Cairo. A peremptory order, however, to appear with his army on the bank of the river opposite Hamdab without delay, and with or without mobilization, put an end to further controversy, and had the immediate effect of reducing the donkeys and camels in the neighbourhood of Merawi in a marked degree.

These arrangements were concluded on the 23rd January, on which date also the last of the four English Battalions arrived at Hamdab. The River Column was now complete, and on the morrow it would begin the forward movement against the renowned Cataracts of Shagghieh.

CHAPTER XIV.

IN WHICH WE ENTER THE UNKNOWN CATARACTS.

AT seven o'clock on the morning of January 24th, the River Column broke up its camp at Hamdab and moved towards the Fourth Cataract. The Stafford Battalion, which had been the first to pass the Cataracts of the Batn-el-Hager, again led the advance. Sixty Hussars and forty Camel Corps covered the movement, moving a couple of miles in front and on flank of the leading boats. It was rough work for both horses and camels and it grew rougher as the cataract was neared.

After passing the base of Kulgaili, we soon got proof that our movements were closely watched. A small party of horsemen showed in the desert eastward of our eastmost flankers, and then disappeared in one of the many "khors" which act as winding covered-ways to hide the advance or retreat of those who know the desert. When last seen, these Arab scouts were retreating in the direction of Bir Sani, an oasis on the track to Berber, lying about fifty miles from the river.

This oasis was a favourite station for the Hassanich Emir El-Zain, a noted Arab raider. A futile attempt had been made a few days before my arrival at Hamdab, to surprise this chief at Bir Sani, by a forced march of the Cavalry and Camel Corps, but it had ended as all attempts to catch a fox asleep must end.

One unfortunate result had, however, followed this abortive enterprise. The little Egyptian horses which carried our Hussars had marched continuously nearly eighty miles without water, and though none had died from this prolonged test, all had suffered from it. As our total force of Cavalry consisted of but eighty troopers, who were now required to cover the boat advance by river, along a country bristling with rocks—a desert, in fact, of trap and granite for many hundreds of miles—the prospects of beginning such a service with animals still showing the effect of this recent severe march were not the most brilliant.

There is not the slightest chance of ever "surprising" an Arab. You may deceive him as to your intentions; you may attack him at some point where he does not expect to be attacked; but as to surprising him by a march requiring length of time for its accomplishment, that is not to be thought of. We will see more of this as we go on.

This security from surprise is nothing more than the survival of the instinct which has saved the Arab from total destruction. Had it been possible to catch the Arab asleep, he would long ago have disappeared in the incessant tribal wars he has waged.

By mid-day the leading boats had reached the spot which I had selected two days earlier as a good camping-place for the Column. Here, opposite Owli Island, and at the foot of the Fourth Cataract, I left the mounted troops and pushed on with a patrol to examine the entire length of the rapids. After an hour's ride we reached the head of the long stretch of broken water, and saw the Nile flowing smooth again between single banks. Rock after rock, island after island, had filled the wide channel throughout a distance of more than four miles, breaking the broad current into many passages, and forming the rapids variously named Tirai, Owli, and Edermih—all of them grouped under the single meaningless title of the Fourth Cataract.

A glance from the imaginary maps we carried with us to the reality of the wild scenes before us, showed that the river and its shores had simply been guessed at by former travellers. In a distance of six miles, no trace of resemblance could be found between map and scene, but a bend in the river brought us all at once in sight of features that could be identified.

Two high projecting rocks stood out from each shore, and on their summits the walls and bastions of ruined fortifications were visible—the castles of Kubinat, these ruins were called. The channel of the river here narrowed to about 400 yards, and between the commanding rocks the stream could be seen for a considerable distance ahead, clear of obstruction. But if the river was clear of rock, the desert at this point was a vast maze of rugged, broken boulders. Tilted and thrown about, these enormous masses of red granite looked as though the Deluge had "ruined along this illimitable inane," and when it had passed away a great earthquake had come to "make hay" of the boulders. We got back at dusk to the camp at the foot of the cataract, where by this time the two battalions had assembled.

Next morning the boats began the passage of the Fourth Cataract, taking the further, or right shore of the river, two miles distant from the left across many islands. While the passage was being effected by the leading battalion, a wing of the second battalion marched to the head of the bad water along the left shore, and took up a position covering the cataract. The mounted troops then pushed on through the defiles of Kubinat, to explore the river and desert to the north.

Beyond the rocks of Kubinat the desert opened out into less rugged features, and for a few miles the soft crunching of yellow sand under the horse-hoofs sounded pleasant after the flinty ring of iron shoes upon endless granite. This interval of open ground was soon passed, and before us rose a ridge of grey granite, closing the forward view.

At the point where this rocky ridge touched the river, the water again showed in waves, and the well-known roar of a "shillal" struck upon the ear.

As we drew near this new cataract two Arabs on camels came up from behind, and I recognized in the leading one the figure of "Malek," or King

Hassan Said of Amri—who had joined us at Hamdab a little while before our start.

Although I had had many previous conversations with his Majesty on the subject of the land we were about to enter, I had gained very little real information from him. He had repeatedly told us that the cataracts lying before us were not formidable, with the exception of Kab'd-el-Abd, which was a bad piece of water. Whenever my questions became too pressing, the Malek pleaded a recent wound received in the attack upon the zeriba at Korti as an excuse for being mentally tired, and unable to continue the conversation. He had indeed had a narrow escape. A bullet had passed through his shoulder, close to the zeriba. He had been borne out of the fight by his faithful followers, and although well advanced in years, Arab blood and desert air soon brought him round again. Although his sympathies were still with the Mahdi, our advance into his country at Hamdab had caused him to throw in his lot ostensibly with us; but I have little doubt his presence in our camp had been of much greater use to our enemies than open enmity would have proved hurtful to his present friends. I stopped the Malek, and made him point out the features of the country. This granite ridge was called Mishami, and yonder rocky island was Omderas, and this cataract to which we were coming was that of Kab'd-el-Abd. I approached to examine it. It was by no means as formidable as the Malek's description led me to suppose, although a very heavy rush of water was sweeping through its " gate."

From a rock above the rapid the Malek pointed out his kingdom. Omderas, Tamra, and Tetami Islands were those rocks and ridges that looked like the opposite mainland, but were in reality large islands overlapping each other, and separated by channels which were dry for half the year. As for the cataract lying below us, there was a narrow passage, hidden by the rocks, at the further side, through which our boats could be taken in single file. So far at least there was good news to tell of the river, for this Kab'd-el-Abd had been pictured in language that made the officer commanding the column fear it might detain us some time. The general had told me he would await my report in the ruined fortress at Kubinat, and thither I returned to tell him it would be easy work for us. Climbing the steep path that led to the castle, I found him, with his second in command, seated on one of the immense walls overlooking river and plain. My story was soon told. The river was clear to Kab'd-el-Abd. . Thence it bent from north towards east, and was lost to view two miles higher up. The cataract about which we had heard so much was easily to be passed. The country was a perfect solitude; not a living thing had we seen. Then we turned to examine the old ruin standing on this isolated ridge. Who built these enormous walls, which were ten and fifteen feet in thickness, and had flanking bastions of still stronger build? Who defended them? Who attacked them? Was this the refuge to which King Samamoun had fled six hundred years ago, when Sultan Bibar first took Old Dongola?

No one shall ever know. The lost island of Atlantis is not deeper buried from the possibility of modern research than are the kingdom and the civilization which were once upon these lonely shores. For these big walls, that time cannot destroy, tell of a day when even this wild " womb of rocks " gave birth to civilized man. This work is no rude piling together of stone on stone. These courses of masonry were laid by skilful hands; these rampart lines were drawn by men who knew a good deal of the craft of defence; and the size of the space to be defended, and the nature of the defences tell of numbers, discipline, and knowledge. Yet numbers mean plenty of food, discipline means government, and knowledge is civilization. And now? A howling waste of granite; a piled-up tangle of desolation; a desert land, where even the shadow of the great rocks falls short at noonday upon a weary world.

Back in the evening to the head of the Fourth

Cataract, where still the two battalions are working up the swift torrents of the Edermeh rapids, and gradually forming at Kabur, at the head of the cataract. The general's headquarters still remained at Owli.

About midnight on this night—the 26th, a spy came into my advanced camp from the front. He brought news two days old from Birteh. I got up from my blankets and questioned him at length. He had left Birteh during the night of the 24th. There were then 3000 Arabs assembled ready for fighting, 1000 of them being Jaalin dervishes. They meant to attack at Kab'd-el-Abd, while the boats were separated by the rapid. They would attack at night, or in the early morning at daybreak. Birteh was only as far beyond Kab'd-el-Abd as Owli was distant from where we now were. They had plenty of men watching us day and night, and they knew everything we did. I put many questions to this man, but could not shake his story. Then, as his news was important, I sent him to the main camp at Owli, and lay down to sleep again.

Daylight brought me an order from the main camp not to move until the General Commanding reached my camp. At nine o'clock he appeared, and immediately after the mounted troops moved forward through the gorges of Kubinat, the boats of the two battalions following along the open water to the foot of Kab'd-el-Abd. Here I found a very strong position for the night's camp, and taking on the mounted troops, was soon on the summit of Mishami ridge.

As the leading scouts topped the long ascent, the solitude through which we had been marching during four days suddenly showed life and movement other than our own.

The ridge fell steeply on its northern side. At its base lay a small plain upon which stood a mosque of sun-dried brick; then a thick wood of mimosa-trees extended for a mile or two along the river, and then the grey rocks came down again to the shore. All at once out of a "khor" or ravine, near the brick mosque, appeared about 130 armed men in line, on foot. Half a dozen horsemen could be seen on the edge of the wood. Presently a shot was fired. The scouts answered by a volley, and the footmen fell back into the mimosas.

Descending the ridge, we crossed the plain, and reached the mosque. The enemy had fallen back through the trees. In a "khor," the bottom of which held a waving crop of dhurra-grass, a couple of figures were visible. There was a rush to secure them. They ran like deer towards the river, reached it, plunged in, and despite a rapid, soon gained an island in mid-stream. The third fugitive—a woman—was caught before she could get to the water. The poor creature, believing her last hour had come, was in great terror, but she was soon assured that no harm would befall her.

As to the enemy, she had either no information to give, or would not tell what she knew. She was a subject of our Malek Hassan Said. She and her people had run away into the desert to avoid the soldiers, and they were now coming to the river along this khor for water. The name of the cataract which we were now abreast of was Um-ha-boa. There was another cataract two hours' journey up the river. The island opposite where we stood was Kandi, and the mosque we had lately passed was called Warrag.

Telling her to go and inform her people that they would be perfectly safe and unmolested if they returned to their homes, we left her to call back her two male friends from the island refuge, and bent our steps again to Mishami ridge, passing along the shore of Um-ha-boa. It was a very rough, long, and difficult cataract, and to pass it with the entire column meant at least four days' labour. These cataract steps grew steeper as we advanced deeper into this desolate land.

It was dark when we reached the camp, still at Kab'd-el-Abd.

Next day—the 28th of January—leaving the first battalion of infantry to pass Kab'd-el-Abd, I pushed on to the cataract next above Um-ha-boa, of which the Arab woman had spoken yesterday. I had the Malek with me, riding on a camel. From the summit of Mishami ridge he pointed out the country. That ridge of serrated rocks was the centre of Ishishi Island. At the foot of these rocks was the Cataract of Rahami, and beyond, where that black hill rose among the sea of grey ridges, stood Birtch. We passed the mosque and wood, the scene of yesterday's first sight of the enemy, and got into more open ground beyond. At Warrag the Malek had protested against going on, but his objections had been overcome. Now, however, at Gamra, he utterly refused to go any further, alleging that it was no reason because he was with madmen he should be compelled to have his throat cut. At the moment I attributed the Malek's refusal to proceed to the shock his Korti experience had given his nerves, but later on we found out he had known more of the exact situation of matters than he pretended to us. Expecting our coming, the Arabs had an ambush in the rocks on a track leading further to our right; but as I was only desirous of seeing the cataract, I had kept the patrol along the shore of the river. Rahami looked as wild as any of its predecessors. How many other cataracts might lie before us could only be guessed at, and as neither the name of this rapid nor that of Um-ha-boa—both long and dangerous

stretches of water—had found mention in the
official map, it was only natural to suppose the
region lying ahead was still less an explored
one.

The following day saw us again at Rahami.
Pushing on through very rocky desert, we reached
a bend in the river, which commanded a long view
up and down the channel. Looking back down the
cataract the river was foaming and flashing amid
a wilderness of rocks; looking forward one saw
the end of the rough water about a mile distant,
and then a smooth reach with a few houses and
"sakeeyehs." While we were surveying this
scene, a woman appeared a little distance ahead,
apparently moving aimlessly about as though she
meant to attract our notice. She was soon brought
in, and at once showed such evident desire to
be communicative that it was impossible not to
suspect some motive both for her presence and
her story. "Birteh," she said, "lay only a short
hour's walk forward—there behind that next ridge
of black rocks the place began. Many thousand
Arabs were there, but how many she could not
say; anyhow, if we wanted to fight them, we
must come far stronger than we now were, or they
would very soon eat us up." Then she volunteered
to show us the path into Birteh. As the ground
was fairly open for more than a mile forward, I
pushed on for a closer survey of the spot we

x

had so long identified with the place where we were to fight the Arabs.

Another mile brought us into very rugged country; the ground by the river was narrowing into space only wide enough to carry the path, while the hills on our right rose some hundreds of feet, broken into ravines and covered with rocks of every size and shape. Not wishing to commit the main body of my little troop to such a tangle of hill and gully, I halted it on ground overlooking a ravine to the right, and pushed on with half a dozen Hussars along the track by the river.

We soon reached the narrow pass leading into Birteh; above it a hill rose steeply on our right hand. Before fully committing ourselves to this defile, between rock and river, I sent an officer [1] up the hill to look over. It had the usual comb, or crest of trap rock, but its slope was clear of obstacle, as the larger stones seemed to have long ago rolled down its steep declivity. From our lower ground I watched the officer as he reached the high crest and looked over it. A single glance seemed sufficient, for without a moment's loss he began vehemently to motion us back with hand and helmet. There could be little doubt that he was looking down upon some movement which was threatening our position in the gorge. I therefore ordered the patrol to fall back clear

---

[1] Lieut.-Colonel F. Slade, R.A.

of the defile at once. If the Arabs had been quick at their work, we might have had a bad time of it, for the ground was all against us. They were drawn up at the further end of the broken ground to the number (as estimated by Colonel Slade) of 3000; they had many standards, and their leading ranks seemed to be advancing towards us. Meanwhile, the half-troop of Camel Corps had got separated from the Hussars in the hills, and following some winding valleys had come upon a scouting party of Arabs; shots were exchanged, and one camel was killed. I had sent a message to withdraw the camels from the broken ground, when we advanced the left along the river, but before they could fall back they had met the Arab scouts and began the skirmish. Moving to our right in the direction from whence the shots proceeded, we met the camel troop emerging from the hills.

It was now nearly sunset; our main camp lay still beyond Mishami ridge, twelve miles distant, and with animals tired by a long day over rough ground, we began our homeward march to Warrag. From this day's reconnaissance it was clear that the Arabs had chosen their position at Birteh with much judgment. Rahami Cataract would prevent our boats concentrating at any point nearer than Gamra, which was a march of six or seven miles from Birtch. The wide circle of rugged hills

x 2

enclosing the Arab position had only, upon our side, the pass between rocks and river leading through them. It might indeed be possible to find a track from the outer desert into Birteh, and although that would entail a march from the foot of Rahami Cataract of some ten or twelve miles over the desert, it would be better to attack the Arabs by such a line than try to force the direct route along the river, which was evidently the road the enemy expected us to follow. This, however, would be a question for the future. Four days must elapse before it would be possible to concentrate even two battalions at Gamra, and for the present at least, the handful of mounted troops, whose work had now for six days been incessant, might take a rest on the morrow.

So, on the 30th, men, horses, and camels had a rest at Warrag, where our advanced camp stood at the head of Um-ha-boa Cataract. This plan of two camps had become the rule of our advance. By noon each day I could tell from the position gained at that hour by the leading half-dozen boats the spot on the river where not less than four companies of infantry would be able to concentrate by nightfall. I then selected the best camping-place that could be found in that vicinity, and having left the crew of the leading boat in possession of the site, would take on the mounted troops for further reconnaissance, return-

ing at nightfall to find four, six, or eight companies
assembled in the camp I had chosen, with a zeriba
of thorns made around it. The main camp would
usually be from two to six miles behind. It is true
that this arrangement gave the Arabs the opportunity of attacking us in detail, but there was no
other way of working up these successive cataract-
steps without making our rate of progress slower
than even it was. As these advanced camps were
certain to draw to them any attack the Arabs
might intend to deliver against us it was necessary
that their selection should be made on ground
suitable for defence; but three other conditions
had also to be provided for, there must be good
anchorage for the boats, cover from fire for the
horses and camels, and mimosa-trees to give thorn-
brush for zeriba. Each day's forward reconnaissance enabled me to judge pretty accurately
where our next night's camp would be, for by this
time one had come to know to a mile what the
boats of a battalion could do over the various
"values" of cataract, rapid, or smooth water. As I
was always sure to have the advanced camp in my
own command, this matter of selection was made
easy by the fact that one had only to satisfy oneself
in the choice. My favourite position was on
ground which had immediately behind it what
we called a high Nile island, that is to say
a ridge of land separated by a dry channel from

the main shore ; this dry channel gave cover to the camels and horses ; the island itself was usually covered with dhukan-grass, or other forage for the animals, and the zeriba on the shore protected all. The men lay down by companies behind the fence of the zeriba, fully equipped, and ready to stand to arms at a moment's warning. A sentry on the flank of each company looked out across the zeriba fence. At the points where the mimosa hedge touched the river a strong picquet was posted, and the centre of the zeriba held a company or two in reserve.

On the evening of the day succeeding the reconnaissance to Birteh our bivouac occupied a strong position above Warrag. It was about three o'clock in the morning when the sound of a shot roused me from sleep ; I rose and went to the sentries nearest the spot from whence I thought the shot had come ; the sentries had heard the shot, but they could not agree as to its direction, one man asserting it had been fired across the river. Although it seemed absurd to put sleeping testimony against waking evidence, I felt certain the shot had been fired about 200 yards from the front of our bivouac in some trees. A small patrol went quietly out to examine. The moon-light was very bright, enabling objects to be distinctly seen in the open. Presently the patrol returned to report all quiet. Tired by their labour

of the previous day in Um-ha-boa, the men still
lay deep in sleep. As another hour would bring
reveille I sat down to wait. There were two
planets at this time, set apparently close together
in the eastern heavens, whose rising always gave
us the morning signal to stand to arms.

Over the rim of the desert, or above the sharp
outline of rock these twin throbbing lights were
always right before us as we stood in the cold
bivouac waiting, ready for the Arab rush, which
we had so often been told would come in the
moments immediately preceding the first streak
of dawn.

But on this morning—as on the mornings
already past—day broke to find our bivouac undisturbed, and the single shot of the earlier hours
unexplained. An hour or two after sunrise the
usual messengers arrived from the main camp;
this time they brought a deserter who had come
in at daylight from the Arabs. The man had once
been an Egyptian soldier in the army of Hicks
Pacha, and after the annihilation of that force he
had joined the Mahdi. In deserting last night from
Birteh he had passed the close neighbourhood of
our camp without being aware of our presence.

"At what hour?" I asked.

" About two hours before dawn, and in passing
through the mimosas in our front he had mistaken
the trunk of a tree that caught the moonlight for

an Arab lying in wait to intercept his flight, and he had fired at the supposed foe." The mystery of the shot was explained.

That day—the 31st—we moved bivouac to the foot of Rahami Cataract, and began to concentrate two battalions at Gamra for a movement upon Birteh.

During the day I made a wide sweep to the east into the desert, and found that it would be possible to approach the Arab position from the east by a march of about eleven miles in length, through ground fairly practicable. So formidable, however, were the difficulties of Um-ha-boa that fully another two days must go by ere even two battalions of infantry would be ready for this movement in the camp at Gamra.

But while all these preparations were being made to attack Birteh the Arab would not stay. A deserter arrived on the night of the 31st, bringing news that the Arabs had abandoned Birteh, retreating northward along the river; but deserters' stories are not always true ones, and it was necessary to test its accuracy. So, on the morning of the 1st of February we pushed on again with the mounted troops through the defiles by the river, General Earle coming with a wing of Royal Highlanders to a position more than midway between Gamra and Birteh. The latter place was empty, not an Arab was to be seen; a rude

breastwork of stone, and behind it, for a considerable distance, the *débris* of an Arab bivouac,
were the only traces left of the large muster we
had heard so much about.

Whither had they fled? A few natives whose
ill-concealed sympathies were all with their late
masters told us the Dervish army had retreated to
Berber, and as the news of the second fight of the
Desert Column, and of that force having arrived at
the Nile near Metemma, must have reached them as
it had reached us, on the 29th, it was not unlikely
that this retirement upon Berber had really been
intended. Scouting four miles further with the
cavalry we found the desert had in store for us
steeper rocks and deeper glens than anything we
had yet encountered; but the river throughout
a reach of six miles lay smooth and unbroken
between impending shores.

Next night the mounted troops bivouacked at
Birteh, and as we had 170 men to nearly 300
horses and camels, the Arabs lost another good
chance of fighting us on terms favourable to
themselves.

Our advanced camp remained at Birteh two
days; during that time the Stafford and Royal
Highlander battalions were working through the
Rahami Cataract, the first-named battalion making
quick work of the north passage, but the Highlanders—committed in error to the southern

channel—had a terrible experience, getting through to Birteh only on the third day, with loss of life and boats. Meanwhile I had fixed my camp seven miles above Birteh, in the only level bit of ground which the river-shore, throughout several miles, here offered. As this new camp formed the base of some curious incidents in our campaign it will be well, perhaps, if we devote a fresh chapter to their story.

CHAPTER XV.

IN WHICH THE MEANING OF OUR MOTTO BECOMES APPARENT.

Y the morning of the 4th February six companies of the Stafford Regiment again took their long-held post in the van of the Nile Expedition, and moved forward from Birteh to a spot which I had chosen for the next camp, about midway between Birteh and Kirbekan. Leaving these companies to form a zeriba, I took the cavalry forward for a further examination of the wild region in which we now found ourselves.

Following a wadi, between high-bordering rocks, we reached a spot where the track—which bore in its sand the print of many hundreds of sandalled feet—forked to right and left, and taking the latter course we again struck a branch of the river, some three or four miles distant from our camp. Then ascending a hill, by what was a natural stairway of stone, we were able to see at last something of an extended view over the rugged granite waste through which we were now groping our way.

The few miles travelled through the rocks had made a strange change in the river. We had left it a single stream, flowing smooth as a narrow Scottish loch, amid steep cliffs of granite. We found it again broken into a dozen channels, filled with immense islands, and spreading out its branches over so wide an area that it was impossible to trace through its ramifications where the islands ended and the mainland again began. Our dream of fair water had been a short one. Below us the Rakabet-el-Gemel ("the Camel's Neck") was brawling as loudly as its namesake at moments of loading, and wherever the eye rested upon water amid the grey and black rocks, it was sure to catch the sheen of rapids, glistening in the evening sunlight. But the most striking feature in the view that lay before us from the great rock above the "Camel's Neck" was a range of black trap-hills, which ran straight from mainland to mainland, across the numerous islands, dropping down at each channel only to rise again in a series of steep wave-crests until lost in the desert on either side. Through the gaps in this range the path of the Nile could be traced by some dark hill-crest, which had already been pointed out by a guide, in days past, as a landmark near which the river ran. Thus the steep black crest, three miles distant, was Gebil Boni, on the island of Boni; and the other ridge, a dozen miles further off, was on the island of Uss. Of the river itself nothing except the broken island-channels below us could be seen. It lay sunken from sight, deep below a world of hill-top, whose black and grey summits were now glistening in the level light of evening.

It was time to get back to camp. We tried to keep the river in sight, but it was not to be done. The shores rose in places 100 feet above the water, and we had to take what openings could be found between these walls of rock. Frequently dismounting and leading the horses in single file, we slowly wound our way in the direction of the bivouac.

At a point where this winding stairway again came near the river we met a very old woman, crawling slowly and with difficulty along the rugged path. She had but the scantiest covering upon her bent and wrinkled body. In one shrivelled hand she held a little mat and a bag of palm-leaf; with the other hand she guided herself through the rocks. She had crawled into a recess, out of the way of the horses. I stopped when I came near her. Despite extreme age and wretchedness, the eyes still shone, but more with the glare of insanity than the light of reason. She muttered incoherent replies to the questions of the interpreter. She will, at least, know the name of the place, I thought. "Ask her the name of this country." There was no mistake about her reply. " El Kirbekan," she answered. If the old hag spoke rightly, then we must be near the Shukook Pass, where it was said the Arabs, who had retreated from Birteh, had again resolved to oppose us. We left this wrinkled wayfarer amid the rocks that seemed a fitting home for such a being, and got back to camp ere the light was gone. The next day would tell us if we had really reached the neighbourhood of the celebrated defile known as " the Shukook."

The following morning brought to our camp a black slave-boy who had run away from the Arabs, near Uss Island. This boy was supposed

to be acquainted with the Shukook country, and
might therefore be of use as a guide. I put him
on a camel, and we set out for the day's work.
We passed our furthest point of yesterday, and
keeping as near the river as the rocks permitted,
gained about mid-day the ridge of brown-
black hills I have already spoken of as extend-
ing right across the Nile and being continued
over the desert.

As we approached this ridge the slave-boy
began to show considerable anxiety. The Arabs
were behind it, he said; and pointing out some
groups of large round granite rocks which lay
close to the river, he declared that a gorge
between two of these groups was the entrance to
the Shukook Pass, and the exact spot where the
Arabs intended to make their first resistance.

We could see in one of the granite clusters
the walls and low straw roof of a small hut,
built of loose stones. We drew cautiously near
this defile, passed through it, and had now the
steep brown ridge on our right, its summit being
about 500 yards from the river. Not a living
being was anywhere visible.

While the horses were being fed and watered
by half-troops at a time, I ascended the brown
ridge for a better examination of the land. The
extreme crest of the hill was composed of a
steep and solid outcrop of trap, which was here

streaked with broad bands of snow-white rock, and smooth and polished by wind, sun, and sand-storm.

From this lofty look-out the river showed at intervals, still deep sunken amid black rocks, the furthest forward glimpse of water being about five miles distant. All the intricate channels and the islands were seen below us on the left, and our boy-guide named them as we looked. Dulka and Boni, further off Uss, where there was yet another " Shellal " rapid, he said, and there at last was the Shukook, where, two days ago, he had left the Dervishes. We were still some two or three miles distant from the real mouth of the pass, whose dark defiles and sombre environments we could partly trace. Lying as an oasis amid the desert of black rock I noticed a light-coloured streak of plain to the right of the Shukook labyrinth, and through the glass I could make out bushes growing upon it. This glimpse was later on to be of use to us. Nearer, and still further to the right, the Wadi-el-Argu led off into a distant desert of grey sand, at whose furthest eastern verge rose a lofty range of blue hills, approaching to the elevation of mountains.

Descending the ridge from this long bird's-eye look at the land before us, we fell back through the granite boulders, leaving the ridge and the rocks to the deep silence from which our coming had for a moment roused them. This was on the 5th of February. Five days had only to pass to find us fighting the Arabs in these very rocks, and to win this now quiet ridge of Kirbekan was to cost us the best blood in the River Column. But many things had still to happen.

Late that night, after I had got back to bivouac, an order reached me from the main camp at Birteh of strange import. I was to halt where I was, make no movement with boats or horses, except the patrols usual around all posts, and await orders. By this evening of the 5th, I had here in the advanced camp two infantry battalions —Stafford and " Black Watch "—and about 100 mounted men. What could this sudden arrest of movement mean? I had not long to surmise.

Next morning brought to the camp the officer[1] second in command of the River Column. He came to tell me the reason of the order. A despatch had arrived from Korti announcing fatal news. The Desert Column had touched the Nile near Metemma; two steamers had reached Khartoum from the column, but it was only to find the town, the forts, and the palace in possession of the Arabs; and, amid a storm of shell and shot, the boats had turned back for Metemma. There were other items of subsequent wreck told in the

___

[1] Brigadier-General Brackenbury.

Y

despatch, but they caught little hold of thought in the terrible news of catastrophe that this short message brought to us. Here was the end of every-thing, not of our labour and our hope, but of our hero. He was gone. It was not said so; but if Khartoum had fallen, Gordon was dead. That was the central point upon which the mind fixed itself, and all the surrounding subjects which grew from that centre were obscured for the moment; for as lesser lights are lost in sunlight, so had minor shadows died out in this all-obscuring gloom.

So I spent the 6th thinking over it all, for the news was still kept secret from the troops.

The following morning brought General Earle to our camp. Half a mile distant a commanding hill-top was accessible by a steep climb. We walked together to this lofty point, and having reached it, sat down to talk over the situation. "What was my opinion?" Sooner or later it must end in a retirement to Korti. The Desert Column was not strong enough to stem the flood which the fall of Khartoum would set loose. It could not afford to get shut up by that flood. If Metemma had been taken, it might risk moving on Berber and forming a junction with us at the latter place; but the possibility of that course would depend upon the state of the camel transport, the supply of food remaining, and above all upon the actual striking power which

the column itself possessed. We only knew that
it had fought twice, that its loss of officers had
been heavy, that it had undergone many hardships. It was true that a splendid infantry
battalion—the Royal Irish—had marched to support it, but behind that battalion there was
nothing. The course of an army is like that of a
river : you must feed it with fresh current, or its
volume will lessen and run dry. On the whole,
looking to the fact that the last card was on the
table, that there was nothing at Korti, and that
the object of the Expedition was for ever lost, I
saw no escape from a retirement. Had we been
at or near Abu Hamad, it would have been
another matter ; we would then have been round
the elbow ; but now, every step we took carried
us further apart. Then we spoke of other
matters. I pointed out to General Earle the wild
panorama before us. There was Boni Island,
and beyond that dark ridge, more to eastward,
lay the Shukook, where the Arabs were still supposed to be awaiting us. He took a long look
over the sea of hill-tops, and then we began to
descend towards the camp. As we came down
the hill he spoke much of early Crimean scenes—
Alma, Inkermann, and the great winter siege—
Alma most of all. What a grand sight it was,
that advance up the long slope, with the music,
the red coats, the epaulets, colours flying, drums

beating, bugles, sunshine, and the rest of it! "It was the last battle of the old order," he said. I remembered all these things later; for when we look back across a grave, it is often easy for memory to see very clearly. And I remembered, too, that among the nameless hills that I pointed out to my companion that day, was the dark ridge at the foot of which, three days later, he was to die.

Early on the 8th, tired of this enforced inaction, I took my boat, which ever during the day had managed, despite frequent cataracts, to keep touch of my night bivouacs, and pulled up the river with the object of trying to reach the foot of the lofty hill of Gebil Boni, whose summit, forming the dominating point in many miles of wilderness, had so often caught our attention. Following the most western channel of the river, we reached a spot some five or six hundred yards from the foot of the hill, left three men in charge of the boat, and took on the remainder to the base of the mountain; then, in company with a staff officer, I began to ascend the hill. The lower part was easy enough, for it was *débris* fallen from the scarped top, which rose as a minature Matterhorn, perfectly abrupt upon three sides. On the fourth, or north side, there was a difficult but practicable way, and following it we gained the summit.

From this lofty point the islands, the river, and the dark mass of the Shukook were all visible; the principal channel of the Nile, filled with rapids, lay below us, between Boni and Dulka islands. On the latter island were the remains of a large town, many graveyards, and the ruins of mosques and churches.

This island of Dulka had evidently been the refuge isle of King Samamouan, and looking back at the world of cataract that lay between it and Dongola, it was little wonder that Sultan Kalaoun and his 500 " harackes," and his 40,000 men had failed to reach him here.

From this mountain of Boni one could see behind the Kirbekan ridge. We had heard on the previous evening that the Arabs had reoccupied that position, but I could see no trace of any force or encampment on island or on mainland. We climbed down from this lofty perch, returned to the boat, and ran down stream to camp—there all was bustle and movement. The order had just arrived for the advance to be continued, and the leading boats were already under weigh.

Into the saddle again and forward over the old ground. Sending on twenty Hussars towards Kirbekan, I turned down a wadi leading to the river above the " Rakabet-el-Gamel " to watch the Staffords passing that rapid; then, directing their commanding officer [2] to bivouac on Dulka Island, I rode forward to join the advanced scouts. Before I reached them an orderly, carrying a pencil note and riding quickly back, met me. "A considerable body of the enemy were lining the ridge we had visited on the 5th."

I cantered on and was soon with the scouts. There were the Arabs at last. On the red granite groups near the river, and on the white-streaked crest of Kirbekan the white tunics of the Mahdi's soldiers were plainly visible. They made no attempt at concealment, but shook their spears and shouted their shrill war-cry along the whole ridge.

Although the sun shone full in their eyes, they soon got the range of our position, and dropped bullets into our group of rocks. Half a dozen dismounted Hussars returned the fire, and for an hour or two a rifle duel went on from rock group to rock group. That our bullets must have been dropping accurately, the disappearance of the white tunics from the front face of the granite groups proved; but the cover in the gorge where we had seen the stone hut on the 5th, was too good to be reached by our fire.

A couple of Stafford boats appeared in sight and soon added their fire to that of the Hussars; but it was now nearly sunset, full time to go

[2] Colonel Eyre.

back and arrange for larger work on the morrow. As the Hussars drew off, falling slowly back upon a second position, the Arabs came out from their rocks and followed us, redoubling their shrill cries; but they halted when they reached our first position, and their shouts of " Allah, Allah " were soon lost amid the desert. It was long after dark when I got back to camp. In reporting to headquarters at Birteh the result of the day's work, I proposed the following movements for the morrow :—Stafford battalion to move from their bivouac on Dulka to a spot I had marked for a camp, close by the scene of our skirmish. Mounted troops to occupy early in the morning the same ground as to-day. Black Watch to move from present camp to same bivouac as Stafford. The first battalion should reach the point of concentration, in front of Kirbekan, by eleven o'clock, the second by two o'clock. I also asked that two guns of the Egyptian mountain battery might be sent to me. A staff-officer— Captain Pirie—carried this report and request back to Birteh. He rejoined me in the middle of the night, bringing the general's sanction to the proposed concentration in front of Kirbekan, at which place he informed me General Earle would also arrive about noon.

At seven o'clock on the morning of the 9th all were in motion. By nine o'clock the mounted troops had reoccupied their position of yesterday, 600 yards from the granite knolls, where the Arabs still showed in numbers. By ten the Staffords were on shore 600 yards behind the cavalry; two hours later saw the Highlanders arriving, and about mid-day General Earle and his staff reached the ground, and came forward to the rocks held by our advanced scouts, to take a closer survey of the enemy's position.

The Arabs were to-day quiet, only a few shots came from the granite knolls; but when one looked through a field-glass, the spear-heads could be seen above the line of rocks, and over the sharp edge of the higher ridge of Kirbekan the heads of many men were visible against the sky-line.

Having described to the general the exact nature of the ground occupied by the Arabs, all of which I had passed over four days earlier, I withdrew, leaving him in company with his second in command to consider the question of attack. After an interval of a few minutes I was again called up. The line of advance had been decided upon. The attack would be a front one. The assault would be made against the left of the granite knolls, and at the right of the high ridge. The ground leading to this portion of the enemy's position was more level than that which approached the right front of the knolls, and over this level space it was proposed to move the two battalions of infantry to cut the centre of the Arab line, and sever the granite knolls from the high ridge. What did I think of this plan? I did not like it, and I said so.

From where we stood, looking straight along the more open ground to the left of the knolls, it seemed fair enough; but I knew that at the very edge of the granite rocks there ran a deep gully, the bottom of which was filled with large blocks of stone; that beyond that again, but also hidden from our present standpoint, there were a succession of ugly places, where formation could not be kept, and that throughout the whole of this ground the column, moving to the attack, must be exposed to a concentrated fire from the knolls, from the ridge, and from the rugged ground between the two.

I thought it would be possible to carry the Arab position by an attack on this central point, but I felt assured that success would be attained at a cost which would cripple the striking power of those two battalions during the remainder of the campaign.

When I had spoken to this effect, I was asked what other line of attack I would propose.

" By the left flank of the Arab position."

From the group of rocks where we then stood a small " wadi " or sandy valley took its course, leading off to our right front in a line which quite cleared the extreme left of the Arab position on the ridge of Kirbekan. That the ground immediately in rear of the ridge was practicable for troops, I already knew, for on the day when I had sat so long in the high rocks that now held the Arabs, I had looked right down upon every square yard of it.

"Follow this sandy wadi leading from where we stand to that low depression in the Kirbekan range, pass the range at that point, then wheel to the left, and take the whole Arab line in rear."

"But can we pass the range at that depressed point?" asked both the general officers.

I felt confident it could be easily done, for the wadi led straight for the hollow in the range, and by this time the rules of the desert had become pretty familiar to me; but to make assurance certain, I proposed to take a patrol that afternoon, out of sight of the sharp eyes on the high ridge, and sweeping round to eastward, approach the valley or depression unobserved. This was agreed to, and it was decided to await my report before finally resolving to attack the centre of the position.

Two hours before sunset I got quietly out of camp with a small party of Hussars, and keeping a course at first right into the desert, and following wadi after wadi, gradually worked round

until, gaining the dip in the range, I stood only half
a mile from the left flank of the Arab line. Here
I left the Hussars, all save four, with whom I
passed through the depression, keeping still on
the sand of the wadi. I had remembered from
the old reconnaissance, a low range of hills that
ran in rear of the Kirbekan range, and at right
angles to it. We reached, unobserved, the
shelter of this low range; then dismounting, I
crept cautiously to the top and looked over. I
stood on the left rear of the Arab line, and could
see every move made along the back or north face
of the Kirbekan range. Many Dervishes were
standing among the rocks, or moving over the
hillside. Groups of Arabs occupied the ground
in rear of the granite knolls, and I could see from
the attitude of the men on the ridge, clearly seen
against the sunset, that there was not the least
idea of any danger from the direction of my
standpoint. The river was only 1000 yards
distant, and the road to it was perfectly practicable along two lines of advance. An easier path
to turn an enemy's flank and gain his rear could
not have been imagined, and all now depended
upon the Arabs not being aware of our intention
until we would have actually carried it into effect,
so far, at least, as to gain with the head of our
column this inner range from which I now
looked.

I crept back to my horse, and keeping low in the little wadi, reached, unobserved, the spot where I had left the Hussars; then we repassed the gap, and made our way towards the camp. As we entered our line of vedettes, the Arabs on the high ridge caught sight of us, and crowding upon the rocks, they shook their spears, and sent their shrill cries ringing after us; but had they known that we were returning from round the rear of their own line, their triumph and jubilation might not have been so demonstrative.

It was dusk when I reached the camp; the general was alone. I told him that in one hour and twenty minutes from quitting the present bivouac, his infantry column might be in rear of the Arab position, marching over ground perfectly practicable for troops. He sent for his second in command. " The account is so good," he said, " that I think we must give up the idea of a front assault, turn the left flank, and attack from the rear." So orders were issued accordingly. Three hours later I was called again to the general's bivouac. The Intelligence officer had just brought in word that his spies reported the retreat of the enemy from the position of Kirbekan.

I did not credit it for a moment. The men who had crowded upon the steep rocks after sunset that evening defying us with voice and weapon, meant to fight on the ridge of Kirbekan.

CHAPTER XVI.

IN WHICH WE FIGHT THE ARABS.

AT seven o'clock on the morning of the 10th February, the troops moved out of their zeriba to begin the turning movement round the enemy's left flank. The advance was led by the Hussars the Egyptian Camel Corps followed, forming a screen between the Arab position and the infantry. The latter—Stafford and Black Watch battalions, less four companies—marched in double column. The zeriba, the baggage, and the boats were covered by two guns of the Egyptian artillery and three companies of infantry; these occupied the group of rocks 600 or 700 yards from the enemy's right, which the cavalry had held during the two previous days.

It took about a quarter of an hour to get the column formed, and then the march began.

We held our way straight towards the gap in the Kirbekan ridge, by the wadi along which I had returned on the previous evening; our movement was therefore in full view of the ridge, although broken ground hid it from the granite knolls near the river. Directing the advance of the Hussars, I kept an eye watching the movements of the Arabs on the high ridge. Now was their moment, if they guessed our intention, to deliver a counter attack upon us. We were passing obliquely across their front, and were they prepared to take the offensive this was their time. But the truth was they never imagined our movement was intended to take their position iu rear, believing that we were only moving further to our right, before delivering an attack upon the front of their line. As it was all-important to us to heighten this impression, I directed the Camel Corps to turn to its left, close in towards the granite knolls, and engage the enemy. This order was quickly executed by the officer in command,[1] and the rapid fire now

[1] Captain Marriott, R.M.A.

opened by the Camel Corps seemed to the Arabs but a prelude to the real attack about to be delivered from the same point.

Meantime following the sandy wadi, we soon reached the gap between the hills, passed through it, and gained the inner ridge on the left rear of the Arab line. Almost at the same moment the first gun fired from near our zeriba; the shell burst among the rocks at the summit of the ridge, and, as a flock of birds will scatter when a shot is fired into them, so I saw a cloud of Arabs rush from the rocks and scatter down the hillside. The greater part of them, however, rallied in a moment, and ran up again into the boulders; a few continued their descent to the foot of the ridge.

Meanwhile the infantry had halted to take a few minutes' breath in the gap between the hills, about 400 yards behind where I stood. The shell bursting in the rocks had shown me two things— first, the Arabs were all in their positions as they had been on the evening before; second, that they were disposed not to stick very closely to them. I judged, therefore, that there was not a moment to be lost if we were to gain the rear of their position while they yet held it. I sent both these messages to the general, and a few minutes later brought the head of the column to the spot where I was standing.

Debouching through this inner ridge, we came at once in view of the enemy. In our front two practicable tracks led towards the river, diverging at an acute angle from each other and striking the river about 300 yards apart.

As we neared the point where these tracks divided, the general asked me which one I thought the infantry ought to follow. I recommended that one battalion should take the left and the other battalion the right; they would both unite in the open ground near the river. "I prefer keeping the battalions together," replied the general. "In that case," I answered, "the left track will be the best one. I will take the right one with the Hussars." At the point of rock dividing the two tracks we separated. On the previous night he had discussed with me the action he wished the mounted troops to take on the morrow. I was to act on the right of the infantry, when in rear of the enemy's position, and if the ground permitted pursuit I was to follow whenever the chance afforded. The leading Hussars had meanwhile proceeded some distance along the right-hand track, and when I caught them up, they had become engaged with detached groups of Arabs who were moving across our front, retiring from the direction of the knolls, along the river. The ground in our front was a succession of rugged rocky groups, with small open spaces between them. Through these openings we could see the rapidly-moving figures of the Arabs, some of them halting behind the rocks to fire at us, but the greater number passing on intent only upon flight. Among these fugitives were a few horsemen and camels. Meanwhile a dropping fire had begun from the top of the Kirbekan ridge, showing that some of the enemy yet held that position. Looking to the left, I saw the infantry 200 yards distant, still in column, occupying a detached mass of rocks, and firing from front and left flank. It was clear that whatever reserves the Arabs had behind their line were now retiring precipitately, leaving the garrisons of the ridge and the knolls to their fate. We pushed on quickly towards the river, and soon reached the track along which the enemy were retreating. The rocks, piled up in detached masses around us, gave countless hiding-places, in and out of which the Arabs kept moving, like rabbits in cover. But our rapid advance prevented any attempt at a rally, while the broken nature of the ground concealed our scanty numbers, and made the fugitives imagine they were being followed by a large force. So strong was this impression in the Arab mind, that prisoners afterwards told us they were convinced we were the mounted troops of the Desert Column, who had crossed from Berber

z

to take them in rear. The idea that they were now cut off by a powerful force from the Shukook Pass was so strong among them that numbers could be seen swimming the river in their haste to get away from this imaginary army, the reality of which did not at this moment equal a full troop of fifty men.

Amid a continuous popping of shots that made much noise but did little damage in this broken ground, we reached a detached mass of boulders in which a body of Dervishes had taken refuge, with the intention of letting our troop sweep by before they took the water to escape by swimming.

As I was very anxious to get exact information of the whereabouts of the main Arab force, I made my interpreter promise life and protection to all who would give themselves up. A few Dervishes came out and surrendered. From them I gathered that the advanced camp was still half a mile ahead of us, at the mouth of the pass; that there was another and a larger camp at Uss, at the further end of the Shukook, two hours' journey distant; and that this main force had not yet been engaged. I therefore determined to push on as quickly as possible to the camp at the mouth of the Shukook, to seize that objective point of all our present operations, and thus hold the outlet through which the main body of the enemy must advance from their camp

at Uss to support their vanguard now surrounded
at Kirbekan.

We soon reached the camp. It occupied a
small level space, near a branch of the river, shut
in on almost every side by steep overhanging
rocks, black as though they had been smeared
with coal-tar. The news of our rapid approach
had preceded us, the level space was deserted—
the last Arabs vanishing into the rocks as we
entered the gorge which led to the camp. At the
further side of the level ground stood a group of
eight or ten Dervish standards of many colours,
and with the usual prayers embroidered upon
them. The ground around these flags was lit-
tered with water-bags, dhurra-sacks, mats, prayer-
carpets, kettles, and all the odds and ends of an
Arab encampment. In the khor, by the river,
about a hundred donkeys and a few camels were
standing or lying around. Behind the camp the
rocks rose into steeper and darker masses
forming fitting portals to the Shukook Pass,
which had here its beginning.

I sent my staff-officer back at once to carry to
the general the largest and best of the standards, to report our capture of the camp,
and to ask if he had any orders to give me.
Then, pushing a patrol along the gorge leading
to the gate of the Shukook, we began to collect the
captured animals. While engaged at this work,

z 2

the black hill-tops around showed signs of life.
The Arabs had found out our real numbers in the
open space, and, climbing into commanding positions, they now opened fire with an accuracy
that showed the distances had been already measured. I sent back to bring up the thirty
troopers we had left half a mile behind, and on
their arrival moved some dismounted men into
the rocks to engage the groups of men holding
the hill-tops over the mouth of the pass. The
staff-officer, carrying the standard, rode hard on
his mission, and in less than an hour he was back
with me again.

He had given the flag to the general, whom
he found with the infantry in rear of the
granite knolls, from which a dropping fire was
kept up by the Arabs—the troops were lying
down in the rocks, near the river; the fight
appeared to be nearly over; a few Arabs still held
the ridge and rocks, but they were completely
encircled by us. The general had no orders
to send me. I had asked for some of the
Egyptian Camel Corps to collect the animals
from the khors and rocks around us, but they
could not yet be spared, he said, from the ridge,
where they still watched the south side of the
position at Kirbekan.

It was now long past noon—the Arab fire
in our front had been silenced, the vollies

which for some time had sounded from our
infantry, in rear, had fallen into occasional
shots, and I gathered from this that the granite
knolls and the ridge were in our possession.
There was no longer any object in holding
this opening from the Shukook. The main
Arab force might now come when it pleased,
and the sooner it came the better, for it would
find us in possession of the ridge of Kirbekan,
with the faces instead of the backs of our infantry
towards the Shukook. I therefore ordered all
the beasts to be collected and moved towards
our camp, then, drawing off the Hussars, we
fell back slowly along the track we had advanced
over three hours earlier.

As we neared the ridge I met a soldier of
the Royal Highlanders fetching water from the
river. I asked him how he had fared. The last rock
group had been taken," he said, " but the general
had been shot dead at the moment of its final
capture." I rode on to the knolls; down the horse-
shoe opening in rear of the central granite group,
half-a-dozen soldiers were carrying a body with
a blanket thrown over it. It was the body of
General Earle. He had fallen at the wall of the
small stone hut, which five days earlier the slave-
boy had shown me in the centre of the granite
rocks. A dozen desperate Arabs holding this
rough building to the last, had sold their lives

very dearly. Their last cartridge had cost the River Column its best life. The straw roof of the hut had been finally fired, and the black and charred bodies of the desperate garrison now lay amid the burning embers.

I rode on to the camp. Two other bodies were being brought in—Eyre, the colonel of the Stafford battalion—Coveney, of the Black Watch. One had been shot on the high ridge taken by the Staffords, the other when the Highlanders first moved against the granite rocks. Altogether exactly a dozen lives, officers and men, had been lost among these stubbornly held boulders.

A week ago this would have seemed a trifling price to pay for any rock or ridge that brought us nearer to Khartoum, but now it was different. Now there was no Khartoum—there was nothing behind that black range whose bare possession would have been dearly won at the cost of the humblest life lost that day, and, looking at these three lifeless forms which a few hours earlier had moved out of this camp the best among our little band, they whose presence through all the long road we had travelled, memory linked with a hundred scenes of service to our lost cause, given without stint of labour, it was impossible not to regret that such bootless victory had cost such brilliant lives.

At sunset we laid them in their sleep. In a

THE BURIAL OF GENERAL EARLE AND COLONELS EYRE AND COVENEY AT KIRBEKAN.

Page 342.

small spot of green, within sound of the waters of the great river, they lie side by side in their long rest. A solitary dom-palm alone marks the spot; around, the rugged rock desert of the Monassir spreads its awful desolation.

It was twilight when all was finished and the guns began to thunder out their last tribute over a darkening solitude. Many a year will go by ere the footstep of a fellow-countryman passes these lonely graves; and even if semi-savage man leaves them undisturbed, the wind and the sun will soon smooth them down into desert level again; but it may be that the tradition of the place will linger long in the native mind, and some old Arab, who as a child-fugitive in the opposite islands listened at nightfall to the roar of cannon that told them the white "Emir-el-Kebir" had fallen, will point out to future travellers the spot where the English strangers lie at rest.

CHAPTER XVII.

AND LAST.

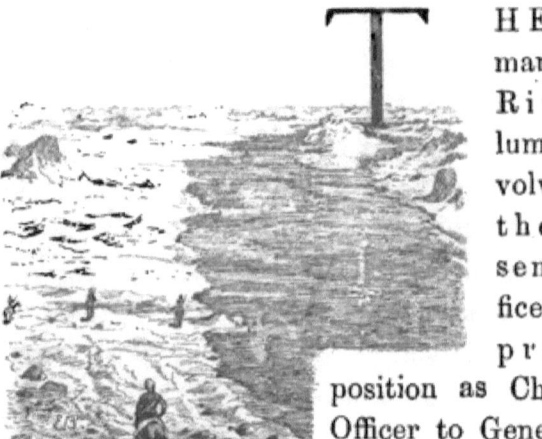

THE command of the River Column now devolved upon the next senior officer,[1] whose previous position as Chief Staff Officer to General Earle had put him in full possession of the orders and objects of the Commander-in-Chief at Korti. There was consequently no alteration in pre-existing arrangements, and the morning of the 11th February found us again moving forward along the old familiar road. Up to this day the Stafford and Black Watch battalions had led the

---

[1] Brigadier-General H. Brackenbury.

advance; the Cornwall and Gordon Highlander regiments were now to take the lead.

As the distance to be traversed this day was a short one, the mounted troops enjoyed a partial rest, and I took advantage of it to go again over the positions which the enemy had yesterday held.

Dead men are said to tell no tales, but the dead of a battle-field are often the most eloquent spokesmen human cause can have, and although in these red rocks and over the lofty ridge the Arab dead did not much exceed one hundred in number, they told plainly enough the story of this revolt. Old and young, grey-bearded veterans, mere boys, and men in life's best years, lay scattered in varying attitudes of fight in the spots they had themselves selected to try to the death the issue against us. Although in taking their positions in reverse we had completely neutralized the artificial defences they had added to the natural strength of their line, they had held their ground for four hours exposed to a terrible punishment, for the boulders among which they lay had given but partial shelter from the rain of lead that had been poured upon them. Our rifle-bullets, striking in continued volleys upon the smooth and sloping sides of those seamless rocks, had splashed lead into every nook and cavity within, cutting and wounding the defenders. The entire outer surface of the rock was marked with bullets, and the cavities were thickly strewn with the bright little lead-splashes, like sharp and jagged coins; while the faces and bodies of the killed showed how terribly they had suffered ere the final moment had come for them to die at their post. Few among them had any ammunition remaining. They lay often in groups of two or three, and the survivor would seem to have used the last cartridge of his comrades ere he himself had fallen.

I do not think that more than three hundred Arabs had held the entire position, and of these probably one-half were killed—the number being about equally divided between the knolls near the river captured by the Highlanders, and the higher ridge which the Stafford had taken.

I have spoken on a previous occasion of the view visible from this ridge of Kirbekan. In all the long waste through which we had come it would not have been possible to match its naked, hopeless nature.

Yet that it was a home worth fighting for, and worth dying for, black and bleak and barren though it was, the clenched fist, the head thrown back, the foam on the open lips of these poor lifeless brown bits of Nile clay, told plainly enough, for after all, these grim realities are the great test, and there is more true love of the home land in one ounce of dust such as this left unburied here in these rocks than in all the well-

turned periods of a century of assertion. Creed
and colour do not alter these things.

Our advanced camp that evening was only a
short distance on the river above the ridge of
Kirbekan. To this camp there came in the course
of the afternoon, the leading companies of the
Cornwall battalion. A couple of small rapids
lying between the camps had rendered tracking
necessary on the way. It chanced that as the
crew of a boat were engaged upon the old work
of towing along the shore, a soldier noticed a
small native wooden saddle lying in a ravine
between the rocks, evidently thrown there by some
fugitive of the previous day, escaping from
the Arab position to the river. A black bag
made of goat's hair was fastened to the saddle. In
the bag there was only a soiled bit of paper which
had some Arabic characters written upon it.
Nine out of ten men would have thrown the
crumpled paper away, but this man brought it
along with him to camp and gave it to his captain,
from whom it passed to the colonel[2] of the battalion.

A couple of hours before sunset I reached the
camp ; the Arabic writing had meantime been
given to the interpreter of the regiment, who was
only imperfectly able to read it. He had made
out, however, that it told " bad news." This was

[2] Colonel Richardson.

the story which that chance-found paper carried to us. It was a copy of an original letter sent from Berber by Mohammed El Khier, the Emir of the Mahdi, to Abdul Majid Wad Le Kailik, head Emir opposed to the infidels in Dar Monassir. After the usual salutations and prayers it ran thus :—

" On the night of the 26th January the army of the Mahdi entered Khartoum and took the forts, city, and vessels in the river: the traitor Gordon was killed. Inform your troops of this signal triumph which God has given to the arms of the Prophet of His Prophet."

On the night of January 26th Khartoum had fallen to the Arabs, and on the forenoon of the 28th, thirty-two hours later, our advanced troops had come within sight of the city. Thirty-two hours too late! Of all the strange incidents in our history, few have surpassed this one.

I got my camel ready and rode back to the lower camp with this letter. It was the first news we had had of the fate of Gordon. The telegram of six days earlier had spoken only of the loss of Khartoum; now there could no longer be any doubt *he* was dead.

By what strange chance had it happened that the first intimation of this death should have come to us almost from the very spot which, twenty-four hours earlier, had been the death-scene of another brave soldier. "Earle does not come up to extricate me, he comes to extricate the garrisons, which affects our 'national honour.' I hope he may succeed, and that the 'national honour' will reward him; but I am not the rescued lamb and I will not be." Thus Gordon had written a few months before—and now ? both had passed through the narrow gate, and were alike beyond the reach of rescue or of reward.

This scrap of paper explained many things to us. It was the news of the fall of Khartoum that had brought the Arabs out of the Shukook fastness and induced them to offer us battle in the wretched position they had chosen at Kirbekan.

In our next day's work we shall see what might have been our task had they adhered to their first intention of opposing us three miles further on.

On the 12th we set out to reconnoitre the country now lying before us; striking away at a right angle from the river, we first traversed a region of hard rock, tilted up like the pointed roofs of old houses, and so hard and solid that if water fell there, it could not have entered the ground; then bending gradually round to the north we reached a broad and deep wadi, running off in an eastern direction. That this must have been the Wadi-el-Argu of the maps was evident from its size and nature. In many places pools of water were along it, and the roots and driftwood at its sides showed that it was frequently the scene of high and rapid floods. It is this valley which cuts the bend of the river, and leads by a line of seventy or eighty miles to the Nile below Berber. Following the Wadi-el-Argu for a couple of miles, I reckoned that we must now be not very far from the white streak of level ground which I had observed from the ridge of Kirbekan a week earlier. We therefore ascended the first opening on our left, and from the top of a neighbouring hill had the satisfaction of seeing the white plain close to us. It was the only bit of good ground our horses had put foot to for three weeks, and as we now pushed quickly over it in a northerly course, it was pleasant to see again bushes and herbage that for once did not owe their existence to the river. At the northern extremity of this plain rose a tall single hill with a white outcrop of trap rock upon its summit. Climbing to this white standpoint, a view was at last obtained over the waste of black roof-top which bore the name of the Shukook. Yet so sunken was the river beneath the granite wilderness that not a vestige of it could be seen even from this lofty point, although its channel was not distant from us to the west much above a mile. Looking northwards one saw distant palms showing across so broad an extent of desert that it was evident the Nile must there become broken again into a series of island channels such as those we had lately passed below Kirbekan. From the base of this solitary hill several " khors " led in different directions, and following one towards the west we gained the river. It flowed smooth and with easy current between high-impending rocks. We halted to rest and water at the river, and then turned our horses' heads towards Kirbekan.

Having no native guide whatever, and our maps being wholly useless, it became no easy matter to grope our way through this black and rugged region. In many of the " khors " or passes in this region of the Shukook the red granite rocks immediately facing the track bear drawings, or rude cuttings of different animals; a stag with wide antlers, long-horned oxen, and camels being most frequently represented. As there are no deer or cattle of the kinds drawn now existing in the country, I believe these figures to be of considerable age, although the grain of the hard rock looks fresh, as though the cutting had been done in recent times. It would have been much too long a route to return by the course we had come; and besides, my object was the Shukook Pass and the course of the river lying near it. The shore was altogether impracticable;

I determined, therefore, to take the first opening in the rocks that led towards the south, and then trust to chance to come out at the south end of the Shukook where, on the 10th, we had taken the Dervish camp. If the long pass was held in any portion of its six miles' distance, we would thus take in rear those who defended it. With many a twist and turn the track led us through rocks that seemed in their wild irregularity to outdo all we had hitherto seen. Often we were obliged to dismount and lead in single file up or down some winding stairway. In many places the walls of the defile could be touched by a horseman right and left at the same moment, and everywhere there were dominating positions where half a dozen men could hold in check ten times their number.

In some parts of the long pass, stone breast-works or " sconces " showed where the Arabs had prepared a succession of positions, one behind the other, to resist our advance.

If the 300 or 400 Robitab and Monassir Arabs who held Kirbekan ridge and rocks against us, had elected to die in this Shukook region instead of six miles further south, the River Column would have found a difficulty in getting clay enough in this wild land to cover the dead it must then have had to bury.

It was sunset when we emerged from the pass

and got upon ground already familiar to us. The new general was waiting at the advanced camp to hear our news, which, though brief, was of good promise. The river was clear of rapids for ten miles forward, and the Shukook held no enemy throughout its entire distance.

Early on the 13th the forward move of the column through the Shukook region began, and by the evening of the 14th the whole force had passed the defiles; but ere Kirbekan was finally quitted, another grave had to be dug beside the three under the solitary dom-palm.

At *reveillé* on the 13th a young officer died of fever, brought on through incessant labour. He had been one of the six officers originally selected to accompany the boats from England to Egypt. For months he had literally lived for his work, and now he had died for it.

Among the deities of the old Egyptian world, Hapi, or the Nile, held high place. If those who die young are the favourites of the gods, then the spirit of the Great River should watch well the spot where Barry Yelverton—Lord Avonmore—lies at rest.

Another wild series of islands and rapids followed the passage of the Shukook, and from the 14th to the 17th the infantry were fighting the old fight with the cataracts of Uss and Sherrari, and the rapid waters that flow between the isles of Shoar, Kamsah, and Sherri. But at the head of the last-named cataract there came a change : the black rocks disappeared ; the old yellow drift-sand of the desert, which for more than a month had been a total stranger to us, was again in sight; and the Nile lay once more a single stream, flowing in broad and even current between banks that held scattered groups of palms and spots of cultivation at intervals along them. We had passed the last rapid of the Shagghieh, and out of 217 boats that had started from Gerf-Hamdab, twenty-six days earlier 215 were here safe and sound at Salamat— "the town of peace"—700 feet above the Nile level of Wadi Halfa.

Salamat was the chief village in the country of the Monassir Arabs, and was the residence of the Sheikh of the tribe, Suliman Wad Gamr, at whose hands Colonel Stewart, Mr. Power, and the Austrian Consul had been murdered five months earlier. That we were now approaching the scene of this deed of blood was made evident to us by the relics of the ill-fated party which were here discovered—pieces of the wrecked steamer, cards, letters, and books bearing the names of the murdered men. Like all other villages on our road, Salamat the peaceful was deserted by its inhabitants, who had followed—man, woman, and child—the fortunes of their Sheikh. A reward of 1000*l* had months ago been put

upon his capture, and while in one way it had
served to illustrate the extraordinary fidelity of the
Arab to his chief, in another respect it had given
us an insight into the manner and method in
which the Turk had been wont to deal with the
natives in these things. Shortly after our entry
into the Monassir country, the Vakeel, or Commander of the Mudir's army, had begun negotiations with the family of Suliman Wad Gamr, to
induce their surrender to him.

Where the law of polygamy obtains, a man's
worst enemies are generally to be found among
his father's sons and relations, so the Vakeel
sought among the uncles of Wad Gamr for the
means of obtaining possession of their nephew
and of the 1000*l* which went with him. There
was only one obstacle—the life of Suliman must
be guaranteed. If Suliman's life were taken, then
the blood feud would rage until it was quenched
in blood. This guarantee could not be given.
In vain the Vakeel remonstrated, pointing out
that it was by no means necessary to keep the
promise of life. "The policies require," he wrote,
"that promise of life be given to the Sheikh; he
will then surrender; you will then take him with
you to Berber, and after you have taken that
place you can deal with your prisoner as you
wish; but the policies now require that you
promise him protection of life, or he will not

surrender himself." When the Vakeel was informed that no promise could be given, he declared that we did not understand the " true policies " at all. There was, however, yet another way of dealing with the Wad Gamr. " You may offer," he said, " any reward you like to his own tribe, or you may punish them as you wish, but they will never give up their Sheikh ; but go on to the next tribe—the Robatab—and begin to punish them ; cut down their palm-trees, burn their sakeeyehs, and destroy their houses, and then say to them, ' We want to get Suliman Wad Gamr, Sheikh of the Monassir, and we will go on at this work of destruction until you bring him to us;' then you will get him." But after all, these " policies " of the Turk are nothing new in history. I am not quite sure that, in looking at them to-day, we may not see a good deal of our own " policies " of two and three hundred years ago, just as in Constantinople at the present time you can find the best examples of the London watches of the 16th and 17th centuries.

In saying that the Monassir would never give up their Sheikh, the Vakeel spoke truly. When on the 15th I reached this town of Salamat, the villagers on the opposite island of Sherri called out from the shelter of their palm-trees, asking for " grace." I replied that we would give grace to all except to those who had murdered the three white men ten miles higher up the river. While this dialogue was going on across the water, two Arabs riding donkeys appeared a little way ahead.

The scouts gave chase, and to save themselves the men abandoned their donkeys and jumped into the river. The current was running strong at the spot, and the men were soon carried down opposite where I was endeavouring to effect the surrender of the islanders, which would have meant to us the supply of many things we stood in need of. I made the interpreter call out to the men swimming for their lives and to their people at the other side, that it was quite in our power to shoot them, but to show our mercy we would not do so. It was impossible not to admire the courage these two Arabs showed.

In their efforts to cross the stream above where we stood they had exhausted their strength, and it was now quite as much as they could do to reach the opposite shore directly in front of us. Yet, with a score of rifles menacing their lives, they would not let drop from their left hands the couple of spears which each carried, though to do so would have given them double strength to stem the current and reach a place of safety. They kept the spears well down in the water, swimming only with the right hand and legs, and when they finally did gain the further shore, they could just drag themselves with difficulty out of the water.

Five miles above Salamat rises another of those solitary hills which give to the wild scenery of the Upper Nile its most striking feature. At the base of this hill the ruins of a Christian church stand amid old graves, and from its summit the eye follows the line of the river through a long distance of yellow sand and grey rock. Now that the boats have all passed the last of the cataracts of Shagghieh and Monassir, our daily rate of progress is doubled, and the camping-places grow far apart.

On the 19th of July we are early at Sulimanéyeh, and in the afternoon reach with a patrol a spot long looked forward to, and often pictured during the past months. It is the village of Hebeh, the place where Colonel Stewart and his companions, Power and Herbin, met their deaths, in September, about ten days after they had left Khartoum. An Arab, whom we had taken in the rocks nearer Salamat, had described the position of the wrecked steamer, and we soon after caught sight of the funnel slanting backwards, and the hull with its bows upraised on the cluster of rocks upon which the boat had struck.

As we rode up opposite the spot, for the wreck lay at the further side of the river, between a small island and the proper right shore, a couple of camel-men started out from behind mimosa-bushes, and rode off towards the north, yelling a war-cry and brandishing their spears. Kirbekan had done a good deal in clearing the Shukook, where resistance might have been offered to us with such effect, but it had not quelled the spirit of these Arabs, and it was clear that at Abu Hamad there would be another gathering of the tribes, prepared to dispute again the road with us.

I sent back for a boat, and while it was coming pushed on a few miles further. Out from a hollow in the rocks two men sprang almost from under the horses' feet, and separating in different directions, ran like deer before the cavalry. The man who made towards the water, reached it, plunged in, gained the opposite shore and escaped; the other was captured. He had little to tell, but that little confirmed previous reports. Suliman Wad Gamr had passed this spot three days before with the fighting-men of his tribe; they had gone to a place called Shamkiyeh near the island of Mograt, where the Robatab and Dervishes from Berber were again going to fight us.

When we got back to the shore opposite the island, the boat had come from below, and we were soon at the wrecked steamer. All around where she lay was now dry ground; the hull was half full of sand, and everything that could be carried off had been taken away. The iron sheeting that Gordon had cased his thin boats in was still fastened around paddle-box, stem and stern, and many hundreds of bullet-marks all over the plates showed how often the *Abbas* had run the gauntlet of Arab fire at Khartoum before she began her ill-fated descent of the river. A few torn pages of books and *débris* of paper lay about the deck. Looking from the vessel to the river-bed in which she lay, it was difficult to believe that the steamer had not been designedly steered into this rock-encumbered side channel. It was, as I have already said, now dry, but even when the Nile had been twenty feet above its present level, four-fifths of the stream must have passed between the island and the shore from which we had come. Beyond the dry channel, on the right bank, stood the group of sand-huts where the murder had been committed.

The next day found the column concentrated on the left shore opposite Hebeh. I had been asked by the general to look out for a good spot to cross the mounted troops and the large convoy of 600 camels from the left to the right bank of the river, and Hebeh seemed to fulfil every requirement of such a place. The shores, the river, the high Nile island, now a peninsula—all were favourable for that operation usually so difficult in war, but here, by our boats, made so easy to us—the passing of cavalry, guns, and transport across a wide and quick-flowing river. Swimming the Hussar horses and Camel Corps took a very short time to accomplish, in the wake of the boats, but the camel convoy was a more protracted work. These 600 baggage-camels had accompanied the River Column for the purpose of enabling it to make an extended flank movement if it should become necessary to do so. As no operation of the kind had been attempted during our march, this large baggage convoy had been quite useless to us, while the provision of forage for its camels had been a source of extra trouble.

It was the afternoon of the 21st before the last animal was towed across the river and the entire force stood on the right shore of the Nile.

On again up stream—pleasant now the change from the rock of the left shore to the soft yellow sand of this right side. Six miles beyond Hebeh a massive ruined fort, El Kab, stands upon a rock by the river. On the opposite shore there is another, but a smaller ruin. Like the twin castles at Kubinat, these old fortresses are the last vestiges of a lost civilization. In the wide and lofty walls, burnt bricks of the best workmanship are visible, telling of forests that once gave fuel in this now treeless desert. What a long, terrible night has descended upon this vast weary world!

Beyond El Kab, a great desert of rolling yellow ridges stretches off to north and east. The boats, now rowing over unbroken water, make easy work of the long river reaches, and the horses no longer stumbling up and down steep tracks of stone, move quickly over the desert. Shoes have become scarce things, and though the sand is deep in places it is soft to hoofs worn very thin with Shukook stairways.

On the night of February 23rd we are all assembled for the first time since the column started from Hamdab, in a single camp ; beneath the sandy bank where we bivouac, 215 boats lie along a quarter-mile of lower shore. We have passed the furthest limit of the Monassir country. We are now moving at the rate of ten miles a day, and are less than three marches distant from Abu Hamad. It was a night, this 23rd, of most brilliant moonlight. The cold winds of a week earlier had given place to sudden heat, and even this night was soft and warm. The place and the moment seemed alike suited to take stock of our past labour and our future prospects. We were here over all the rapids of the Shagghich and Monassir. We had ascended these cataracts so long regarded as utterly impassable, at the worst time of the year, during a season of exceptionally low water, the river being five feet below its ordinary

February average, and in the whole of those long
and intricate torrents our loss had been two
boats—217 had started one month earlier from
the foot of the Fourth Cataract—215 were lying
here at Huella, carrying still two months' food for
our entire force. Throughout the first half of the
advance we had been always within striking distance by an active and watchful enemy, while the
length of our line, separated by cataracts which
imposed upon our boats passage one by one
through their numerous " gates," rendered our
power of striking that enemy a slow and difficult
process—in other words the weak *head* of our
advance was day and night within reach of the
strong *body* of our enemy, while our body could
only get at his through a concentration more or
less protracted. He knew every rock in the
river—every " Khor " and wadi in the desert.
He could approach us by day or night, along a
hundred hidden passages, while every move of
ours was exposed to his keenest scrutiny. We
knew nothing of the road before us, but had to
feel our way through defile and over ridge, finding
our own track along the shore, and discovering
that for the boats in the river. The work would
have been a difficult one had the strength of our
mounted force in advance been four times what it
was, but to our little troop of forty horsemen and

thirty camel-riders,[3] the task of covering such a
movement, through such a country, had taxed to
the utmost limit the strength and endurance of
men and animals. So much for the past—and for
the future? Well, we were here five-and-twenty
miles from Abu Hamad, where two important acces-
sions of strength would reach us. The north wind
would there again become our friend, and with
sails spread before it the labour of the river would
be reduced three-fold. At Abu Hamad we would
also receive the long-planned convoy of 800 camels
which under an officer noted for his desert rides,[4]
was waiting ready to start from Korosko.
That the Arabs would attempt to fight us again
at or near Abu Hamad was very probable, but
we were now in an open sandy country, where
resistance could be of little avail to them. Once
round that turn at Abu Hamad, every step would
be taking us directly nearer to the Desert Column,
whose latest reports described them as being
about to take Metemmeh, under the leadership
of the officer who had succeeded to the command
upon the death of Stewart.[5]

---

[3] From sixty to seventy was the usual strength of the force
scouting in front, and covering the advance of the boats. The
remainder of the Mounted Troops were kept with the convoy
and the main camp ten or twelve miles behind us.

[4] Major Rundle, R.A.

[5] Sir Redvers Buller, late chief of the staff.

From Metemma that column was to move down river to Berber, where the two wings would again unite, and as our distance from that point of meeting was now not more than 130 miles, with three cataracts, none of which were described as being at all as formidable as those we had crossed, we might fairly expect to join hands with our long-separated brethren in three weeks' time. As for the physical condition of our own troops, it would have been difficult to show anything finer, disease was entirely absent; and so far from the long-endured labour of the cataracts having injured or broken down the health or constitutions of the men, they had come forth from the wilderness of the Monassir almost the perfect models of hard and seasoned soldiers.

So, looking back and looking forward that moonlight night at Huella, seemed our retrospect and our prospect. The morning of February 24th came; I was riding out of camp to push forward with the mounted troops another dozen miles, when a call from the General's bivouac caused me to stop. A native foot messenger had just arrived, bringing a cypher despatch from Korti of great moment. The man had come through with much rapidity, as well he might, for the reward of his flying feet was set at 50*l*. The message he carried was our recall. The Desert Column had abandoned all attempts upon

Metemma, and was already in full retreat upon Korti. The Arabs were following, and threatened to harass it on its march. When the last despatch had left they were firing heavily into the camp at Abu Klea, where General Buller was waiting for fresh camels. We were to return at once, if not actually in Abu Hamad or in presence of an enemy formed to oppose us. Such was the purport of this message. "What did I think of it?" In these things one reads a good deal between the lines. It was plain the end had come. The Desert Column was no longer in a condition to advance, to strike, or even to sit still. It must fall back. Its camels were gone; that meant marching, abandonment of stores, difficulties with sick, hardships, and, perhaps, want of water. That it meant no more than this I felt almost sure of, because in the Royal Irish battalion I knew that the officer commanding the column possessed a compact and powerful body of men, unshaken by previous losses, and able, as a rear guard, to keep back twenty times their numbers.

While the General was issuing his orders for a retreat, I took a score of Hussars forward on a last patrol. We passed the solitary group of dom-palms which marks the end of Dar Monassir, and entered the long sand wastes of Dar Robitab. The Nile bent more and more to the east. We

had reached the beginning of its great turn.
Amid the sands near the river many very old
mimosa-trees grew at intervals, giving occasional
patches of shade in fiery sunlight. Holding on
for two hours, we passed out from the last of
these old giants and saw the river lying six miles
before us clear of rock, flowing blue through a
blinding waste. At its furthest extreme the
channel divided at the end of a large island, the
left branch flowing south of west. We were in
sight of Mograt Island. Not one living, moving
object marked the vast silent desert. Upon a ridge
that overlooked a long expanse we halted for a last
look forward. Amid the toil and heat of this life
of ours there had been scant time to give to the
sentiment or the enthusiasm of travel. Ever
since the fatal news of the 6th of February it was
only too clear that all our labour had been in
vain, and that the great cheque we had drawn
upon future history had come back to us un-
honoured by Destiny. But now—all our old
hopes, all our past labours, all our strivings and
our losses seemed to gather into this last view of
the Nile before us.

It lay a blue belt amid the waste of yellow
drift, far stretching to the east, with a rugged
outline of purple mountain in remotest distance.
A few red and black hills rose in the bare level
of the middle distance, and one lofty rock, shaped

like a gigantic sphinx, stood looking at us from across the river.

It was noon. The sun burned fiercely overhead. Around lay a vast silence, broken only by the north wind rustling low in the dry leaves of the dom-palms, as we turned back over the desert.

The Campaign of the Cataracts was over. Ten days later we reached the foot of Gebil Barkal, recrossed the river opposite Merawi, and there set up our tents, while the remainder of the column passed down stream to the province of Dongola.

During the months that followed one had time to see many things with clearer vision than the strife of our effort had before permitted.

There are sermons in the stones of these lone places; the palm "reeds shaken by the wind" have far-off meanings.

The man we had "come out to seek in this desert" was gone, and only the echoes of his "voice crying in the wilderness" reached us through the darkness. "I have done the best for the honour of our country. You send me no information, although you have lots of money. I am very happy. I have tried to do my duty. God rules all, His Will be done. Good-bye." These were the last messages he sent us, uttered as the light of earthly hope was flickering low.

Like the rustle of the wind-shaken reed they reached a long way over the desert.

"In the flood of many waters they shall not come nigh unto him." What does it all now matter?—

> We dig a grave and carve a name—
> The name of one who tried in vain
> To lift a load and break a chain ;
> The Prince—the Pauper—all the same.
>
> Yet, from this mystery of man,
> Out of Life's travail and its tears,
> Through all the anguish of the years—
> Clearer and clearer grows the plan.
>
> For, building with our grief and pain,
> Sifting each soul through Life's brief day,
> Casting aside the baser clay,
> God gathers at the grave again.

THE END

B   b

APPENDIX A.

NOTES ON THE ADVANTAGES OF THE USE OF SMALL BOATS FOR THE ASCENT OF THE NILE.

LORD WOLSELEY,—There are four distinct methods by which boats of from twenty-six to thirty-two feet in length, six to seven feet beam, and eighteen to twenty-four inches draught, when loaded, can be moved against stream ; these are sails, oars, poles, and track-line. All four means can, in some conditions of water, be used at the same time ; but, as a rule, tracking is resorted to when the current is too strong for oars or sails. The track-line and the pole are, in fact, the means by which rapid water can best be stemmed. In a large river the lower stages of water are essential to the best use of these two methods. In high water the pole will not reach bottom, and "tracking" has to be done along the outer, or main, banks of the stream, which are usually rough, broken with fissures, or encumbered by a growth of trees, bushes, or by drift-wood, rendering progress slow, laborious, and exhausting ; but in low season the sand-banks, left bare by the receding waters, become admirably adapted to the use of the track-line. The margin close to the water is usually firm under foot, and is clear of obstruction. Where these lower banks end, recourse is had to the oar ; or if the current be sharp, to the pole until another sand-bank is come to which will permit the track-line again being run out ; and at all times the sails are available to take advantage of any favourable wind ; in fact, it may be said that boats of the dimensions stated, carrying crews of ten or twelve men, can always make some headway against a stream, except where actual barriers of rock cross the channel, or where the water becomes too shallow to float the boats.

In the case of the rock-barriers the stores and boats can be lifted over. Shallowness of water would, of course, be fatal to progress if the shallowness existed for any considerable distance. In the case of the Nile, however, this contingency is not to be feared with boats of light draft, for the following reasons :—

The Nile differs from all other rivers on the globe in the fact that the higher it is ascended from the sea through 1500 miles of its course the greater becomes the volume of water found in it. In that immense distance the river receives no tributary streams, while the evaporation caused by the sun, and the loss through percolation into the sand, amounts to nearly thirty per cent. in volume of water.

The difference in volume between highest Nile in October and lowest Nile in May is as fifteen to one, but although the fall is rapid from that highest point in October, a stage of water is reached in December which does not seriously diminish during the next two months.

Thus in mid-December the river has five times its lowest volume; in the middle of January it has more than four times, and in the middle of February it has just three times its lowest May volume.

Commander Hammill, R.N., visited the Nile between Wadi Halfa and Hanneck, during the lowest stage of the river, in May and June. This portion of the Nile is undoubtedly the worst for navigation in the entire course below Khartoum ; the descent is nearly fourteen inches to the mile. It has the largest number of cataracts and rapids, and the longest stretches of continuous strong water, yet the report of that officer only speaks of the river being sometimes fordable at one spot—Koheh— and he regards the east shore as absolutely secure from attack from the west side, which could not be the case if the river had been fordable at intervals. It has been taken for granted, in many papers and reports on the Nile, that because trade between Wadi Halfa and Dongola is carried on by means of camels and not by boats that the river is necessarily impassable for boats in that distance, but it must be remembered that there are many other reasons why the natives should find it easier to use camels than boats. Almost alone among the rivers of the world the Nile has no timber on its shores suitable to build craft to navigate its waters. Boats on the Upper Nile must be costly articles. In one of the intercepted letters from the French Army in 1799, the Comptroller of Finance in Egypt writes to the Directory thus :—" Since our arrival (fifteen months earlier) a prodigious number of Nile boats have been cut up and burnt for want of other fuel—these neither have, nor can, by any possible means be replaced." The wood to build them had to be imported, and the sea was closed.

The Arab, too, is only a boatman when current or wind is in his favour. He does not like the work of the oar, and knows nothing of the American-Indian and half-breed system of tracking, poling, and portaging. The country from which he came has no rivers in it, but the camel has been his ship for thousands of years, and it is little wonder that he should prefer it to any other means of movement.

It has also been said that the Nile would not be found adapted to the use of poles on account of the soft mud at the bottom of the river ; now, I have already stated that poles can only be of use in very rapid, and, comparatively speaking, shallow water. These rapid and shallow places are precisely those where the bottom *must* be hard, stony, or rocky, because the very rapidity of the stream washes away the softer substances, as a quick-flowing tide will scour the mouth of a harbour of mud and sand.

A great deal has been said upon the difficulty, almost the impossibility of ascending the Nile Cataracts, but the question appears to have been judged altogether upon the assumption that large boats must be used. When once we come to deal with the kind of boats I have specified, all the conditions change. If the north wind blows, these boats can take advantage of it as well as can any larger craft ; if the water prove rapid, they have pole and track-line to overcome it ; if the current should be deep, and there should be no wind, oars are available.

Finally, if rocks should form a continuous ridge across the river, the stores can be portaged and the boat lifted over the obstruction.

I have not seen the Nile above Cairo and its neighbourhood, and, so far, I labour under a disadvantage in writing these rough notes, but I have had considerable and varied experience in ascending rapid and dangerous rivers. Water is water, and rock is rock, whether they lie in America or in Africa; the conditions which they can assume towards each other are much the same all the world over.

I take the broad fact that the Nile has an average fall in 1800 miles of about nine inches to the mile. The river Saskatchewan in North America, from Rocky Mountain House to Lake Winnipeg—a distance of 1200 miles by river channel—has a fall of more than two feet to the mile.

The Winnipeg river, from the Lake of the Woods to Lake Winnipeg, has a fall of nearly three feet to the mile, yet it was this last-named river up which the 60th Rifles worked their way in September, 1870, at the rate of sixteen miles a-day, having actually to lift their boats out of the water below rocky interruptions, and launch them again above these rocks and rapids twenty-seven times between the two lakes. It may be said with truth that the entire trade of that vast region of North America, until recently known as the Hudson's Bay Territory, was carried on river conditions very much more unfavourable than those of the Nile.

(Signed)   W. F. BUTLER,

Colonel.

Plymouth,
    4th August, 1884.

APPENDIX B.

Submit calculation of time from delivery of boats in England to their being launched at Sarras and ready to start. Give all details.

10th *August*, 1884.   W.

Reply.

10th *August*, 1884.

Date of delivery of boats in England one month		
from date of order . . . . say	15th September	
Shipping in Transports . . . ,,	17th	,,
Sailing of Transports . . . . ,,	18th	,,
To arrive at Alexandria . . . ,,	30th	,,
Boats leave Alexandria. . . . ,,	2nd October	
Arrive Assiout . . . . . ,,	3rd	,,
Leave Assiout for Assouan . . . ,,	5th	,,
Arrive Assouan . . . . . ,,	13th	,,
Arrive Wadi Halfa . . . . ,,	20th	,,
Arrive Sarras . . . . . ,,	25th	,,
Ready to start . . . . . ,,	1st November	

W. F. B.

The above dates, given before the first boat-keel was laid, were meant as approximate mean averages, showing when the two-hundredth boat might be expected to arrive at the various points named. As a matter of fact 130 boats were at Wadi Halfa on the 18th October. There the original plan was changed; the native craft were given the right of way, and during ten days our boats remained at anchor at the foot of the Second Cataract.

APPENDIX. C.

BOATS CONSTRUCTED FOR NILE EXPEDITION.

Name and Address of Contractor.	Dimensions of Boats.			Number of Boats Contracted for.	Price per Boat.	Place of Delivery.
	Length.	Beam.	Depth.			
John Elder & Co., Fairfield Works, Govan, Glasgow	30 feet	7 feet	2 ft. 6 in.	20	85l.	Glasgow
John Read, Junr., Heaving-up Slip, Portsmouth	30 feet / 30 feet	6 ft. 9 in. / 6 ft. 6 in.	2 ft. 6 in. / 2 ft. 6 in.	10 / 1	85l. / 100l.	Portsmouth / Portsmouth (specimen boat)
D. & W. Henderson and Co., 30, Lang field Quay, Glasgow	32 feet / 30 feet / 30 feet	6 ft. 10 in. / 6 ft. 6 in. / 6 ft. 9 in.	2 ft. 8 in. / 2 ft. 6 in. / 2 ft. 6 in.	17 / 16 / 17	78l. / 74l. / 74l.	Glasgow
Forrestt & Son, Norway Yard, Limehouse	32 feet	7 feet	2 ft. 8 in.	100	90l.	30 Liverpool / 70 Woolwich
John White, Medina Dock, Cowes	32 feet	7 feet	2 ft. 8 in.	30	88l.	Portsmouth
T. W. Woolfe & Son, Shadwell, E.	30 feet	6 ft. 9 in.	2 ft. 6 in.	6	78l. 15s.	Woolwich
Watkins & Co., Orchard Yard, Blackwall	30 feet	6 ft. 9 in.	2 ft. 6 in.	20	85l.	14 Woolwich / 6 Portsmouth
Symons & Son, Falmouth	30 feet	6 ft. 9 in.	2 ft. 6 in.	10	70l.	Portsmouth
M. Robson & Son, North Quay, Monkwearmouth, Sunderland	30 feet	6 ft. 9 in.	2 ft. 6 in.	15	75l.	Woolwich
F. Hedley, West Hartlepool	30 feet	6 ft. 9 in.	2 ft. 6 in.	4	80l.	Woolwich
J. E. Scott, 13, Rood Lane, E.C.	30 feet	7 feet	2 ft. 6 in.	25	80l.	13 Glasgow / 12 Woolwich
W. A. Black & Co., Hatcher's Yard, Southampton	30 feet	6 ft. 0 in.	2 ft. 6 in.	5	85l.	Portsmouth
Waterman, Bros., Cremyll Yard, Devonport	30 feet	6 ft. 9 in.	2 ft. 6 in.	10	74l. 5s.	Portsmouth
Earle Shipping and Engineering Co., Hull	32 feet	6 ft. 9 in.	2 ft. 6 in.	20	78l. 5s.	Woolwich
F. Pounder, 77, High Street, Hartlepool	32 feet	6 ft. 0 in.	2 ft. 6 in.	4	80l.	Woolwich
John Preston, 59 and 60, Cornhill, E.C.	32 feet	6 ft. 9 in.	2 ft. 6 in.	35	85l.	Portsmouth
Cochran & Co., Duke Street, Birkenhead	32 feet	6 ft. 9 in.	2 ft. 6 in.	14	85l.	Liverpool
J. & G. Thomson, Clyde Bank, Glasgow	32 feet	6 ft. 9 in.	2 ft. 6 in.	10	85l.	Glasgow
Camper & Nicholson, Gosport	32 feet	6 ft. 9 in.	2 ft. 6 in.	10	88l.	Portsmouth
Copeman				1		
				400		

The second series of 400 boats, under charge of Colonel Grove, followed closely upon the first series.

APPENDIX D.

TRANSPORTS FOR FIRST 400 BOATS.

Ship.	Officer.	Number of Boats.	Where Shipped.	Sailed on.
Pelican	Lieutenant Peel	32	Royal Albert Docks	8th Sept.
President Garfield	Lord Avonmore	56	Surrey Com. Docks, Portsmouth	10th Sept.
Naranja	Hon. F. Colborne	56	Woolwich, Portsmouth	15th Sept.
Aston Hall	Major Boyle	80	Royal Albert Dock	18th Sept.
Frutera	Major Crofton	65	Glasgow	16th Sept.
Magdala	Lieutenant Pirie	44	Liverpool	13th Sept.
Bulimba	Sir G. Arthur	17	Portsmouth	16th Sept.
Scheldt	Lieutenant Orde	22	Woolwich	21st Sept.
Cruigton	Major Dickson	28	Glasgow	20th Sept.

APPENDIX E.

LIST OF BOAT EQUIPMENT.

Every boat carries—

2 masts.
2 sails and yards.
12 oars.
2 boat-hooks.
6 pushing poles.
2 grapnels, 6 fathoms rope.
12 rowlocks.
3 hardwood rollers.
5 spare planks, besides usual footboards.
2 spare knees.
1 awning
2 awning-poles.
1 rudder and yoke-lines.
1 towing rope, 120 fathoms.
1 coil of cordage, 50 fathoms.
1 snatch block.
1 leading block.
1 bell tent.
3 bags, waterproof, blankets.
1 bag, waterproof, accoutrements.
6 boxes ammunition.
2 axes, felling.
1 axe, pick.
1 balance, spring, with pan.
3 buckets, leather.

3 canisters, tin.
12 cups, tin.
12 plates, tin.
1 dish, baking.
1 dredger, pepper.
1 fork, flesh.
12 forks.
12 knives.
12 spoons.
2 knives, butchers'.
2 tin openers.
2 kettles, camp.
1 ladle, soup.
1 lamp, in box.
2 gallons colza oil.
2 mops.
1 pail, iron.
1 pan, frying.
1 portable stove.
2 spades.
6 sacks (with strings).
1 sponge.
6 slings, webbing.
2 canvas, slings.
1 sheet, lead, 2 ft. by 2 ft.
4 lb. pitch.
32 lb. paint, in tins.

1 paint brush.
4½ yards thick canvas.
3½ yards sail canvas.
1 coil spunyarn.
1 filter.
1 tin reserve charcoal for do.

1 lb. tow.
1 hammer.
1 bag nails.
Corks.
Sandpaper.
Hooks and lines, fishing.

One boat in Six carries—

1 coil of cord.
10 lb. pitch.

6 axe handles.

One boat in Eight carries—

1 tool chest.
1 adze.
1 auger.
1 axe.
4 bradawls.
4 chisels.
12 screwdrivers.
2 files.
3 gimlets.
2 hammers, claw.
1 hatchet.
3 knives.
1 mallet.
48 needles.
7 palms, sailmakers'.
2 pincers.
1 jack plane.
1 punch.
1 rule, 2 feet.
1 saw.
1 scissors.

1 saw set.
2 stones, sharpening.
1 tape, measuring.
2 brushes, paint.
1 axe, felling.
5 shoes, pushing-poles.
6 lb. copper nails.
4 lb. iron nails.
4 gross brass screws.
10 sheets tin.
2 lb. marline.
1 marline spike.
5 lb. twine and sail thread.
1½ gallons oil.
25 lb. lead, white.
2 lb. paint, white.
½ lb. beeswax.
6 axe handles.
10 lb. tow.
4 bottles oil (tin).

One boat in Twenty carries—

1 grindstone, complete.
1 luff tackle.

30 lb. iron nails.

Fifteen Boatmen divide between them—

2 cans, soup.
1 dredger, tin.
15 forks.
1 fork, flesh.
3 kettles, camp.
2 kettles, tin.
2 knives, butchers'.

15 knives.
1 ladle, soup.
15 plates.
15 tin pots.
15 spoons.
Spare lines, hooks, and fishing nets.

APPENDIX F.

LIST OF SUPPLIES TO BE SENT IN EACH BOAT PROCEEDING UP THE NILE, CALCULATED FOR 12 MEN IN A BOAT, AND TO LAST 100 DAYS.

Net total for each boat.	Article.	Packed in. No. of cases.	Contents of each.	Proposed daily issue.*
799 lb.	Preserved corned meat	1 / 10 / 4	60 lb. / 54 ,, / 49½ lb.	1 lb. 4 days out of 6
192 ,,	Preserved fresh meat	4	48 lb. average.	1 lb. 1 day out of 6
168 ,,	Bacon†	4	42 lb.	,, ,,
48 ,,	Boiled mutton†	1	48 ,,	
66 ,,	Cheese	4	2 cheeses, 16½ lb.	⅔ oz.
770 ,,	Biscuit, Navy	22	35 lb.	1 lb. 5 days out of 6
240 ,,	,, Cabin	8	30 ,,	
200 ,,	Flour	2 / 2	60 ,, / 40 ,,	1 lb. 1 day out of 6
52 half-pint bottles.	Pickles	2	26 bottles	¼ oz. 4 days out of 6
17 tins	Jam	1	17 tins	1½ oz. 2 days out of 6
17 ,,	Marmalade		17 tins	
80 lb.	Tea	2	40 lb.	1 oz.
240 ,,	Sugar	4 bags	60 lb.	3 oz.
19 ,,	Salt	1 bag	19 ,,	⅓ oz.
80 ,,	Preserved vegetables	1 / 1	48 ,, / 32 ,,	1 oz.
7½ gallons	Lime juice	3 / 1	5 bottles / 4 ,,	₁⁄₁₆ gallon
432 rations	Erbswurst	2	216 rations	1 ration every 3rd day
40 lb.	Cocoa and milk	1	40 lb.	Extra for occasional use
1½ gallons	Vinegar	1	5 bottles	₁⁄₁₆ gallon
40 lb.	Rice		20 lb.	⅜ oz.
40 ,,	Oatmeal	2	20 ,,	⅓ oz.
10 ,,	Baking powder		5 ,,	
2 ,,	Pepper		1 ,,	₁⁄₁₆ oz.
40 ,,	Tobacco	1	40 ,,	On repayment at 1s. 4d. per lb.
27 ,,	Soap (common)	1	27 ,,	On repayment at ¼d. a piece
9 ,,	,, (carbolic)	1	9 ,,	On repayment at 1d. a piece
192 boxes	Matches	1	192 boxes	...
	Field hospital supply case.‡	1	Sundry	...
		88		

* The column for the daily issues shows the data upon which the supplies of each article have been calculated, but, provided the total ration is not exceeded, the various articles may be issued in such proportion as may be considered advisable by the Officer Commanding.

† If the supply of bacon is sufficient, five cases containing about 200 lb. will be sent in each boat. In that event the supply of boiled mutton will be omitted.

‡ Containing—
3 bottles brandy
3 bottles port wine.
12 4-oz. tins Liebig's extractum carnis.
½ lb. mustard (in tin)
1 lb. yellow soap (in tin).
1 lb. candles (in tin).
1 tin alum.
2 lb. arrowroot.
¼ lb. salt (in turned box).
4 tins condensed milk.
6 tins cocoa and milk
2 boxes safety matches.
½ lb. compressed tea.
1 corkscrew.
1 opening knife.
1 bottle permanganate.

INDEX.

www.ingramcontent.com/pod-product-compliance
Lightning Source LLC
Chambersburg PA
CBHW050902130726
47900CB00015B/1682